DAN

Versus

NATURE

DAN
Versus
NATURE

Don Calame

CANDLEWICK PRESS

First paperback edition 2019

Library of Congress Catalog Card Number 2015954529
ISBN 978-0-7636-7071-9 (hardcover)
ISBN 978-1-5362-0059-1 (paperback)

21 22 23 24 25 TRC 10 9 8 7 6 5 4 3 2

Printed in Eagan, MN, U.S.A.

This book was typeset in Utopia.

Candlewick Press
99 Dover Street
Somerville, Massachusetts 02144

visit us at www.candlewick.com

For my dad, who taught me to fish —
I love you and miss you

CHAPTER 1

Charlie and I are getting our asses punched.

That's right, *punched*.

It's the wrestling team this time. The fists come fast and furious — to the back of my head, my kidneys, my shoulders.

And, yes, my ass.

I don't know who the hell's punching my ass, exactly, because I'm rolled up on the gymnasium floor like a pill bug. When you're sickly skinny, in a school rife with steroid abusers and future ax murderers, and you happen to be best friends with a wiseass like Charlie Bungert, you learn fairly quickly to protect your face and vital organs when you're taking a beating.

Particularly if you don't want to be grilled for details when you get home.

"What did you call us, you little snot socket?" someone asks, punctuating his sentence with another stinging slam to my ribs.

I didn't call them anything. It was Charlie who referred to them as a bunch of "uriniferous homunculi." I was merely a bystander.

A bystander who made the fatal mistake of snorting at Charlie's creative slight.

Which they deserved, by the way. Charlie was only trying to take a team photo for the school paper, and the guys wouldn't cooperate. They kept flipping birds, picking their noses, and flashing their hairy butt cracks just as Charlie was about to snap the picture.

Coach Pullman started muttering stuff about how "artistic types" don't know how to take command of a situation and that he had "much more important things to deal with." Then he grabbed his *Sports Illustrated* and headed to his office.

And that's when things really got out of control.

Charlie lowered his camera and stared at the team. "I wonder," he said, "if it might be possible to feign—for the fleetest of seconds—a mere soupçon of decorum."

Of course, no one on the wrestling team had any idea what Charlie had just said. But instead of admitting this, one of them called him a "snobby crotch waffle," which got a big laugh from the team.

And then someone started chucking tape balls.

And dirty jockstraps.

And ratty wrestling shoes—one of which knocked the lens off Charlie's camera.

"Stick that up your decorum!" somebody shouted, sending another wave of laughter through the squad.

Charlie's face darkened. There's nothing in the world he cares more about than that camera. His parents gave it to him for his tenth birthday—the last birthday they ever got to celebrate with him.

"It's funny," he said far too loudly, examining the body of his Nikon. "I didn't know uriniferous homunculi could actually speak."

And that's when I snorted. *Big* mistake.

"Excuse me?" Rick "'Roid Rage" Chuff spat, his caveman forehead jutting. "What was that?"

"I said . . ." Charlie replied. "You're surprisingly articulate for a bunch of uriniferous homunculi."

Rick glanced at his nine buds, each of whom shrugged.

"Would you like me to translate?" Charlie offered.

"Aw, fuck, Charlie, don't," I begged under my breath, taking a step backward.

"Yeah," Rick said. "Why don't you do that for us?"

"Urine. Bearing. Trolls," Charlie said, pushing his glasses back onto the bridge of his nose. "Trolls who carry around sacks of their own piss. Certainly explains the unwashed vagrant smell wafting off of you."

Then they rushed us. Like lions pouncing on a couple of wounded gazelles.

And now here I lie on the gritty gym floor. Taking yet another beating with Charlie.

"Who smells like piss now, Bungert?" Rick Chuff says,

hauling Charlie up by his camera, the black-and-yellow Nikon strap wrapped around his neck like a noose.

And damn if Charlie doesn't sniff the air through his bloody nose as he dangles there.

"Hard to tell," he rasps. "Your fecal-scented breath is overpowering every other odor at the moment."

Rick quickly yanks the camera higher into the air, lifting Charlie off the ground, the tips of his toes barely brushing the floor. "Not so easy to make jokes when your windpipe's being crushed, now is it?"

Charlie wheezes, his eyes bulging, his face turning blue as he desperately claws at his neck.

I don't have time to think. I quickly roll away from my attackers, reaching out and grabbing whatever's close at hand—a jockstrap, as it turns out. I stumble to my feet and hurl the dirty, limp thing at Rick.

It whiffles in the air and lands right on Rick's hand, the one holding Charlie's camera, where it dangles for a moment like an ornament, the nut-brown ass stain on the thong in full view.

Everyone freezes.

"What the Christ?" Rick drops the camera like it's on fire and shakes the athletic supporter off his hand.

Charlie crumples to the floor.

Rick turns to me, his eyes full of all the world's hate.

"You've just signed your death warrant, bitch," Rick says. "Grab him!"

The entire wrestling team lunges at once, gripping my arms, my legs, my shirt, my hair, stretching me out like da Vinci's *Vitruvian Man*.

4

Someone wraps the jockstrap around my face, the molded plastic cup covering my nose and mouth like a respirator. Several curly pubes cling to the cloth, tickling my cheeks.

"Breathe deep, shithead," Owen Rocco says.

I try breathing through my mouth, but it's impossible not to smell the horrible, farty stink of sweaty sphincter.

I gag and choke back some vomit.

'Roid Rage Rick towers in front of me, his fist clenched and cocked.

I squeeze my eyes shut and brace for a horrible pounding.

"Hey! Screwheads!" Mr. Pullman calls out from somewhere. "Cut the crap already. Save it for the meet."

Not exactly the response I would have hoped for—a few years in San Quentin would have seemed more appropriate—but at least it's enough to stop the onslaught.

I peek through one squinted eye. Rick's fat finger is in my face.

"This is not over, dicktard," Rick says. "Not even close." He flicks my nose hard. "I can see the future, and yours is filled with blood and pain."

And with that, the Willowvale High School wrestling team releases me. I drop to my knees and pull the filthy jockstrap from my face as Rick and his buddies lumber off toward the gym doors.

"You OK?" I ask Charlie, struggling to my feet. I flip my left wrist and check the black face on Dad's old Timex, make sure the crystal isn't cracked. It's the first thing I always do after taking a beating. Even though the thing hasn't worked since he took off six years ago.

Charlie clears his throat. "I've had worse." He runs his tongue over his blood-rimmed teeth. "No money from the tooth fairy this time, but it was still worth it."

I laugh, which sends a screaming pain shooting through one of my ribs. "Shit." I wince and clutch my lower back. "You've got to stop doing this, Charlie. I don't know how much more my body can take."

"You can run, you know," Charlie says, picking up his camera lens and his glasses. "It's not a precondition of my friendship that you take these beatings with me."

"It's not like I had time to consider my options."

Charlie replaces the lens on the Nikon and checks for damages. "Oh, please. A Magic Eight Ball could have predicted that was coming. And yet you stood by my side. *And* you took a soiled jock to the face for me. I am forever in your debt. If you require something—help with a paper, an adjustment of your report card grades, porn site passwords, anything—you just let me know."

I shake my throbbing head. "You don't owe me anything, Charlie. We're friends. That's what friends do." I rub my sore ass. "Is it really worth it, though? Just to get a dig in?"

Charlie laughs, then coughs, droplets of crimson spraying from his mouth. "I like being the thorn in their collective paw. Besides, it's an adrenaline rush. Makes me feel alive." He pounds his fist against his chest like a warrior, then grimaces in pain.

"Couldn't we just go to Six Flags and ride the Barracuda?"

"Daniel, Daniel, Daniel. Always looking for the easy way out." He pulls out the bottle of Purell that's permanently tucked into the front pocket of his pants, squirts a quarter-size blob into his palm, then waves the hand sanitizer at me. "Decontaminate?"

I shake my head. "I'm good. Don't you think it'd be more sanitary not to get beat up in the first place?"

Charlie laughs. "You can't avoid germs, my good man. You can only destroy them." He slathers the alcoholic goo all over his hands and then proceeds to dab some on his split lip. "You should really take some of this. I need you alive and healthy if you're going to be fighting by my side during the coming zombie apocalypse."

"Right. We can't even fight off regular people. You think we stand a chance against zombies?"

"It's all in the planning, my apprehensive friend. With enough ammunition, food stores, and an impenetrable bunker, I'm pretty sure we can handle the undead."

"Don't be so sure," I say. "Besides, my aunt Agnes says we need to be exposed to lots of bacteria so our immune systems can grow stronger."

Charlie rolls his eyes. "Sure. Believe that. Then Google 'necrotizing fasciitis' and let me know if you still want to take your chances."

CHAPTER 2

I trudge up my driveway, past Mom's white Nissan, and check my reflection in the side mirror. I tug a strand of hair over my right temple to cover the red welt that's blossomed there. The only conspicuous evidence from this afternoon's thrashing.

The nice thing about being a klutz is that Mom buys my excuses every time. But at this point I'm running out of things I could have "bumped into" at school. With any luck Mom'll be too busy—doing dishes, practicing her fly-fishing cast, or studying hockey box scores—to notice my head wound.

"That you, honey?" Mom calls out the second I step through the front door.

So much for being preoccupied. I sigh and dump my backpack on the floor of the entryway.

"Yeah," I call back. "It's me."

"Could you come into the kitchen for a sec?"

There's a warm ginger scent in the air. Mom's been baking. Which means either she's happy about something or wants to bribe me. Possibly both.

I tug off my coat and hang it up. Kick off my sneakers and proceed to trip over the stupid things as I step into the family room. Typical. I hobble past the couch and TV, this afternoon's beating settling into a dull, full-body throb.

"Dan?" Mom calls out.

"On my way. I'm a little sore today." I turn the corner and step into the fluorescent glow of the kitchen. "Stupid me, I fell down the stairs at school again and—"

I jerk to a stop. There, standing next to Mom, is Wolverine. Or a very reasonable facsimile.

"This is Hank," Mom announces, beaming, her hands outstretched like she's presenting me with a fabulous prize. "I told you he was coming over today, remember?"

"Oh. Yeah." Of course I didn't remember. Otherwise I would have come up with a more manly excuse for my injuries.

"Hey," I say, stepping forward, swiping my sweaty palm on my pant leg before I extend it. "Dan."

"Right," Wolverine says, his voice a radio baritone. "Hank. Langston." He takes my hand—his palm desert-dry—and shakes it a little too firmly as he meets my eyes with his piercingly clear baby browns. "Great to meet you."

9

"You too," I lie, flexing my fingers to make sure nothing's fractured.

Jesus. Mom's flashed me a picture or two on her phone, but I sure didn't expect this . . . this Men's Wearhouse model.

"Your mom's told me tons about you," Hank says.

"Same." I force a smile, trying to recall this one's particulars. Hank Langston. The world's most attractive dentist. College football star. Mountain climber. And fearless bear hunter. Terrific. I wonder how many scrawny graphic novelists *he* beat up when he was in high school.

"Well, hopefully she speaks as highly of me as she does of you." Hank gazes lovingly at Mom. "She's super proud. Brags all the time about what an amazing artist you are. I'd love to see some of your work. I'm impressed by anyone who can draw. I can barely doodle a stick figure."

Hank chuckles at his little quip, but I'm not buying the chummy act for a second. I've seen it *way* too many times before.

It's unfortunate, really. They actually look halfway decent together, Hank and Mom. They have a sort of Outback Ken and Barbie thing going on. But it won't last. Hank will turn out to be a deadbeat. Or an alcoholic. Or an adult baby.

Or just a plain old dick.

They always do.

Poor Mom. It started in high school with Dad—a deadbeat *and* an alcoholic—and hasn't gotten any better in the fifteen years since she birthed me. I feel bad for her. Beyond being not so bad-looking—for a mom, anyway—she's also good-hearted. She deserves to find someone who appreciates her.

Of course, she doesn't help her cause any with her chameleon act—studying up on things she never cared about before, all in an attempt to get a guy to stick. She's clawed her way through *Ulysses,* tried learning to speak Mandarin, downloaded and listened to hip-hop music, subscribed to *Stained Glass Quarterly,* taken square-dancing lessons. She even got a tattoo of a baby meerkat on her ankle when she was dating some schmo from the Kalahari Meerkat Project.

You'd think she would have learned by now.

But it doesn't seem like it. Not if the new teeth-whitening kit, copies of the *Hockey News,* and *Man vs. Wild* Blu-ray box set are any indication.

"So," I say, just to say something.

"So," Mom echoes.

The awkwardness in the kitchen swells like a septic boil.

I force another smile. Tuck my hands into my front pockets and rock back on my heels.

"I made cookies." Mom gestures at a platter of marshmallow gingersnaps in the middle of the table. Three small plates and three glasses of milk have been strategically set out on flowered place mats. "Your faves."

"Cool," I say, though my stomach tightens. Why do I feel like I'm about to be told our dog just died? Even though we don't have a dog.

"Shall we partake?" Hank suggests, stepping toward the table.

Mom nods. "Let's."

They slide out chairs and take their seats in perfect sync, almost like they've rehearsed it.

I don't want to be rude, but honestly, the last thing I want to

11

do right now is sit down with Mom and the macho dentist and make small talk over milk and cookies.

But I don't see as I have much of a choice.

"Sounds good," I say, pulling out my chair and plopping down. I grab a cookie and immediately take a huge bite so I don't have to talk.

Mmm. I always forget how they melt in your mouth, Mom's gingersnaps, all sweet-spicy goodness. Definitely bribe-worthy.

Depending on the request, of course.

Hank reaches over and takes four cookies. He places two on Mom's plate and the other two on his own.

How gallant. I bet he's got a wife and brood stashed away somewhere. Or has a prison record. Or likes to sit on your head and rip toxic buck snorts.

"As someone whose whole world is oral hygiene," Hank says, "I should probably be a better example here. But I have a sweet tooth the size of a blue whale. Let's just say we'll all brush afterward." He laughs, and then he does something so unspeakably disgusting that it's all I can do not to bolt from the table and barricade myself in my room: he crumbles his cookies into little bits and submerges them in his milk.

What. The. Hell?

"You'll have to excuse me," Hank explains. "I'm an extreme dunker. I know it's not the classiest thing in the world, but I've done it ever since I was a kid. You let 'em get real mushy and then you drink them down with the milk. Sort of like a cookie shake."

I retch. "Or *baby* food," I say, glancing at Mom for a reaction.

But she doesn't get the reference. Nor does she seem revolted by the desecration of her special cookies.

Instead, she just smiles and says, "This is cozy, huh?"

"Mmm-hmm." I shove the rest of my cookie into my mouth so I can get the hell out of here.

"So, Dan. We have something we wanted to tell you." Mom takes a deep breath. She looks over at Hank. "Do you want to—?"

"No, no." Hank shakes his head and wipes a blob of milk-soaked gingersnap from his lip. "You go ahead. It's your . . . you know."

"OK." Mom laughs nervously, shifting her cookies on her plate. "Well. All right. So. As you know, Hank and I have been dating for a while now . . ."

Oh, Christ. Is that what all this is about? This cookie defiler is going to be moving in with us? That's just what I need—another one of Mom's freeloading man-child boyfriends eating all our food, shedding body hair in the shower, and stealing money out of my change jar.

"I realize this is the first time you're meeting Hank," Mom continues, placing her hand on his woolly arm. "But things between us have gotten pretty serious, and . . ." Mom takes another deep breath.

"*And?*" I say, because, really, I'd like to get this over with as quickly as possible so I can go hide in my room. Maybe search for the earplugs I haven't had to use since the last grunting loser took off, leaving cigarette burns in our couch and a thousand-dollar pay-per-view porn bill.

"And . . ." She glances over at Hank and smiles. "Well . . . we're engaged."

I blink hard. "I'm sorry. What?"

"Hank and I . . . are getting married."

Her words punch me in the gut. A mass of gingerbready hurl rises in my throat.

I shake my head. "Wait. You guys . . . You've only been dating for a couple of months."

"It's three and a half months, actually," Mom says. "I know it seems fast, but I told you from the very beginning that I thought Hank was the real deal."

Right. Like I haven't heard that before. "When did this happen?"

"Last night," Mom says. "During our Valentine's Day dinner. It was totally unexpected, but it all just felt so *right*." She thrusts her left hand at me to display the ginormous diamond ring on her finger. Jesus, how did I miss that? "Isn't it gorgeous?"

"It's . . . um . . . big." And fake, probably. Hank claims he's a dentist, but a thousand bucks says it eventually comes out that he's involved in something only *vaguely* dental related.

A receptionist at a dentist's office. Or a toothbrush sales rep. Or the ever-popular "No, no, no, I never said I *was* a dentist. I said that I *go* to the dentist. Because I'm concerned about good dental health."

I look over and stare at my future stepdad. College football star. Extreme cookie dunker. Alligator wrestler.

Rick Chuff all grown up and ready to make my life a living hell.

I clutch the edge of my chair, the kitchen becoming a Tilt-A-Whirl.

"I realize this may seem fast to you, Dan," Hank says.

"What? Fast? No, it's—it's great. Three months is . . . plenty of time."

"The thing is," Hank says, "when you get to our age, you sort of know what you want in a partner."

"And what you don't," Mom adds.

Hank smiles shyly at Mom. "And you recognize pretty quickly when you've found someone truly special."

"Yeah. No," I say, the back of my neck sweating. "It's great. I mean, it's a little . . . surprising and all, but . . . if you both think—"

"We'd like your blessing, of course," Hank says.

Now? You'd like my blessing now? What about before you bought the ring, jackass? What about before you freakin' proposed?!

"No. Yeah. No. I mean, if my mom's . . . happy, then . . . I'm . . ." I swallow my scream. "Congratulations."

I glance at the window over the kitchen sink, tempted to make a run for it. Dive through the glass and race all the way down to Mexico or Peru or wherever the hell Dad's disappeared to, so I can beat the piss out of him for leaving us and making me have to deal with this crap.

"And I'd greatly appreciate it," Hank says, "if you'd be my best man."

"Your—" I cough. "Your best man? Why? Don't you have any friends?"

Let me guess: You're a loner? A loser? A drifter? The quiet neighbor who buries bodies in his backyard?

Hank laughs. "Of course I have friends. And they'll be in the wedding party. But I thought . . . well . . . I thought it might be nice if we all stood up at the altar together. As a new family."

Hank shrugs. "Only if you'd like to, though. No pressure. I don't want you to be uncomfortable."

"No. Yeah. It's . . ." I look over at Mom, who's beaming, all hopeful. "That'd be . . . great."

Mom swats Hank's arm. "See. Didn't I tell you? Dan's the greatest. You guys are going to get along like gangbusters."

CHAPTER 3

Hank is making dinner for us. To celebrate the big announcement.

The menu is a surprise—as if I need any more of those tonight. The only hint Mom would give me is that the meal would center on the spoils of one of Hank's hunting trips. So, rancid game meat, I guess.

And really, should a guy who spends all day with his hands in people's mouths be allowed to prepare food? Charlie would *not* approve.

I shift the sketch pad on my desk and drag my pencil down the page in a long, swooshing arc, trying to make the cloak of the Night Goblin flow behind him. The scene is Temple Araxia, home of the Sacred Scarab, one of the seven Bewitching Amulets belonging to Warrior Princess Erilin, supreme and benevolent ruler of Melifluose.

The Night Goblin has already stolen three of the Amulets: Godstone, Noble Birth, and the Onyx OxSkull. If he gets his hand on a fourth, the balance of power will be tipped in his favor.

In this next panel, the Night Goblin is headed for the Temple keep, where he will be confronted by a sword-wielding Princess Erilin, who has been alerted to the threat by Sir Stan Stalwart of Summerhall.

I'm basing my drawing of the princess loosely on this girl I like at school, Erin Reilly. I needed a model, someone who was beautiful and strong but not intimidatingly so, and Erin was the obvious choice. It's been a bit of a challenge getting her look just right because I don't have the balls to ask her to sit for me in person, and I *certainly* don't want to be caught staring at her from across the room for long stretches of time like some creepy stalker. As a result, I have to work off of a combination of memory, stolen glances at school, and Erin's Instagram feed. She really likes to make goofy faces in her photos, which, while super cute, doesn't exactly scream Warrior Princess.

I swipe my phone, click the Instagram app, and find a shot of Erin making googly eyes and a fat tongue at the camera. Not great, but better than the one where she's wearing giant heart glasses and pulling up her nose in a pig snout. At least I can get the shape of her ears and the swoop of her neck.

"Engaged!" I mutter to myself as I draw. Un-freakin-believable. How did I not see that coming?

Well, you never met the dude. Perhaps that had something to do with it?

Yeah, but there must have been signs. I just wasn't paying attention. I got complacent. And why wouldn't I? All of Mom's dates tend to blend into each other. Ryan, Ted, Allan, Jesse, Peter, Hank. Such gentlemen. So funny. So sweet. "The real deal this time." And me nodding, smiling, and zoning out as Mom blathers on giddily.

Until the day the truth comes out—the other girlfriends, the mean streak, the fur suit fetish—and Mom comes home crying.

Unless they've moved in. Then I come home to find her crying on our couch. Or in her bed. Or locked in the bathroom.

But there's always crying. And yelling.

I don't see how she didn't give up years ago. If I were her and my taste in guys was so bad, I'd probably try being a lesbian.

But that's just the way Mom is, eternally optimistic.

Me, I conceded defeat on the surrogate dad front a *looong* time ago. And honestly, it hasn't been such a big loss. All that father/son crap—learning how to shave, tying a tie, dribbling a basketball—you can pick up off the Internet, no prob.

It'd be nice, though, if Mom found someone she could rely on before I leave for college. A real partner. Like you see in the movies or on TV.

Unfortunately, this Hank character is *not* that guy. I can just tell. It's the "too perfect" angle. It's a dead giveaway.

But clearly he's got Mom totally snowed.

I sigh and press my graphite-stained palms into my tired eyes. I pull my hands away from my face and look at my sketch pad.

I blink at the picture I've drawn. What the—? The Night Goblin has a tuxedo on! And Princess Erilin is wearing a wedding dress and is clutching a bouquet of flowers!

And they're holding hands!

No. No way. I snatch my eraser and scrub out both their faces. I start redrawing the heads. We're not at Temple Araxia anymore. Nope. We're in another part of the city completely, a church miles away where Sir Stan's mother, naive physiotherapist Sarah Stalwart, is about to wed the evil Lord . . . Fang Plaqueston.

And now Sir Stan is faced with a dilemma: go help Princess Erilin battle the Night Goblin and save all humanity, or race to the church in order to thwart this unholy union which threatens to destroy his entire family. . . .

"I think you're going to like wild boar, Dan," Hank says, placing two more platters of food on the table. He's wearing Mom's pink cowgirl apron and somehow is able to make it look macho. "It's what pork used to taste like before pigs were domesticated."

"Everything smells delicious. You've outdone yourself, Boogabear," Mom says.

Ugh. Cue the string of sickeningly sweet pet names I'll now have to endure. The last loser was "Crumpkin" and Mom was "Taffy," whatever the hell *that's* supposed to mean.

Mom's broken out her favorite multicolored Fiestaware for the occasion. She takes generous servings of everything: boar chops, stuffed mushrooms, green beans amandine, homemade coleslaw. "My mouth is watering!" she says.

"Yeah," I say. "It all looks so . . . hot." I spear the smallest of the boar chops with my fork. I add a single mushroom cap, three green beans, and a tiny lump of coleslaw to my blue plate.

"Not hungry, Dan?" Hank asks, reaching for the largest chop.

I shake my head. "Charlie and I hit the deli after school, and we had chips and stuff."

Mom laughs. "Dan's not the most adventurous of eaters. His comfort zone is more spaghetti and meatballs than haute cuisine."

"That's not true," I say, my face prickling with heat. "I eat lots of other things. It's just that tonight I'm not feeling so well."

"Hey, listen," Hank says. "Don't sweat it. I'm honored that you're even trying it. When I was fifteen, I wouldn't touch anything that didn't have 'burger' or 'McNugget' in the title."

Wow, patronizing much?

Mom raises her water glass. "To new beginnings," she says. "And to togetherness and family."

Hank grabs his glass and clinks Mom's. "Cheers to that."

They hold their glasses out toward mine, which remains on the table. "Sorry," I say with an apologetic smile. "It's bad luck to toast with water."

"Oh." Hank looks at me, then at Mom. "I didn't know that."

"Yeah," I say. "It's from Greek mythology. They thought the dead left their physical bodies behind after drinking from the rivers of the underworld. So a toast with water is basically a toast to death."

"Huh. Interesting. Well." Hank laughs. "Uncheers, then." He does a little reverse motion with his water glass.

"Uncheers," Mom echoes, waving her glass in the air.

"I don't think it works that way," I say. "It's like trying to unbreak a mirror." I scrunch up my face, like I'm embarrassed at having to be the bearer of such bad news.

"Well, I don't believe in superstitions," Mom says. She takes a big bite of boar chop and chews with her eyes closed, a look of rapture on her face. "Oh my God, Boogabear, it's so tasty."

"Oh, good." Hank sits up tall and proud, a goofy smile dimpling his stubble-covered cheeks.

I cut the skinniest sliver off my wild boar chop. Examine it on the end of my fork. Sniff at it. Dab it on the tip of my tongue. Then, finally, slip it into my mouth and chew.

I so want to hate it. I want it to taste like rancid pig slow-poached in an old man's colostomy bag, so I can make a show of "furtively" spitting it out in my napkin.

But it actually tastes good. Really good. Like, the best pork chop I've ever eaten. It's sort of sweet and nutty and smoky.

Goddamn it.

"So, what's the verdict, Dan?" Hank asks. "Is it yea or nay on the wild boar?"

I knew he was eyeing me. I hate it when people watch me eat. I should have grimaced a little as I swallowed. Gagged a bit.

"It's . . . um . . ." I trail off. "Interesting."

Hank grabs his heart like I just speared him. "*Interesting?* That's the kiss of death right there."

"Sorry. I'm sure it's great. It's just that I'm not that hungry, like I said."

Hank wipes his mouth with his napkin. "No apologies necessary. If you don't like it, you don't like it. I'm not one of those clean-your-plate kind of guys. My father was like that." He

22

shakes his head. "Had to finish everything you were served or he wouldn't let you leave the table. He liked to give you extra when he knew it was something you really hated. True story, I once fell asleep in a giant plate of liver and wilted spinach. Nothing you ever want to eat. But it does make a pretty comfy pillow."

Mom chuckles at his joke.

I push some food around on my plate, trying to ignore the siren call of the boar chop. *Eat me, Dan. Eeeaat meee.*

I turn to Hank, eyes wide with innocence. "Is it true that dentists have the highest rate of suicide in the world?"

"Dan," Mom admonishes.

"What?" I shrug. "It's what I heard."

Hank laughs, nods, takes a bite of mushroom. "It's OK. I've heard the same thing. Everyone has. People think because nobody likes coming to the dentist that we have an inferiority complex. But actually, psychiatrists have a much higher incidence of suicide than dentists."

"But dentists are still pretty high up there," I say. "Right?"

Mom gives me a cold stare.

"If you look at the data," Hank explains, "which most dentists have, I guess you'd have to admit there is a slightly elevated percentage of suicide. Though not by much. Certainly no higher than other doctors. And in reality, we tend to live several years longer than the general population."

"Huh," I say. "Interesting."

Guess I can't count on Hank taking himself out of the picture.

"So, Dan," Hank says, after chewing and swallowing a piece of meat. "That's a nice watch you've got there. You don't see many kids wearing watches these days."

I glance at Dad's scratched-up Timex, wondering if he's making fun of it. "Thanks," I mumble, taking note of the gargantuan man-watch Hank is wearing.

"Maybe that's what I can get you for your birthday," Mom says. "A new watch—one that actually works!"

I instinctively slide my left hand off the table, like Mom might actually rip Dad's watch from my wrist.

"I didn't know you have a birthday coming up," Hank says.

What you don't know could fill a book, buddy.

"Next week," Mom says. "The big one-six!"

"We should celebrate!" Hank says, like he's just invented the idea of birthday parties. "Maybe you guys can come over to my place for a movie night or something."

A movie night with my mother and her boyfriend? I'm not sure I'm ready to party quite that hard.

"He *does* have the most incredible media room," Mom gushes. "Just wait till you see it, Dan!"

Suddenly, another terrible thought drops into my mind.

I look at Mom. "We're not going to have to move, are we? When you guys get married."

"Oh, honey." Mom says gently. "We can't stay here. There's barely enough room for the two of us."

"What are you talking about? We've made it work before," I insist. "With Randy and Steve and Frank and Tony and—"

"We get the point," Mom says, laughing nervously. Hank puts a reassuring hand on her arm. "But Hank's house is a *home*, Dan. We were thinking that I could move my physiotherapy practice to the studio in the backyard. Plus, you'll have a much bigger bedroom—"

"The second-biggest room in the house," Hank cuts in. Obviously they've talked about this at length.

"And there's not only a studio in the backyard," Mom continues. "There's also a tree house in one of the big elms. You're a bit old for tree houses, maybe, but it could be a nice place to sit and work on your graphic novels. We could have offices side by side." She laughs. "Anyway, it's a really great neighborhood. Very family-friendly. Not like here with Mrs. Nosy-Body next door."

My stomach drops. "Where is it?" I ask.

Mom glances at the table. "It's . . . east of here."

"How far east?" I ask, my heart racing. Silence. "Would I have to move schools?"

Hank forces a smile. "We don't have to discuss this right now. We're celebrating, right? Why muddy it up with details we can work out later?"

"I'm not moving schools," I insist. "No way." I can't imagine finishing up high school without Charlie. And then there's Erin. I'm the closest I've ever been to actually talking to her, which means there's a chance that by the time graduation rolls around, I might have worked up the nerve to ask her on a date. I'll be damned if Hank "Fang" Plaqueston is going to stand in the way of me and my dreams.

"Let's talk about this another time," Mom pleads. "Tonight I just really want to focus on our happy news."

I nod numbly, but my mind is whirring. This isn't just an assault on my life, it's a full-out nuclear explosion. I need to stop this thing before it's too late. "So," I say, a heavy pulse in my right temple. "When are the nuptials, anyway?" Translation: Just how much time do I have to disarm this bomb?

Mom looks over at Hank. "We were thinking . . . mid-May, right?"

Hank nods. "No reason to put it off too long."

"Wait. *May*?" Jesus Christ, three months? "Hold on a second." I turn to Mom. "Are you pregnant?" I ask, fairly sure that she isn't. Mom has made it pretty clear she isn't interested in having any more kids.

"What? No." Mom's cheeks flush. "I mean . . . why would you think that?"

I give her a look. "Why else would you be hurrying to the altar?"

"Not because your mother's pregnant, certainly," Hank blurts a little too fast. He coughs into his first. "Not that . . . it would be a . . . bad thing . . ." He furrows his brow at Mom, obviously trying to gauge her feelings about this.

"No . . . I mean . . . yeah," Mom says, laughing nervously. "But I'm not, so . . ."

"Yeah," I say, waving my hand. "Well, I wouldn't worry about it, anyway. I'm sure no one else will suspect that you're having a baby. And really, who cares what other people think. So what if everyone's watching everything you eat and drink from now until the big day. Or if, you know, people are whispering behind your back. It's none of their business, am I right?" I raise my glass of water high in the air. "To a joyful marriage in May."

CHAPTER 4

"Wait a second," Charlie says. "Back up a moment here. So, is this guy *your* dentist?"

"God, no. That'd be even weirder," I say, glancing over at Erin Reilly's table across the cafeteria, sketchbook propped on my thigh, pencil in hand, trying not to be too obvious as I detail the blunt cut of Erin's bangs, the slight curl of them curving into her forehead. "My mom's his physical therapist. They met three months ago when Hank twisted his ankle playing squash or something. She gave him a rubber resistance band, and he asked her out to dinner."

"Surely that's some kind of code-of-ethics violation," Charlie says. He pulls a square Tupperware container from his backpack like a rabbit out of a hat. He won't touch cafeteria food with a ten-foot fork, what with all the "festering bacteria" and "lunch-lady germs." "What if you reported them to APTA?"

"What the hell is APTA?"

Charlie squirts some hand sanitizer into his palm with a little wet mini-fart. Rubs it in. "The American Physical Therapy Association."

I stare at Charlie. "Why do you know that?"

"There is very little I do not know, Daniel," he says, prying the lid off his sandwich container to reveal a neatly cut and Saran-wrapped peanut butter and jelly, no crusts. "And I believe that if you lodge a formal complaint, you might just be able to halt this marriage. Of course, your mom might lose her license in the process, but at least you wouldn't have to move. Well, unless your mom could no longer pay the bills, then instead of living in a nice big *new* home, you wouldn't have *any* home at all."

"Yeah, I'm not doing that," I say. "Being homeless isn't exactly the endgame here."

I shift my gaze back to Erin. She and her friends are cooing over the Baby-Real-A-Lot doll that Erin's been tasked with caring for this week in our Life Skills class. She's named him Baby Robbie. I wonder if that's what she'll want to name our baby when we get married and have kids someday.

God, she's so gorgeous. Her long eyelashes. Her beautifully silky, cinnamon hair. Her rosy cheeks. Her little swooped-up nose. It's hard to take, really. Like someone reaches into my chest and crushes my heart every time I see her.

It's been like this ever since third grade. It was during silent reading when my eyes were first opened to her true beauty. We were seated side by side, the last seats in our respective rows.

Erin was surreptitiously sucking on a butterscotch lollipop, flipping the pages of *Charlotte's Web*. Out of nowhere, she leaned over, held out her lollipop, and whisper-asked if I'd like a lick.

And even though Charlie had already been on me for years about the dangers of germs, I *did* want a lick—more than I'd ever wanted anything. But I couldn't bring myself to take one. Instead, I gave my head a quick jerk, flushing heat all the way to the roots of my hair. I turned back to my ragged copy of *Goosebumps*, my breath hitching as I read the same sentence over and over again for the next fifteen minutes, until Mr. Falaxus announced that it was time to get out our math textbooks.

Erin and I have exchanged twenty-seven passing smiles and thirty-two *Hey*s since that fateful day. Around town. In different classes. In various hallways. And she's also appeared, in one form or another, in every single comic I've drawn over the last seven years.

But that's all. Nothing more.

Even though an hour doesn't go by without me thinking of her.

I nearly mustered the courage to ask her out last year, after having practiced in the mirror for two months, but I botched it by choking on the wintergreen Altoid I popped in my mouth right before I approached her. The mint finally came up after I punched myself in the stomach, but it flew out of my mouth and stuck to the front of her shirt. I stared with growing horror at the ring of spit blossoming around the partially dissolved Altoid, then turned on my heel and fled.

I haven't been able to face her since.

One day I'll have the balls to talk to her again.

For right now, though, I have to be content with using Erin as the inspiration for Princess Erilin. Sorceress. Warrior. And all-around master of bad-assery.

"Please tell me that's the cartoon for this week's *Willowvale Oracle*," Charlie says, lifting the hermetically sealed sandwich from the Tupperware and carefully peeling back the plastic. "We go to press in two days. We can't miss another deadline, not with Mrs. Horvath looking for an excuse to shut down the paper. If that happens, my college portfolio will end up severely anemic."

I look up from my drawing and force a smile. "Sorry. I'll get it to you. I promise."

Charlie cranes his neck to peek at my sketch pad. "Ah yes, the continuing adventures of the Night Goblin and the Desert Princess. Much more important than the *Oracle*."

"I just have to get some final details down so that I can finish this chapter," I tell Charlie. "Then I can give my full attention to this week's cartoon."

"I don't see how you can even concentrate on the Night Goblin, anyway," Charlie says. "Shouldn't you be formulating some sort of stratagem to stop this wedding before you have to memorize a new zip code?"

"Believe me, it's all I've been thinking about." I flip the cover of my sketchbook closed, set my pencil down, and sigh. "I just can't figure out how to do it."

Charlie rolls his eyes. "Oh, Daniel, must I do everything for you? It's quite simple, really: the first step is to find some dirt on him—you know, check his wallet, his phone, his laptop, his vehicle for pornography, lurid text messages from mistresses, receipts from hotels. Anything that will freak your mother out, make her question his morals."

"That's the problem," I say. "If there *is* any dirt on this guy, I imagine it's going to be nearly impossible to find. I've never heard my mom go on *quite* so much about someone before. What a great guy he is, with his great job, his great friends, his great sister who loves him, and his adorable nieces and nephews who are crazy about him."

"Why do you want him gone, then?" Charlie asks. "He sounds perfect."

"Exactly," I say, pointing at him. "And if we've learned nothing else from my mom's tragic love life, it's that there is no such thing as a perfect guy. The other shoe is going to drop eventually. I'd rather it be *before* we sell our house and are trapped in Hank's hunting lodge a million miles away from here."

"OK, so, if character assassination is out"—Charlie takes a bite of his sandwich—"I suppose you'll just have to scare him off."

I laugh. "Scare him off? The dude who hunts bear with a bow and arrow?"

"Look, he's only just met you. You're the wild card here. You can use that to your advantage."

"How?"

"Let's think about that for a moment." Charlie takes another bite of PB&J and chews thoughtfully. "All right. What about this? What if you pretend to really like him? Play the kid desperately looking for a father figure. You can start out by asking him to help with simple things. Father-and-son stuff: Homework. How to fix a flat on your bike. How to tie a tie or throw a curveball. That sort of thing."

"How's that going to scare him off?"

"It won't, at first. He'll think it's great, like you're accepting him. But then you begin to push the boundaries. You become needier and needier. You pull him aside and ask him things that'll make him wildly uncomfortable. Like about coitus—but not your conventional teen boy proclivities. More like weird fetishes and things. And about drugs—the really hard ones: opioids, dissociatives, hallucinogens."

"I don't know if I can do that."

"I don't know if you can afford *not* to."

"He'll tell my mom."

Charlie shakes his head, an evil-genius glint in his eye. "That's the beauty of this plan. You make him promise, as your soon-to-be stepdad, not to. Explain to him that these are things that you could *never* discuss with your mother. Things that you never got a chance to ask your father. Make him buy you glow-in-the-dark condoms and some really weird-flavored lube, then confess that you don't have a girlfriend—or a boyfriend. Ask him if it's normal to get an erection when you see pictures of baby kangaroos."

"I don't do that!" I insist.

"You do now. The more awkward your questions, the better. You need to convince Hank that he's in *way* over his head with this stepdad thing. Be creative. Have fun with it."

"It doesn't sound like a whole lot of fun," I say.

"Are you kidding?" Charlie says. "I'd give my left nut to have a stepdad I wanted to frighten off. And I'm not just saying that because I'm an orphan."

I squint at him. "You really think it could work?"

"Would you want to deal with that kind of crap if you didn't have to—some needy, clingy teenager with a seemingly endless stream of awkward problems? This guy has a short window of opportunity to bail on this situation. Once the papers are signed, he's committed. All you have to do is give him a reason to grab the parachute and leap from the plane."

"Huh," I say, tapping the cover of my sketchbook. "Could be worth a shot, I guess."

"Of course it is. What do you have to lose? Except maybe another miscreant muscling in on your life."

"True, true." I take a deep breath. Let it out. "OK. But you're going to have to help me come up with some stuff. You're way more Machiavellian than me."

Charlie grins big. "I'd be absolutely delighted to."

I pick up my pencil and flip the cover of my sketchbook open. I feel a tiny glimmer of hope. Charlie's plan could actually work. Sure, it'll be uncomfortable to have to say this stuff to Hank, but it'll totally be worth it in the—

Hukkkk-THWAH.

A giant green gob of quivering phlegm splats on my drawing, landing smack-dab in the center of Princess Erilin's face.

"Nice picture, asshat," Rick Chuff says. "Just needed a little color."

He laughs hysterically, then reaches over and grabs the other half of Charlie's perfectly cut sandwich. He squeezes it into a big dough ball and drops it into the open Tupperware container.

"Enjoy your lunch, boys," Rick says, wiping his hand on Charlie's shoulder.

I can see the wheels turning behind Charlie's glasses. He slides his Tupperware aside and is about to stand, to shout some obscure but withering insult at Rick and get us beat up right here and now.

I shake my head sharply. "Don't, Charlie. Please." I reach for a napkin and wipe Rick's thick mucus from my sketch pad, smearing Princess Erilin's features beyond recognition.

"You want to let him get away with this?" Charlie says. "With no response?"

"I just . . ." I swallow, glancing over at Erin's table. "I've managed not to get beat up in front of Erin for this long, and I'd like to keep it that way."

"You realize that acquiescence is a form of consent," Charlie says. "By not rebelling, we are thus agreeing to be tormented."

"I know, but . . ." I say. "Another time. Please."

Charlie takes a long, deep breath and nods. "OK, Daniel. I will keep quiet. I will go hungry for you today. But we will need to exact retribution in the near future." He smiles. "And I have a most excellent idea on just how to do that."

CHAPTER 5

"Woo-hoo!" Hank leaps to his feet along with Mom and the other eighteen thousand screaming fans in the hockey arena. "Right through the five hole!"

A tugboat horn sounds to announce the goal and then "Rock and Roll Part 2" starts pounding over the PA system. All around us fists are pumped, bellies are squashed together, hands are high-fived, and popcorn kernels fly from their containers.

I fumble with the precariously balanced grease-stained box of stale nachos on my knees, nearly dropping the small plastic sputum cup of cyber-orange cheese. The seating is airplane-tight here, and it takes a contortionist's dexterity to try to bend over and place my items on the floor so I can stand up and "hurrah" with the beer-swilling masses. I finally get all of my foodstuffs settled safely onto the sticky concrete, unfold my body, and wrestle myself out of my chair into a standing position—

Just as everyone else is settling back down again.

Great. Nice timing, Dan.

People stare. I make a big show of stretching my arms above my head—elongating my body, rolling my shoulders—like this was the plan all along.

This is how I'm spending my sixteenth birthday. A hockey game with Mom and her fiancé. In case you care, the San Jose Sharks are now tied with the Anaheim Ducks two to two. We're four minutes and forty-five seconds from the end of the second period—I've been promised there are only three—and I've got a splitting headache and a full-blown cheese-sauce-and-soda stomach churn going on.

Could life get any more tragic?

Mom is now a huge sports fan. Hockey, mostly. Because Hank loves hockey. Three months ago she purchased *NHL GameCenter LIVE* and subscribed to the *Hockey News*. Since then she's been studying up on the lingo and learning all the star players' names and stats.

Whatever else it's accomplished, Mom's intense desire to be liked has made her the most well-rounded and oddly knowledgeable person I know. She can talk fantasy football, sea-glass collecting, antique books, DNA testing, tai chi, vintage cars, ghost hunting, the stock market, cooking, gardening, dog training, cosplaying, decoupage, magic, sailing, model railroading, ventriloquism, rock stacking, poker, disc golf, pigeon racing, shortwave radio, falconry, paintball, robotics, beekeeping, and, yes, even gongoozling.

I don't think Mom's boyfriends have any idea how hard she works at trying to incorporate their interests into her life. If they did, they would either be incredibly touched or seriously creeped out.

Before I sit again, I glance down the aisle, contemplating a wander in the quiet of the pre-intermission concourse. But two seats away a pregnant man with a peanut-shell-flecked beard shoots me a don't-you-dare scowl. He and the other spectators in our row are getting pretty pissed at me for leaving so many times during the game already. Probably because I can't seem to scooch my way out of the aisle without crushing toes or accidentally kicking over beers.

I can't help it. I'm antsy. I could chalk it up to all the caffeine coursing through my veins. The deep-dimpled girl at the concession stand hard sold me on upsizing my Coke, and in my boredom I've managed to suck the mop bucket of soda completely dry.

But really, I'm on edge because I've decided to implement Charlie's scare-Hank-away-with-inappropriate-questions plan. While I've been able to pull off Part One of the operation just fine—ingratiating myself with him by asking for tips on everything from how to shave to how to fold a handkerchief—I haven't worked up the courage yet to push things to the next level.

But I'm going to have to up the stakes soon before Hank goes and buys himself a "World's Greatest Dad" mug.

The universe seems to agree, as just then Mom's cell phone plays "The Hockey Song," her latest ringtone. She reaches in her purse, checks who's calling, and frowns. "It's Bonnie, from work. I've got to take this, sorry." She swipes the screen, plugs one ear, and stands. "Hey, Bonnie. What's up?"

"That's the artistry of the sport right there," Hank says to me as Mom disappears down the aisle. "The way that guy handles the puck. That was a dirty little dangle. You can't teach that kind of thing."

"Totally," I say, trying to simulate interest. "The dangling . . . dirtily . . . Pretty amazing."

Hank unholsters his huge phablet and snaps a picture of the player who just scored.

"Hey, did I show you my new gadget?" He turns the screen toward me. "It's a real beaut. It's got a quad HD-plus display. A sixteen-megapixel camera. A fingerprint scanner. A heart-rate monitor. And I don't know what the heck else. It's crazy. I love it."

I can tell he loves it because he's gazing at it the way he gazes at my mom. I may vom.

"Wow, that's . . . pretty sweet," I say.

"You can't even get these right now," he says. "They're sold out everywhere. I had to stand in line for thirty-nine hours for this bad boy, but it was worth it."

"Wow," I say again.

"I'm ashamed to admit it, but I do adore my tech." He gives his phone a kiss, then wipes away his lip prints and reholsters the phone. "The key to upgrading is to save all the materials and keep your equipment super clean. That way you can maximize the resale value of your old phone and subsidize your new investment."

"Right." I nod. "Good idea." I wipe my sweaty palms on my pant legs and look up at the clock. Three minutes twenty-four seconds left in the period.

I lean over. "Can I talk to you a sec, Hank? Out on the concourse?"

"Sure, bud," he says, chin-gesturing toward the ice. "Period's almost over." He rubs his hands together. "Sharks are on a power play. They could take the lead here."

"I know, but . . . it's kind of important. And . . ." I lower my voice. "I don't want anyone else to hear. If we go now, we'll beat the crowds."

"Oh, OK." Hank's eyes flit to the ice, where the Sharks are passing the puck around like crazy. "If you're, uh, sure it can't wait a few minutes."

"It really can't."

Hank nods. "Right. Yes. Let's do it." He slaps his thighs and stands, then starts to gracefully sidestep his way down the aisle, his eye on the game as he goes. I trail Hank, making my way down the row. I trip on someone's foot, fall, and brace myself on the pregnant man's oddly firm belly. He grunts and shoves me away, causing me to butt bump the heads of the people in front of us.

"Sorry, sorry, sorry," I say as I stumble on.

Finally, I make it to the stairs and follow Hank, who scales the steps like a mountaineer. He glances back over his shoulder one last time, catching a final glimpse of the game before heading through the doorway to the concourse.

"So," he says when I catch up to him in front of Panda Express. "What's going on?"

I look around. "Actually, I feel a little exposed out here. Could we maybe talk in the bathroom?"

"The bathroom?" Hank asks, his eyebrows shooting up.

39

I nod.

He sighs, which means I'm starting to annoy him. Excellent!

"OK," he says, forcing a smile. "Sure. I can use the bathroom. Sounds good."

The men's restroom is all blinding white tiles and gray Formica. The whole place reeks of malty whiz, the ammonia cakes having raised the white flag sometime during the first intermission.

Hank quickly moves over to the urinals, unzips, and angles his ear, listening to the radio play-by-play of the game being piped in over speakers.

"Fifty-five seconds left on the power play," the announcer calls. "The Sharks break out of their zone."

There are a few other crowd-beating bathroom-goers straggling about, but the row of urinals is mostly vacant, leaving plenty of options for me. Still, I take up a position right next to Hank. He gives me a little acknowledging nod while still managing to keep his gaze directly forward.

I unleash myself and stare at the perspiring chrome urinal handle.

"Shot from the point, hits the crossbar," the announcer shouts.

Hank winces. "Damn it."

Do it now, I hear Charlie's voice in my head. *Right now. What we discussed.*

Aw, crap. My heart hammers inside my chest, the back of my neck prickling.

I lean over slightly and whisper, "So, anyway, the . . . uh . . . thing . . . that I wanted to ask you . . ."

Hank's eyes dart over to me, though his head remains dead straight. "Yes?"

"It's . . . kind of embarrassing," I say.

The sportscaster suddenly bellows, "He shoots, he scores!"

Hank's shoulders slump.

"Oh," I say. "We missed it. Sorry."

Hank takes a breath. "It's OK. This is more important. What's on your mind, bud?"

Oh, good Christ. All right. Here goes.

"So, you . . . know . . . your, uh . . ." I say, glancing downward. "A guy's . . . you know his . . . his . . . testicles?"

I look over at Hank. A mortified pink climbs his neck like the red in a thermometer.

"Yes," Hank says with a curt nod. "What about them?"

Just then a middle-aged Indian guy in an age-inappropriate team hoodie steps up to the urinal next to Hank.

Abort! Abort! Abandon ship! Cut bait! Cease and desist!

No! Charlie's voice drowns out my inner coward. *Witnesses are a good thing. The more humiliating it is for you, the more embarrassing it is for Hank.*

"Um, well . . ." I clear my throat, which is rapidly closing up. "I was just . . . wondering . . . are your"—I lower my voice—"you know . . . are they supposed to be . . . really small?"

"Really small?" Hank's eyes dart over to the Indian guy.

"It's just . . ."

Oh, shit, I can't go through with this. Charlie, what the hell were you thinking?

Do you want this man out of your life, or do you not? Say it. And say it convincingly.

41

"I'm just . . . sort of . . . worried," I croak. "Like . . . what size . . . is normal? For a testicle? Like . . . the size of a peanut? Is that normal?"

Hank squints one eye. "A peanut? Like, in the shell?"

Oh, Jesus, I think I might faint. Or throw up. Or both. I'm sweating through the pits of my shirt. Hank may be embarrassed, but I am beyond mortified.

"No . . ." I swallow. "A . . . cocktail peanut. That's tiny, right?"

Hank blinks. "Listen, bud, maybe we should, uh . . . you know . . . Maybe we should talk about this later, in private."

"Never mind." I shake my head, starting to hyperventilate. "It's OK. Forget it." I zip up and head to the sinks.

A moment later Hank steps up next to me. I look in the mirror. I can't tell whose face is burning redder, his or mine.

"Listen, Dan," he says, soaping his hands. "It's all right. You can talk to me. About anything. It's good. That's what, you know, a father—stepfather—is for."

"It's nothing," I rasp. "I didn't . . . it's fine. Really."

"We can take you to the doctor," he says. "If you're concerned."

"No," I squeak. "I mean. I'm fine. I'll just . . . I'll ask the doctor about it next time I see him. I'm probably just being paranoid." I turn to him. "Please don't tell Mom. Seriously. I'd die. Promise me. Please."

Hank nods. "Sure, bud. Absolutely. Between you and me. As long as, you know, you're sure you're OK."

"Totally, yes, I'm good, thanks," I say, then bolt from the bathroom.

CHAPTER 6

I take a tour around the entire concourse to try to gain my com-
posure, pushing through the crush of people to buy a bottle of
water. Letting the blood drain from my face.

That was *way* harder than I thought it was going to be. Stupid
Charlie and his stupid ideas. I can't believe I let him talk me into
doing that. When I get home, we're going to need to regroup and
rethink our strategy.

When I finally return to my seat, Hank and Mom are pointing and laughing at the two guys dressed in giant plush sumo
suits, battling on the ice. The referee counts one of the wrestlers
out and a cheer goes up from the intermission-thinned crowd.

"Oh my God," Mom says, shaking with laughter. She sniffles
and wipes a tear from her cheek. "That was hilarious."

I watch her carefully to see if she gives me any kind of are-you-OK-honey-I-didn't-know-you-had-such-tiny-testicles look, but there's nothing. So Hank must have kept his promise.

"Hey, do you want to open your birthday present from me?" Mom asks.

I shrug. "Uh, yeah. Sure. Sounds good." I kind of assumed that this hockey night was a present from both of them, but I guess we're not playing the whole one-present-from-the-parents game yet. Which is good. It means the cement hasn't completely hardened on this relationship, and I still have time to wedge my crowbar between them.

Mom reaches into her purse and takes out a gold envelope. She leans over Hank and hands it to me.

It's light. Almost weightless. Which is curious because Mom's not a check writer. She usually puts a lot of thought into her gifts. Even if they don't always hit the mark. Like the time she bought me a framed *300* movie poster. Sure, I read the graphic novel, watched the film. But did I want a life-size shot of a totally ripped dude in a loincloth hanging over my bed? Not really. Still, it's sweet of Mom to actually pay attention to my interests.

"Go ahead, hon," she says. "Open it."

Inside the envelope is a green sheet of paper, which I unfold. It's a homemade gift certificate of sorts, the message written with gold Sharpie in Mom's greeting-card-quality cursive.

Mom is vibrating with excitement. "Read it out loud."

I smile, her enthusiasm contagious. "OK." I clear my throat: "'Happy Birthday, my beautiful boy.'" I roll my eyes. It's her standard birthday-card opening, and it's getting a little old. Just like I am. I continue, "'I know you're sixteen now, but in my heart you will always be my adorable little baby bundle.'" I glare at her over the paper. "Thanks, Mom."

She flushes. "Sorry. But it's the truth. Keep going."

"'That being said, I love and adore the man you are becoming and continue to become. And it is with this knowledge that I have organized a very special trip: a survivalist camping adventure for you and Hank to share together.'"

My heart nosedives. Seriously? A camping trip? With Hank?

"A camping trip?" Hank says, sounding as flabbergasted as I feel. "You didn't mention anything about—"

"Shh, Boogabear." Mom pats Hank's arm. "Let him finish."

I keep reading, though I'm no longer here. No longer in my body. "'Over Easter break, my two favorite men will get to know each other as you spend five days exploring the undisturbed backcountry of Idaho's Frank Church–River of No Return Wilderness. There you can bask in . . .'" There's a parenthetical CONT'D and a tiny arrow at the bottom of the page. I turn the sheet over and resume reading, "' . . . two point three million acres of untouched forest and prairie, which is home to untold wildlife including mountain lions, gray wolves, black bears, coyotes, elk, moose, lynx, big horn sheep, and countless others. No tents, no prepackaged food, no electronics, no modern conveniences at all. Just you and nature!'"

In the small blank space under these words, Mom has attempted to draw some trees, a few blades of grass, a campfire, and what look like puffy clouds with four legs, eyes, and half-moon smiles, which I'm pretty sure are meant to be the big-horned sheep. A few tiny floating hearts pepper the bucolic scene like loving pixie dust.

Tear it up. Rip it into a million pieces, throw them into the air, and let them rain down like confetti. She doesn't know you. If she knew you, she never would have done this to you—embarrassed you like this, put you in a situation like this. Invited this asshole into your life.

"Oh dear." Mom bites her lower lip, her eyes big. "Did I goof up? I thought you'd be so excited."

Ah, shit. She looks so vulnerable. Worried. Like I just told her I was thinking about spending Christmas at Charlie's house.

"No. Yeah," I say, twisting a smile onto my face. "I am. Totally. I just . . . wasn't expecting something so . . . awesome. It's great, Mom. Really. Amazing."

"Oh, phew." Mom lets out a relieved sigh, the excited glow returning to her face. "I mean, it took a lot of research, let me tell you. And quite a bit of money. But I found a company online that organizes the whole thing. The shuttle, the floatplane reservation, the guide, the permits, everything."

Hank turns to Mom. "You really should have run this by me, Sweetums. I have work and patients and appointments and—"

"I wanted it to be a surprise. For both of you. Your receptionist, Sally, helped me arrange it. She's rebooked all of your appointments that week, so you won't even be missed! Except by me, of course." Mom laughs.

"You talked to Sally?" Hank says, sounding dismayed. "She really shouldn't have—"

"It's going to be great," Mom insists. "You boys'll get some quality guy time in—you know, male bonding. Five days of hanging out, sleeping under the stars, fishing, cooking over a campfire. I'm telling you, I was pretty tempted to come along myself!"

Hank rubs his face. "It sounds . . . incredible. I just . . . I wish we could have spoken about this."

"I didn't want to ruin the surprise." Mom's body slumps a little. "I don't know, I thought you'd be happy about it."

"I am," Hank backpedals. "Absolutely. I just . . . didn't expect to be included in Dan's birthday present, that's all."

That makes two of us.

"It was incredibly sweet and thoughtful of you." Hank pats her arm. "It's going to be amazing." He turns to me. "Right, Dan?"

"Totally," I deadpan.

Hank laughs. "I mean, who doesn't love the great outdoors?"

Um, me. The birthday boy. I do not love, nor have I ever loved, the great outdoors. And I'd just assumed my own mother knew that about me. But I'm not going to be the one to break Mom's heart. I'll just have to find a way out of this: too much homework, the flu, a disfiguring bicycle accident. Something. Anything.

Mark my words: A survivalist camping trip with Hank is *never* going to happen.

Ever.

CHAPTER
7

"Is your mother insane?" Charlie says. "Is she not aware of the innumerable ways a person can die out in the wilderness?" He's hunched over a keyboard in the back corner of the dimly lit Computer Lab, the blue glow of the computer screen reflecting in his glasses. "We're talking an incredibly high probability of parasitic infection: giardiasis, cryptosporidiosis, and toxoplasmosis, just to name a few."

It's an hour before first bell. Charlie and I have come in early and are scrambling to make this week's newspaper deadline. Though I doubt anyone really cares. Circulation for the school paper is at an all-time low. Ninety percent of the copies wind up in the recycle bin, never having been picked up off the stacks in the lunchroom and library. The *Oracle* is on life support, and unless we find a way to turn things around, our principal, Mrs. Horvath, is going to pull the plug.

Not that it would be any skin off my nose. But it would completely devastate Charlie. He's beyond passionate about photography, and the *Willowvale Oracle* is the one avenue he has to get his work out to the public.

Hence Charlie's willingness to stoop so low as to start covering school athletics again.

"She was trying to be thoughtful," I say, furiously finishing this issue's comic. "But don't worry, I'm not going. I just have to figure out a way to bail without hurting her feelings."

"Wise decision." He pushes his glasses higher up on his nose and goes back to work, typing away like a madman. "Seriously. Think about it. You accidentally drink contaminated water, inadvertently touch some infected animal excrement and rub your eye, get stung by a West Nile–infected mosquito, and it's Happy Fucking Birthday, Dan. Enjoy sixteen because you can kiss seventeen good-bye." Charlie removes an SD card from his shirt pocket and slides it into the side of the computer. "And infection is just the tip of the iceberg. We haven't even discussed mud slides, hypothermia, flash floods, quicksand, lightning, snakebites, heatstroke, animal attacks, or—maybe worst of all—fecal impaction."

I grimace. "Do I even want to know?"

Charlie glances over at me. "Let me put it this way. People don't like egesting in the woods. They much prefer sitting on toilets and playing Angry Birds while they defecate. So they hold it when they go camping. For *days*. Combine that with extended bouts of physical activity, limited water intake, and

49

the consumption of unfamiliar, high-fiber foods, and you get a GI tract full of hardened excreta much too big and fossilized to void. Thus, fecal impaction. And blocked bowels equals loss of circulation, which leads to a slow, agonizing—not to mention humiliating—death." He grabs the mouse and starts uploading his photographs. "It's nothing you ever want to experience."

I erase an errant line. "Once again, your knowledge of the obscure and disgusting absolutely astonishes me."

"*Although*," Charlie says, clicking on the picture of the wrestling team. "It *would* be the perfect thing to completely freak out your future stepdad. Nothing will have him screaming 'I want no part of this family' quicker than having to dig rock-hard feces out of his future stepson's rectum with an index finger."

I glance over at Charlie, who is going to town on the wrestling team photo with the healing brush tool.

"What the hell are you doing?" I say.

"If Rick can make you suck on a jockstrap, the least I can do is make him appear as ill-endowed as a Ken doll."

I laugh and return to my drawing.

"You know," Charlie says after a while. "The more I mull over this camping trip of yours, the more I'm thinking that it might just be exactly what the good dentist ordered."

I look up from my sketchbook. "What are you talking about?"

"Think about it for a second. You'd get to spend almost an entire week with Hank. *Alone*. It's uninterrupted freak-out-the-future-stepdad time. Perhaps your mom actually *did* give you the perfect gift."

"You just got finished telling me I was probably going to

die on this trip," I say. "And now you're telling me you think I should go."

He shrugs. "It's a gamble, for sure. But if you're careful—and forearmed, which I can certainly help you with—it might be opportunity knock, knock, knocking on your door."

Charlie grabs the mouse and starts scrubbing again.

"I don't know. I barely survived trying to talk to Hank about my tiny testicles. I'm not sure I'm up to this scheme of yours."

"Embarrassment is good, Dan," he says. "The more embarrassed you are, the more believable your issues will seem. That's why this plan is ideal for you. It works to your strengths."

Charlie continues enacting revenge on the team photo: giving the players the slightest of potbellies, receding a few hairlines, adding some acne and a bit of protruding nose hair. As he does, he continues to talk about the opportunity that this wilderness trip could provide. And the more he talks, the more I realize that he might be on to something.

This *could* be the chance of a lifetime. Five days where Hank couldn't check in with Mom. Where he wouldn't be able to say anything to her about the uncomfortable things I ask him about—or ask him to do. How long till he comes to the realization that he just doesn't have the knack for this parenting thing?

Sure, I'm not exactly a fan of the natural world, but I might be willing to brave the elements for five days if it would mean slaying the villainous Fang Plaqueston once and for all.

But could I actually pull it off? Could I say and do the outrageous things Charlie will come up with—all of which I'm betting will be way worse than copping to having a microtesticle?

The solution hits me like a repulsor blast. "You have to come with me."

Charlie coughs. "I'm sorry, what? I don't think I heard you correctly."

"I said—"

"I was being facetious, Dan. I heard you quite clearly." Charlie swivels his chair away from his masterpiece. "And there's not a chance in Judecca I'm coming camping with you."

"It isn't camping," I correct. "It's a survivalist week in the wilderness. We're going to learn skills to keep us alive without any modern conveniences. With all your talk of end times, I'd think you'd jump at the chance to learn how to subsist off the land."

Charlie rolls his eyes. "I am not risking death by dysentery for information that can easily be obtained on the Internet. You, on the other hand, have a real reason to roll the diarrheal dice."

"You said you owed me, remember? 'You require anything, let me know.' I believe those were your words."

"Well, yes . . ." Charlie mumbles, shaking his head. "But I meant . . . help with a paper or putting in a good word with Erin." He waves a hand at the screen. "Revenge via Photoshop. That sort of thing."

"You said 'anything,'" I repeat.

"Yes, but—"

"You like my mom, Charlie, don't you?"

"Of course. Sarah has been like a second mother to me. But what does—"

"Do you really want to see her get her heart ripped out by some thug dentist?"

"Of course not. Which is why I—"

"And you care about the school paper, right? The floundering *Oracle*?"

"Sure, but I really don't see what that—?"

"Just think of the photo-essay you could publish based off our trip! To say nothing of the additions to your portfolio. Come on, Charlie. Come on this trip with me. Be my wingman and help me scare Hank away—and save me from getting Montezuma's revenge. Do it and we can call it even. What do you say?"

Charlie stares at the wrestling team photo. His mouth is moving but no words are coming out.

"Awesome," I say, clapping him on the shoulder. "I'll take that as a big yes."

CHAPTER 8

"OK," Charlie says, flipping open his spiral notebook and writing TORMENT CRUSADE: SUPPLEMENTARY MEASURES on the top of the page. "I've procured all of the supplies we will need for our larger-scale incursions next week. But we still have to put together a list of smaller strikes: more embarrassing questions you can ask Hank on a moment's notice, things like that."

"Don't you think the pranks we already came up with are enough?" I say.

"No, I do not." Charlie takes off his glasses. Rubs his eyes. "We want to systematically wear this fellow down." He puts his glasses back on. "The bigger salvos will put the cracks in the foundation. But sometimes it's the tiniest breeze that finally brings everything crumbling to the ground."

We are sitting in eighth-period Life Skills class, in the back of the room. It's the last day before Easter break. We're supposed to be working on this week's assignment: putting together a monthly household budget so we can learn the costs of living in the real world.

Instead, Charlie has decided that this would be the perfect time to put the finishing touches on our campaign of terror. Though, the way things are starting to shape up, I'm not sure who's going to be more terrorized, Hank or me.

"So," Charlie says. "Let's brainstorm." Charlie writes the word "COITUS" in his notebook. "We'll begin with the one subject everyone's ashamed of."

"I'm not sure if I can ask him any more sex stuff," I say, glancing over at Erin, sitting beside Gail. She's hunched over her notes, writing away furiously, casually scratching the side of her beautiful little nose. "It makes me feel too . . . skeeved out."

"Exactly," Charlie says. "Which is why you'll definitely want to hit the genitalia questions hard. It doesn't have to be too deviant—at least at first. For example, have him explain the difference between latex and lambskin condoms. Ask him how to do a proper foreskin cleaning or if you ever grow out of obsessive masturbation. Then later you can move on to things like penile implants and scrotal piercings."

Charlie excitedly adds these to the list.

"I really don't think I can do that."

"You can and you must," Charlie insists. "If *you're* embarrassed, just think how mortified *he'll* be. Parenting is not for the faint of heart. We need to teach him that."

"What else?" I say. "Besides sex stuff."

"All right, moving on." Charlie writes DRUGS AND ALCOHOL on another line. "At some point you'll want to ask him if he's ever smoked pot. Or done LSD. Or tried magic mushrooms. Ask him if he ever got drunk as a teenager. Then ask him how often. Parents hate talking about that kind of thing with their kids because they usually have to lie. And if we can catch him in a lie, we can use that as ammunition later."

I shift in my seat, my stomach gripping up.

"What about things I can *do*?" I say. "I'm much better at that than talking about stuff. Like getting him to leave the hockey game early because I had 'a stomachache.' That was fun."

Charlie nods. "OK. OK. You're more of an actor than an orator. We can work with that. How about biting your toenails when we're sitting around the campfire? Picking your nose and eating it? Constantly playing pocket polo?"

I sigh. At first, I really wanted Charlie's help. But I didn't expect him to get so into the whole thing. And now that he's committed himself to the trip—gotten over his initial terror of the contaminated wilderness—Charlie has been on a tear, arming himself with an arsenal of disinfectants and concocting countless pranks for me to pull on Hank.

"OK, class." Ms. Drizzler clears her throat. "We only have a few minutes left, so we'll go over your budgets when we return from vacation. In the meantime"—Ms. Drizzler opens her desk drawer and pulls out the little plastic baby carrier with the Baby-Real-A-Lot doll lying inside—"we need to decide who gets to care for our little class cutie over the break. Do I have any volunteers?"

Erin shoots her hand up immediately. "I'll take Baby Robbie, Ms. Drizzler."

Ms. Drizzler smiles. "You've already had your turn, Ms. Reilly."

"I know, but I love him so much," Erin says.

Several people in the class laugh. I grin dopily. She is so adorable.

"Yes," Ms. Drizzler says. "It certainly was evident by the perfect Care Score on your ID bracelet. And the fact that you named him. And printed up a birth certificate. And made a baby book. Not to mention the beautiful sweater you knitted. I have no doubt you will be an exemplary parent someday, Ms. Reilly. But I'm afraid it's time for one of your classmates to have a turn."

Ms. Drizzler turns to the rest of us. "Now, before you all go raising your hands at once, let me remind you that this assignment constitutes fifty percent of your final grade. So"—she holds up the baby—"who would like to volunteer?"

Nobody makes a move.

Erin bites her lower lip.

"Come, now," Ms. Drizzler says. "Don't be shy. You each have to watch the baby at some point. Do *not* make me have to assign a parent. I'll grade you much harsher if I do."

I stare down at the desk, classic I-can't-see-you-so-you-can't-see-me. There is no way in hell that I'm taking a baby—pretend or not—on a survival trip.

"I'll give you to the count of five," Ms. Drizzler says. "Then I'll simply stab my finger at my attendance roster, and that will be that. One . . . Two . . ."

Suddenly, I feel someone kick my ankle. I look over and see Charlie giving me a nod.

I frown at him.

"Do it," he whispers.

"What?" I mouth.

"The baby." Charlie lifts his chin toward the front of the room. "Volunteer."

I shake my head. "No way."

"Three," Ms. Drizzler calls out. "I'm not kidding about the harsher grade. I'll take two points off for every missed care or mishandled event. Four . . ."

"Do it for Hank," Charlie says under his breath. "We can foist the baby on him. It's the perfect I-never-want-to-be-a-parent tool. Go on! Before she assigns it to someone else."

"Aaaaaand, fi—"

I fire my hand into the air, instantly regretting it.

"Mr. Weekes." Ms. Drizzler smiles. "Excellent. Thank you. Now come on up here and collect your new son and your ID bracelet."

Charlie gives me a thumbs-up.

I stand and trudge to the front of the room, my head bowed, my eyes on the floor. I can't believe this. Why did I listen to him? This is going to make our trip so much more miserable than it was already going to be.

I grab the handle of the baby carrier and take the plastic ID bracelet, which will track how well I've looked after the doll.

"Take good care of Baby Robbie!" Erin calls out.

The class cracks up again.

I glance over at her. Her eyes are wide and moist, like she's just given up her only kid for adoption.

I force a smile and croak out a muted "I will."

I turn back to Charlie, who's rubbing his hands together like a cartoon villain.

My heart sinks as I suddenly realize that I've just told my first lie to Erin.

I will not be taking good care of Baby Robbie.

Because Charlie intends to destroy this child.

CHAPTER 9

"Baby-Real-A-Lot, Baby-Real-A-Lot," a child's soprano lilts as a girl cradles a tiny plastic infant in her arms. "He cries. He coos. He pees. He poos. Feed him. Cuddle him. Change him when he's wet. Baby-Real-A-Lot, as real as real can get!"

Out of nowhere, the girl hurls the baby across the room, its head banging against the door and exploding in a shower of plastic shards.

Jesus!

I bolt up in bed, my eyes flying open. The room is a Vaseline smear, mostly dark still. A slash of light coming from . . . somewhere.

Tap, tap, tap.

I turn my groggy head toward the sound.

"Time to get up."

What?

"Come on, guys." Hank's loud whisper comes from the hazy glow by the door. "We've got to grab some breakfast and get going. I've got doughnuts and coffee downstairs."

My mind starts to chug awake, like a train pushing away from the station. Oh, that's right. It's the first day of my birthday punishment—I mean, present.

"What time is it?" I croak.

"Four fifteen," Hank says. "Our shuttle'll be here in twenty. So, chop-chop. And remember, no electronics. I'm bringing my cell phone but only for emergencies."

"Yeah, OK," I say. "Be right there."

"Your mom's still asleep," Hank says. "So keep it down."

I roll over and click on my bedside lamp, the blast of light stinging my sleep-crusted eyes. I haul my legs around and place my feet on the floor. The room tilts a little. It feels like I've been clubbed over the head.

I yawn and rub the back of my cramped-up neck. God, I'm so tired. I would gladly give my *Sandman* box set for another ten minutes of sleep.

I reach for my dad's old watch and strap it on above the Baby-Real-A-Lot ID bracelet. The band on the watch is getting worn, floppy. I'm going to have to replace it soon.

"Wake up," I say to the mass curled up in the forest-green sleeping bag on my floor.

Charlie pokes his head out from inside the bag. "I never went to sleep." The low light from his iPad casts a blue glow on his smudged glasses. "I've been reading every survival book I could download: *No Doctor, No Problem: The Survivor's Guide to Wounds and Infection; The Ultimate SAS Survival Handbook; The U.S. Army Survival Manual;* and a dozen others."

"Why'd you bother? Between the guide and Hank, we'll be well taken care of."

"You can never be too prepared, Daniel. Speaking of which, I'm wondering if we might have time to swing by the twenty-four-hour pharmacy so I can pick up a few more supplies."

"We have to go straight to the airport."

He sighs. "OK, well, I guess we'll just have to make do with what we've got." He throws back the sleeping bag flap—he's fully dressed, never having gotten out of his street clothes—and starts rummaging inside his backpack, pulling out and stacking various boxes, tubes, and pill bottles: six bottles of alcohol gel, three types of analgesic, an intestinal sedative, oral antibiotics, antibiotic cream, two kinds of antihistamine, anti-diarrheal, anti-malaria tablets, potassium permanganate, Dramamine . . .

"You leave any room for clothes in there?" I ask.

"Mock all you like," Charlie says. "We'll see who's laughing at whom when you're hunched over a hole in the ground, violently voiding your watery, blood-soaked stools and pleading for a sip of my Kaopectate."

I laugh. "We're going to a national park, not the Australian outback."

"Ignorance is the silent killer, Dan," Charlie says, carefully repacking his medications. "And instead of worrying so much about me, I suggest you make sure that you're fully prepared to engage the enemy."

"Don't worry," I say. "I'm all set."

"You've got your dummy sketchbook?" he asks.

I nod.

"And your carry-on items?"

"All packed."

"Did you memorize the list of code words I gave you?" Charlie asks.

I sigh. "Yes, Charlie. I'll listen out for them."

He cocks an eyebrow. "And Baby Robbie?"

"Locked and loaded." I hold up the Baby-Real-A-Lot doll, clad in a fresh diaper and the blue-and-white baby sweater that Erin made, and press the initiate button on my ID bracelet.

The doll's eyes flutter open. It makes a little cooing noise. I grab the tiny bottle and begin feeding it.

Charlie spent a few hours yesterday working on the baby. He managed to hack into the doll's programming so he could increase the frequency and force of its "biological" functions. Then we replaced the colored water in the baby's bottle with a chocolate yogurt drink. Finally, Charlie loosened the joints at the baby's shoulders and hips.

Charlie has triple-promised me that he'll be able to alter the Care Score on my ID bracelet before we go back to school. I'm praying he's right, or I'm going to fail big-time.

I look down at the little bundle in my arms. It's probably just my imagination, but I do see a bit of Erin in his features: his nose, his mouth. I feel a twinge of guilt for what we're about to do.

"Are you sure this is going to work?" I ask, squeezing the bottle to get the rest of the thick brown goo into the baby's mouth.

"Trust me," Charlie says. "That kid's a ticking time bomb."

And, as if on cue, Baby Robbie blows a massive, sputtering cheeser, his instantly full diaper vibrating in my hands.

"Jesus," I say.

Charlie grins and waggles his eyebrows. "Let the games begin."

CHAPTER
10

"I'm not really sure how this works."

Hank has the wailing Baby Robbie on the kitchen table. He fumbles with the loaded diaper, trying to figure out how to get it off. Some of the "poo" is starting to leak down its legs. "Is there any way to keep him quiet while we do this?" Hank glances at the ceiling; Mom's bedroom is directly above us.

"Not until we've got him cleaned up," I say.

Charlie is busy snapping photos of the scene with his camera. The flash blasting our eyes with each shutter click.

"Could you please stop with that?" Hank says, blinking hard. "You're blinding me."

"I am a photojournalist, Mr. Langston," Charlie states, rifling off several more shots. "I have vowed to document our entire trip for the school newspaper. The photo-essay from this excursion could be the very thing that saves the *Willowvale Oracle*."

"Yes, well." Hank squints, holding up his hand. "Could you maybe turn off the flash?"

"Would you ask Martin Parr or Diane Arbus to turn off their flashes?" Charlie asks, exploding another burst of light in Hank's face.

"I don't know even know who—"

"Trust me, you wouldn't," Charlie says, blasting Hank yet again.

"Jesus Christ." Hank rubs his eyes and peers down at the squawking baby. He exhales loudly. "All right. There's got to be a trick to this."

"They showed us how to do it in class," I say. "But everyone was crowded around and I couldn't see very well. I thought you'd know how."

"I haven't had much experience with this sort of thing." Hank flips the baby onto its belly, then onto its back again. "It can't be that hard. Let me look it up on my phone." He wipes his hands fastidiously on his pants, even though he hasn't actually encountered any of the yogurt surprise yet, then unclips his gleaming phablet and starts typing. "OK. Wait. Yes. Right. Got it." Hank lays down his phone well away from the doll and finds the clear sticky strips at the waist, pulls them back, and carefully slides the soggy, brown-stained diaper off.

Finally, Baby Robbie stops crying.

Hank breathes a deep sigh of relief. "Thank God." Then he tilts his head as he notices Baby Robbie's tiny plastic penis. "Wow. They really went all out on the verisimilitude, huh?"

And just like that, the baby sprays a gusher of whiz into Hank's eyes.

"Jesus," Hank splutters, grabbing a Duke of Donuts napkin and swiping at his face.

Charlie quickly raises his camera and snaps a dozen more shots. "Good thing my Nikon is waterproof."

The doll is screaming again, shrieking like we're stabbing it repeatedly with a butcher knife.

Another one of Charlie's hacks: making the cries infinitely louder and more shrill.

"Hank," I plead, pointing to my ID bracelet. "We have to get him dry and dressed."

"We will, we will. Give me a clean diaper," he says, blinking wildly as he mops the baby's nether regions with the doughnut napkin. "Quickly. Before he erupts again."

I hand him the disposable diaper that Charlie and I superglued shut. Hank snatches it from me and starts to wrestle with it, trying to pull apart the cemented tabs.

Baby Robbie lets out a long, hoarse screech that sounds like a Godzilla roar.

"Goddamn it." Hank's face is red, his fingers contorted. "Something's . . . not . . ." He yanks the diaper hard, tearing the thing in two. "Another one." He holds out his shaking hand. "Hurry. Before it wakes your—"

"What's going on down here?" Mom stands in the doorway,

her eyes half shut, her bathrobe clutched around her. "Did we have a baby that nobody told me about?" Her voice is groggy. And more than a little annoyed.

"It's OK, hon." Hank waves the diaper at her. "Go back to sleep. I've got it covered."

"It's a school project," I say. "I have to take care of a Baby-Real-A-Lot doll for a week."

"*This* week?" Mom says. "On your trip?"

"Believe me," I say. "I wasn't expecting it."

"*Hah!* Got it!" Hank shouts, flicking the diaper open. He makes fast work of getting the baby swaddled.

And finally Robbie is silent once more.

"Well," Mom rasps. "Good luck with that. I'm going back to bed. Have a safe flight."

She starts to go.

"Sarah, wait," Hank says. He looks at me, then looks at Mom, who's turning back toward us.

"Yes?" Mom says.

"Uhh, I'm just . . . thinking out loud here, but . . ." Hank looks at me again. "What if . . . what if your mom looked after the baby this week?"

"Excuse me?" Mom says, her eyes suddenly wide.

"Yeah, what?" I say. Mom can't take Baby Robbie. That'll ruin everything!

"It *is* Dan's birthday present," Hank explains. "This trip. And I can't imagine this is what you had in mind when you set it up. So maybe, well, maybe you taking care of the baby could be part of the gift."

"I have work, Hank," Mom states. "I can't be looking after a toy baby."

"It's just a little feeding." Hank says. "A little changing."

Mom laughs. "Tell that to your sweaty brow."

"Well, that's just because I've never done this before," Hank says. "But you have. And I bet you were great at it!"

"I don't know." Mom looks at me sympathetically. "I suppose I could. Since it is your birthday gift—"

"I'm sorry, Ms. Weekes, but I can't let you do that," Charlie interjects, pushing his glasses up onto his nose. "I hate to put a damper on these plans, but, technically, it would be cheating for you to take care of the doll."

Hank laughs. "Come on, Charlie. You have to admit that we have extenuating circumstances here."

"Yeah, Charlie," I say. "If Hank's OK with cheating, then I'm OK with it."

"Now, hold on." Hank raises his hand. "I didn't say I was OK with cheating."

Mom smirks and crosses her arms. "What *were* you saying, Boogabear?"

"I was saying . . ." Hank wafts his hand in the air. "That . . . given the situation we're in . . . and the fact that we were afforded no prior notice of having to look after this baby . . . I think that we have just cause in making other arrangements for . . . little Robbie."

I stare at Hank long and hard, well past the point of comfort, trying my best to look like I'm searching my soul. Finally, I shake my head and turn away, like I'm ashamed. "Charlie's right. I'm supposed to look after this baby. A little help is OK, but the main responsibility has to fall on me, or I won't be learning anything." I look at Mom. "I appreciate you considering it, Mom. But I can't just take the easy way out when things get hard."

She smiles at me. "That's very mature of you, Dan." She gives Hank the stink eye before heading back upstairs.

Mature? Right! If she only knew . . .

CHAPTER 11

I stand with my arms outstretched and my legs splayed as a shark-eyed TSA officer runs his scanner wand up and down my body. I've already been through the metal detector four times. Each time the beep went off and the red light flashed. Each time I removed some piece of metal I "forgot" I had on me.

Keys. Nail clippers. A bottle opener. A piece of hematite that Charlie gave me.

Charlie and Hank wait off to the side, Hank checking his humongous watch for the umpteenth time. When the TSA dude finally waves me through, I go to grab Baby Robbie and my sling bag from the conveyor belt.

"May I look in this?" a bushy-browed guard says, gripping my carry-on with his blue-latex-gloved hands.

I'd been worried that they wouldn't flag my bag for inspection and that all of our careful planning—and packing—would be for naught. But obviously I worried for nothing.

"Why?" I ask, cradling the whimpering Baby Robbie.

"The machine is showing some suspect items inside," he says.

"Suspect? Like what?"

"That's what I need to identify." He lifts my bag. "May I?"

Hank and Charlie approach.

"What's going on?" Hank asks.

"Can you hold Baby Robbie, please?" I say, thrusting the doll into Hank's arms.

"Uh . . . sure," Hank says, reluctantly. "But what's the holdup?"

I gesture at the TSA officer. "This guy wants to look in my bag."

"Well, let him," Hank says, holding the baby in one arm and glancing at his watch on the other. "We don't want to miss our flight."

"Yeah, come on, Dan," Charlie says. "What's the big deal?"

"It's just . . . There's . . . I don't . . ." Finally, I sigh. Throw my hands in the air. "Whatever. Fine. Go ahead."

The guard unzips my bag, reaches inside, and pulls out a Swiss Army knife.

"We're going on a survivalist camping trip for five days," I say. "That's gonna come in real handy."

Hank winces. "You can't take that on the plane, Dan."

"What? Why?" I say, looking between Hank and the TSA officer.

"It's a prohibited item, sir," the officer explains. "No sharp objects allowed."

"But . . . it's my dad's," I lie.

The officer looks over at Hank, who laughs nervously.

"His . . . other dad," Hank says. "I'm the step- . . . or . . . will be . . . soon . . . eventually."

The agent puts the knife aside and reaches into my bag again.

This time he removes a large bottle of Jergens Soothing Aloe hand lotion. Followed by . . . a second large bottle of Jergens Soothing Aloe hand lotion.

The TSA officer gives me a look.

I swallow nervously, gesturing at the lotion. "That's—"

"An *emollient*," Charlie interjects.

"I have . . . eczema." I stare at the ground. My insides twisting up.

"Eczema?" The officer raises his thumb-thick eyebrows as he puts the two full bottles of lotion next to the knife.

"It's a skin condition," Hank says. "I told you to put those in your checked baggage, Dan."

Well played, Hank. He's keeping it surprisingly cool. But I'm struggling to hold up my end of the performance. My toes curl thinking about what's coming next.

The TSA officer says nothing. Just peers back into my bag, then pinches up a giant wad of stuck-together tissues, the crumpled mass doing a little slow-motion pirouette in the air. The officer wrinkles up his nose.

I wrench a smile onto my face. "Those are . . . my, uh . . ." I sniffle. "I've got, you know, bad allergies."

The agent drops the clump of tissues onto the metal counter with a muffled thump. He scans the inside of my bag and removes a family-size box of Kleenex Ultra Soft.

"I like the, uh, the softer ones," I mumble, my chest tightening up. "They're gentler on my . . . nose." Another swallow.

I glance over at Hank, whose face is bright pink. He's looking down, acting like he's tending to the baby's needs.

The TSA officer clears his throat.

I look back at him. Force a laugh.

"We're going to have to confiscate the knife," he says. "And the bottles of lotion. You can keep the box of tissues and"—he looks down at the mass of stuck-together Kleenex—"that. But everything else has to stay here."

"What?" I blink. "I get the knife. I wasn't thinking. But . . ." My head starts to spin. I feel like the whole world is staring at me. "How am I supposed to, you know"—I lower my voice—"moisturize?"

"I'm very sorry," the TSA officer says, not sounding sorry at all. "But the bottles far exceed the permitted three-point-four-ounce limit."

Just then a no-nonsense female voice comes over the loudspeaker: "This is the preboarding announcement for Alaska Airlines flight number two-four-zero-four to Boise. Those passengers with small children and anyone requiring special assistance should begin boarding at this time through gate twenty-eight. Regular boarding will commence in approximately five minutes."

Hank finally looks at me, his face still cherry-pie-filling red.

"Come on, Dan. Just leave it. We don't have time for any more delays."

And just like that, Robbie rips a mighty wet rumbler, the entire contents of his belly slopping from his ill-fitting diaper all down the front of Hank's pants.

CHAPTER 12

We are running. The three of us. Tearing through the terminal at top speed, dodging suitcase draggers, sunglasses kiosks, shoe-shine stalls, and special-offer credit-card vendors.

We've each got our carry-on bags in tow, and Hank, the front of his pants drenched from the clean-up, has the yowling Baby-Real-A-Lot doll tucked under his arm like a football.

Once again it took much longer to change Baby Robbie than it should have—thanks in large part to several more doctored diapers. Hank was practically pulling his hair out with frustration as the three of us stood around the changing table in the men's room, tossing aside diaper after useless diaper, all while

Baby Robbie screamed bloody murder and I fretted loudly about the neglect points I was racking up on my ID bracelet. I've never seen Hank so close to losing it.

"This is the last and final boarding call," a female gate attendant announces, "for Alaska Airlines flight two-four-zero-four to Boise. All passengers should board at gate twenty-eight. Final checks are being completed, and the captain is about to order the doors of the aircraft closed."

"Hurry!" Hank shouts, pumping his arms faster. "We miss this flight, we miss the trip."

I look down at my ID bracelet strapped below my dad's old Timex. "You're shaking Robbie too hard. I'm getting mistreatment points."

"Aw, Christ." Hank takes the baby from under his arm and holds him against his shoulder, like a real baby.

Baby Robbie immediately stops crying.

We sprint past gates seventeen, eighteen, nineteen . . .

"Jesus," Hank huffs, his head twisted toward the gate numbers. "It has to be at the end of the terminal, of course."

Just then Charlie trips and goes flying, his body and his backpack tumbling over each other like he was thrown from a speeding car.

I stop. Look back.

Charlie reaches a hand in the air like he's drowning. He wheezes, "Go on . . . without me! Don't miss . . . the plane! I'll get . . . a taxi home."

"Like hell!" I race back to Charlie, grab his outstretched arm, and yank him to his feet. "You're not bailing on me now."

"Stop messing around!" Hank hollers over his shoulder, still trucking it toward the far end of the terminal, the baby jiggling on his shoulder. "Move!"

"You have . . . the list. And my . . . supplies," Charlie says. "You don't . . . need me anymore."

"That stuff is useless if I freeze up," I say. "I need you egging me on. Besides, you owe me, remember?"

Charlie sighs and hoists his backpack onto his shoulders. "I guess . . . it's nice to be needed."

I stagger off once more, dragging a stumbling Charlie behind me.

"Wait!" Hank bellows to the Alaska Airlines agent as she's shutting the doors to gate twenty-eight. "Don't close that! We're here. We're here." Hank turns and waves Charlie and me forward toward the empty waiting lounge. "Come on, guys."

The agent *tsk*s us. "Cutting it pretty close, aren't we, fellas?" But she pulls the glass door open again, then stands behind the podium to scan our tickets.

"Thank you . . . so much," Hank says, trying to catch his breath.

"Cute . . . doll?" the attendant says, furrowing her brow.

"Oh." Hank flushes. "Yeah, it's, uh, a school project. My stepson's. Here." He passes Baby Robbie to me, then pulls our boarding passes from his pocket and hands them to the agent. "Thanks again. We really appreciate it."

The agent takes the tickets, scans them, and gives him a twinkling grin. "My pleasure."

I guess these are the times when it really helps if you look like a handsome movie star.

"Holy moly." Hank huffs and puffs as we head down the

Jetway and wipes his sweaty brow. "That was too close for comfort."

"Truly," Charlie says, fastening a surgical mask over his nose and mouth. "Let's just hope this doesn't augur a disastrous trip."

"What's with the mask, Charlie?" Hank asks.

I guffaw. "Yeah, you planning on performing an operation on the flight or something?"

"How very amusing, Daniel," Charlie says as we step onto the plane, his voice muffled through the mask. "Airplanes are one of the world's largest breeding grounds for bacteria and germs. You're one hundred and thirteen times more likely to catch rhinovirus or influenza during a flight than during your normal daily life." He tugs a pair of rubber gloves from his pocket and snaps them on as we make our way down the aisle. "I'm just taking the proper precautions."

I shrug, watching the other passengers stare at him. "I guess if you don't mind looking like a freak."

"Yes, Daniel, I'm the freak." Charlie shoots me a look over his shoulder. "This from the person cradling a relentlessly defecating toy child. The same individual who tried smuggling a year's supply of hand lotion onto the plane."

"All right, guys," Hank says. "Enough. How about we just relax and have some peace and quiet for the rest of the flight, hmm?" He rubs his temple. "I could sure use a break."

Fat chance of that, buddy. We're just getting started here.

CHAPTER 13

We find our seats and strap in. Charlie takes the window so I can sit across the aisle from my future stepdad.

I settle Baby Robbie in my lap, then take out another bottle filled with chocolate Yo-Gulp and shove it into his mouth. He starts to drain the thing dry almost immediately.

Meanwhile Charlie is swabbing his video screen, tray table, seat belt, and armrests with a handful of disinfectant wipes. The harsh bleach smell burns my sinuses.

I cough. "Jesus, Charlie. Really?"

"You should do the same," he says. "Sanitizing your surroundings is the first line of defense."

I give my seat belt the tug test as the plane backs away from the gate. "I'm more worried about falling out of the sky than catching a cold," I say, loud enough for Hank to hear me.

"Excuse me?" A female flight attendant with big hair and too much makeup stands over me. "I'm going to have to ask you to put your little dolly either in the overhead compartment or under the seat in front of you."

"Oh," I say, flushing. "Yeah. This isn't a doll. It's a Baby-Real-A-Lot. It's for school. If I put him under the seat or in the overhead, he'll start crying." I hold up my wristband. "And I'll be docked compassion points."

"I see." She fake-smiles at me, her makeup mask cracking at the corners of her mouth. "Well, then, I'll have to ask you to hold him like a real baby when we take off, OK? In the burping position, with your hand supporting his head. Would you like me to show you how?"

I shake my head. "Nah, I got it."

Another foundation-fracturing grin. "Excellent." She pats my shoulder and continues down the aisle.

I pull the empty bottle from Robbie's mouth and return it to my bag. Then I turn to Hank. "Can you show me the burping position?"

Hank's got a camping magazine open in his lap. He looks over at me. "I thought you told the flight attendant you knew how to do it?"

"Yeah." I twist around and look back down the aisle. Then whisper, "But that's because I was embarrassed."

"Well, just turn him around," Hank says. "So he's looking over your shoulder. Hold him to your chest. Support his head and bottom with your hands."

I furrow my brow. "I don't get it." I hold up the baby. "Can you just show me, please?"

Hank exhales. Shuts his magazine. "Sure." He reaches out and takes the doll from me. "I've never really done it myself. But I've seen my sister do it." Hank turns Baby Robbie toward him and does exactly what he told me to do. "See. No big deal."

"Why does she want me to hold him like that?" I ask, stalling for time.

"I don't know," Hank says. "I guess so he doesn't go flying across the plane if we stop suddenly."

Baby Robbie starts to whine.

"Dang it. Again?" I look at my ID bracelet. "Could you pat his back a little? Before my neglect score goes even higher."

Hank gives the baby's back a few taps. Baby Robbie whimpers even louder.

"You have to jiggle him a bit," I instruct.

Hank holds the doll out to me. "Why don't you do it? We wouldn't want to cheat you out of the experience, now would we?"

The plane starts picking up speed. Racing down the runway.

"Oh, boy," I say, pressing back into the seat. "We're going." I clench my eyes shut. "Could you hold him for takeoff, please? I have to . . . focus. I don't really love flying so much." I swallow. "I'll take him back when we're in the air. I promise."

I sit stock-still. Eyes closed. Doing my best to look terrified.

To my right, I hear my baby crying. Louder. And louder.

I open one eye and see Hank frantically jiggling and patting the weeping doll.

Hank looks at me with a pained expression. "He's not wet. And you just fed him. I don't know what he wants."

And just like that, Robbie blows his baby brack all over Hank's shoulder, the snotty, sepia spew oozing down his back.

"Lovely," Hank says, cringing.

I reach my hands out. "Here, I'll take him."

"Sure," Hank says, looking into the infant's suddenly silent, sick-smeared face. "After I take the barf shower and get him all settled down."

In response, Baby Robbie shoots another powerful geyser of hurl all over the front of Hank's shirt.

"Jesus." Hank holds the baby out like it's radioactive. "It's like this thing's possessed or something."

The lady in the powder-blue jumpsuit sitting next to Hank looks even more horrified than he does. She hugs the window, trying to avoid any collateral damage.

Charlie's got his camera out, snapping a series of action shots, the flash popping over and over again. "This is exactly why Ms. Drizzler wants us to do this exercise," he says. "To show us just how difficult it is to be a parent."

Hank pulls a face. "Yeah. I can see how it would be an effective mode of birth control. Here. I've done my tour of duty for the day." He hands the baby off to me, then removes the barf bag from his seat-back pocket and uses it to wipe the brown sludge from his doused shirt. "At least it's a short flight."

Yes, but it's going to be a long week, Hank.

A very long week.

CHAPTER 14

When we arrive at carousel number three, everyone from our flight is greeted by someone—with hugs, kisses, and whoops of delight.

We, however, are met by no one. Our representatives from My Woodland Trek Adventures—the grinning, chapeaued, and bevested greeters from the website—are missing in action. According to the description, they were meant to meet us "with snacks and smiles" before dumping us off at some lake where our "beautifully restored" bush plane is awaiting our arrival.

"They'll be here," Hank says, reading my mind. He flips his wrist to check his mega-watch. "Maybe they got caught in traffic."

"Or were killed in a fifty-car pileup," Charlie offers as he removes his surgical mask and gloves.

"Right," Hank says. "Though, unlikely."

"Not as unlikely as you'd think," Charlie corrects. "There were nearly six million car accidents last year in the United States alone. That's one every five seconds."

"I'm sure our people are fine."

"And I was sure my parents would be fine," Charlie says matter-of-factly, "when they drove off for their anniversary dinner. But forty thousand people die in the United States from automobile accidents every year. That's over a hundred people a day. One every fifteen minutes. It's almost like a plane crash every twenty-four hours. Ponder that a moment. If a plane crashed every single day, do you think anyone would want to fly ever again? And yet we get into these rolling death machines willy-nilly. Even if our hosts *do* arrive, it's entirely possible we'll be killed on the drive to our next destination. It might actually be better if they *don't* show up."

Hank's eyebrows are squished together. "Wait, what was that about your parents?"

"Charlie's parents died in a car crash," I say, feigning impatience. "Five years ago. I told you that."

"What? No. I don't . . . think so." Hank swallows. "Jesus, Charlie. I'm so sorry." He looks at me. "I really don't think you ever said anything about that—"

"Yes, I did," I lie. "When I asked you if Charlie could come on the trip, I said it would be really good for him to be around a father figure, since Mom's been his only real parental influence for the last five years. Well, and his grandparents, of

85

course, but they're, you know, old." I sigh. "I guess you weren't listening."

It feels wrong using Charlie's parents' accident as a way to make Hank feel terrible. But it was Charlie's idea, and he claims they would've fully supported us in our efforts to rid the Weekes family of the detestable dentist.

Hank turns to Charlie. "I really am very sorry. I honestly don't recall . . . I mean, I think I would have remembered that . . . God . . ." He runs his hand through his hair. "I feel awful—"

"It's OK, Mr. Langston," Charlie says. "I'm sure you've had a lot of things on your mind lately, what with the wedding planning and the fun camping trip and all."

Just then the conveyor belt on the baggage carousel groans to life. As Hank hauls our packs from the conveyor, Charlie digs around in his carry-on, finds a small brown dropper bottle, and surreptitiously hands it over to me.

"I'm going to the bathroom," I announce as soon as I pocket the bottle. I hold the Baby-Real-A-Lot out to Hank. "Can you take Robbie?"

Hank grimaces. "Maybe Charlie would like a turn."

Charlie holds up his hands. "I'm going to have to respectfully decline. I took my turn the very first week of school, before the filthy masses got their paws on it. And even then I wore rubber gloves the entire time. But now that thing is a festering petri dish teeming with untold quantities of bacteria. I'd sooner suck on a kitchen sponge."

"Right." Hank sighs. "OK. Give it to me." He yanks the baby from me.

"Careful," I say, glancing at my ID bracelet. "Abuse points count double."

"I'm not abusing him," Hank says. "However, if he poops his diaper again, I won't be changing him. He'll have to wait until you get back."

"But that'll raise my neglect score," I say.

Hank cocks his head. "Well, then, you'd better make it quick."

"Jeez," I say, raising my eyebrows. "I sure hope you and Mom aren't planning on having kids."

If Hank isn't questioning his parenting abilities now, just wait until I treat him to a lungful of Liquid Limburger.

CHAPTER 15

On my way back from the bathroom, I stop by the newsstand to pick up some supplies for a future incursion: a mini-sleeve of sour-cream-and-onion Pringles, some Skittles, a bag of barbecue Fritos, some beef jerky, a pack of peanut butter cups, and a 3 Musketeers bar. The trembling old man behind the counter screws his face up and gags when my cheese-scented armpit stink hits him, but I pretend to be oblivious.

By the time I return to Hank and Charlie, the baggage claim area is nearly empty and they've taken up a perch on a bench by the door.

I plop my bag of goodies on the seat beside Hank, making sure not to stand too close—not yet.

"He started fussing again," Hank says, leaning forward and handing Robbie over to me. "Didn't soil his diaper, though. I checked. He probably just needs some rocking or burping."

"Thanks," I say. I glance at the blank screen on my ID bracelet and saucer my eyes. "Holy crap! Did you . . . Did you hit him? Or drop him or something?"

"No," Hank says, shaking his head. "No way."

"Why am I'm getting a 'gross mistreatment' warning?" I lie, tapping the empty bracelet display. "Apparently, I'll be receiving a visit from child services."

"Nothing happened," Hank insists.

"Well, *something* happened," I say, unwrapping the blanket to check Robbie for damages. As soon as the blanket's removed, the doll's left leg falls off, clattering to the floor. "Jesus Christ, Hank! You dismembered him!"

"I did nothing of the sort. I swear!" Hank looks over at Charlie for support. "We just sat here, right? Tell him."

"Hank held the baby very gingerly, Dan," Charlie says.

Hank looks up at me. "See?"

"At least whilst I was here," Charlie says. "Of course, I did spend five minutes hacking the 'Healthy Choices' vending machine. They were pretty tricky with their codes but, as Benjamin Franklin once said, 'Energy and persistence conquer all things.'" Charlie holds up a pack of apple chips and an organic pomegranate juice.

"I can't believe this! I'm totally screwed. Not only am I going to fail Life Skills, but I'll probably get detention for damaging him." I snatch up the leg and try to fit it back into place. As I do, one of his arms drops off.

The three of us stare as the little baby limb rattles on the linoleum.

"OK," Hank says, rubbing his face. "Obviously, the doll is defective."

"He was fine when I took him home." I glare at Hank. "Are you *sure* nothing happened? Maybe you bumped into something. Dropped him when you were putting him down."

"I never put him down," Hank says, exasperated. "I held him gently the entire time."

"Sure, OK," I say, my voice laced with suspicion. I bend over and snatch up the arm. "Although . . ." I gesture with the tiny appendage. "Now that I think about it, you were pretty annoyed when I asked you to look after him. I'm just saying."

Hank blinks at me. "I'd never hurt your baby, Dan. Doll or otherwise. He must be damaged from all the students handling him."

"Yeah, maybe." I push the limb back into its socket, then wrap the blanket back around the baby and sit down next to Hank. "Though I doubt Ms. Drizzler will buy that excuse."

I lean back and start rocking the baby in one arm. "So, any word from our escorts?" I scoot closer to Hank and rest my free arm on the bench back behind him.

"I tried calling the number I have, but—" Hank's nose spasms. He coughs and shifts over a bit. "I just . . . got their voice mail. We should be OK, though. I confirmed everything before we left." He coughs again, then "casually" looks over his shoulder at the teeming rain outside—away from my *eau de armpit*. "Probably just got held up by the weather."

"Over a quarter of all car crashes are weather related," Charlie informs us.

Hank nods. "All we can do is hope for the best." He grabs his copy of *Outdoor Life* and opens it. "Let's just relax and . . . enjoy the nice Muzak for a while." He turns so that most of his back is to me.

After a couple of minutes, I manage to get Baby Robbie to sleep. I place the doll on the seat beside me, then pull out my dummy sketchbook and pencils from my bag. Might as well get some work done while we wait.

I turn to a clean page near the back and start in on some drawing, angling the sketchbook so that Hank can't see my real sketches if he glances my way.

The next set of panels is going to be a kick-ass action sequence: Princess Erilin and Sir Stan leading the Royal Infantry into battle with the Night Goblin and his army of Hobgobblers.

This scene is key. Every graphic novel needs a few really spectacular eye-catching moments. If I can get the details right here, I think I have a real chance of getting this book published. And wouldn't *that* be supremely impressive to an art school admissions board.

Not to mention to a certain gorgeous girl I know.

I glance over and smile at the slumbering Baby Robbie, swaddled in the tiny sweater Erin knitted. With yarn she held in her very own hands.

And once again, I get a serious pang of guilt. If Erin had any idea what we'd done to her child so far—what we *plan* to do to him—she'd never forgive me. Charlie had better be right when he said he can reprogram my ID bracelet to make it look like Baby Robbie was nothing but pampered the entire week.

I'm about to return to working on my sketch when Charlie clears his throat dramatically, like he's got a five-pound hairball stuck in his windpipe.

Hank and I turn and stare at him. Charlie smiles apologetically. "Sorry. This canned air is murder on my *cilia*."

Hank turns back to his magazine, but Charlie holds my gaze, giving me a loaded look.

"You don't want to harm your *cilia*," he says, sniffing loudly. "That could be quite unpleasant."

I gulp and put my sketchbook back into my bag.

I take a deep breath. "Hank?"

"Hmm?" Hank glances up from his magazine.

"I was wondering . . ." I start. "Do you . . . do you know how to dance?"

"Dance?" He peers at me. "What do you mean?"

"Dance," I repeat. "You know. Like, with a girl."

He laughs. "Well, I wouldn't say I'm *Saturday Night Fever* good, but—"

"I don't know what that means," I say.

"Before your time." Hank shakes his head. "Anyway, I do know a step or two. Why?"

"Can you show me?" I ask.

His eyebrows shoot up. "Show you?"

I stare down at the ground. "I just . . . the thing is . . . there's this dance at school. And there's this girl I'd like to ask, only I've never slow-danced before. So I was wondering . . . Can you show me how to do it?"

92

"Sure thing, bud," he says. "Your mom and I'll give you a lesson when we get home. We'll have you in school-dance form in no time." He leans back and raises his magazine again, like the subject is closed.

"Yeah, the thing is," I say, "the dance is the night we get back." I swallow. "Is there any way we could do it, like, now?"

Hank slides his eyes toward me. "*Right* now?" He glances around at the near-empty baggage claim area.

I nod. "If it's too much of a bother . . ."

"No," Hank says, clearing his throat. "It's just . . . Well . . ."

Charlie leans forward. "I wouldn't mind getting a few pointers myself."

Hank sighs heavily. "I, uh, I guess I can show you guys the basics." He places his magazine down and stands. "All right, let me think here." He pinches the bridge of his nose. "OK. So. You want to have very good posture. That's key." Hank straightens up and elongates his neck. "You'll position yourself so you're looking over the girl's right shoulder. Then you want to get into hold. So the man's left hand takes the woman's right hand, palms facing each other."

"Unless, of course it's two men dancing," Charlie corrects. "Or two women. We do live in the twenty-first century, Mr. Langston."

"Right, well, in that case," Hank says. "Whoever's the *lead* dancer will use their left hand, while the non-lead dancer will use their right. Then the lead dancer's right hand"—he curves his arm around his imaginary partner's shoulder—"is placed on the non-lead dancer's left shoulder blade. And the non-lead dancer puts her—or his—hand on the lead dancer's right shoulder.

Then you guide your partner in a simple box step in time to the music." Hank starts dancing to the canned version of "Piano Man" playing over the airport speakers. "One-two-three, one-two-three, one-two-three, one-two-three." He stops and lowers his hands. "Just like that."

"I'm not really sure I get it," I say, standing and stepping into his personal space, my gamy bouquet billowing around my body like a stink cloud. "Can we practice it together?"

"Oh, um . . ." Hank says, blinking hard and taking a step back, casually rubbing his nostrils with the tips of his fingers. "Well . . ."

"I'm more of a hands-on learner." I take a step closer and hold up my arms like I'm ready to dance with him, exposing my putrid pits to his face.

"I don't think, uh—" Hank retches a little. "I'm not sure that . . ."

"You don't want to help me?" I say, dropping my arms.

"It's not . . . th-that," Hank stammers, hacking. "It's just that . . . It's . . . Did you, um . . . This morning . . . When you got up . . . Did you put on . . . ?"

"Did I put on what?" I ask, the picture of innocence.

He rubs the back of his neck. "You know what? Never mind."

"I get it," I say dejectedly. "It's too much of a hassle. No big deal. I just won't go to the dance. She probably wouldn't have said yes anyway."

"Wait, Dan," Hank says, his voice all nasal, like he's mouth breathing. "It's OK. We can do this."

"You sure?" I ask, looking all bright-eyed and hopeful.

Hank nods. "Mmm-hmm. But, uh, let's make it quick, OK? In case our escorts show up." He grabs my arms and repositions my hands, all the while holding his breath. "You be the non-lead first. Then we can switch." He turns his head away from me, breathing the air from another direction. "That feel OK?"

"It's a little awkward," I say. I step even closer to him. "There. That's better."

"OK. Good." He gags and clears his throat like he's just sucked in an insect.

"Are you all right?" I ask.

"Fine, fine," Hank says. "So, just follow my lead. As I step, you do the reverse. Got it?"

"Yeah. I think so."

"Good." Hank's brow is beading with sweat and his complexion is pale. "Let's . . ." He swallows. "Let's give it a try."

Hank starts to move me backward, then sideways. I make a point to step on his feet. We stumble. I fall forward and press my cheese-tainted body up close to his.

"Don't fight me," Hank says, wheezing.

"Sorry," I say, and raise my elbows high like chicken wings.

Hank suppresses a dry heave. "Just follow my lead."

As he guides me forward, I take an exaggerated step and "accidentally" knee him in the balls.

"*Ooof!*" Hank folds over and hacks.

"Oh, God," I say. "Sorry-sorry-sorry. Are you OK?"

I lean over to help, planting my polluted underarm in his face.

"I'm fine," Hank rasps. "Please. Just . . ." He staggers backward. "I think we . . . should stop."

"I can do better," I say, taking a step toward him. "I just need to practice."

95

Hank holds up his hand to ward me off. "It's not your dancing." His whole body shudders. "Listen to me. I don't . . . I don't mean to offend you or . . . insult you in any way, but . . . we seriously need to talk about your . . . your body odor."

"Uh-oh," a girl's voice says from behind me. "Is someone suffering a bout of apocrine bromhidrosis?"

I whip around and come face-to-face with one of the cutest girls I've ever seen in my life. She's got geek-chic black specs, has a blunt-cut hairdo, and is wearing a skintight Himura Kenshin T-shirt.

It's as if someone plucked the perfect girl from my mind and plopped her down in front of me. The kind of girl you dream about running into at Comic-Con.

The kind of girl who makes glasses look hot.

The kind of girl who will talk to you for hours about Hayao Miyazaki's films, and *Fullmetal Alchemist,* and the influence that medieval history has on *Game of Thrones.*

And I have just made the world's worst first impression on her.

CHAPTER 16

"If I were you," the girl says, arching a heavy brow, "I'd be less worried about your disagreeable pong and more concerned with those two left feet of yours." She nods at Baby Robbie on the bench. "Nice doll, by the way."

"It's not a doll," I explain, blushing as badly as if she'd caught me looking at porn. "It's a Baby-Real-A-Lot."

The girl looks me up and down. "Smelly, clumsy, *and* puerile. Now there's a winning trifecta."

A short, stocky woman with stringy bottle-blond hair and the face of a bull terrier clomps into the baggage claim area. She's wearing a bulging backpack like a turtle shell and is hugging another giant bag in her arms. "Please forgive my daughter. Besides being lazy"—the woman drops the bag to the ground for emphasis—"Penelope has a unique affliction whereby she is unable to filter her thoughts before they reach her mouth."

"Ah, yes," Charlie says. "An acute lack of discretion, the absence of social skills, and the use of an inflated vocabulary. Medically, I believe that's known as Asperger's."

"Oh," the woman says, smiling. "So you have that condition too."

"I don't have Asperger's, *Mother*," Penelope snaps, then turns on Charlie. "And neither does this ass burger."

Charlie smirks. "How exceptionally witty of you. Perhaps you can take your insolence and your homonym-heavy humor to another part of the airport."

"Homo*phone*-heavy," Penelope says, crossing her arms. "A homonym is a word that's *both* pronounced *and* spelled like another but has a different meaning."

Charlie laughs. "I suppose you know better than the *OED*, which *clearly* states that a homonym can be either a homophone *or* a homograph." He cocks his head defiantly.

Penelope sneers disgustedly. "Seriously? *The Oxford English*? You're not *actually* referencing that overblown, outdated abortion, are you? Not when the unabridged *Merriam-Webster* is the most respected *American* English dictionary in the country."

Charlie cough-mutters, "Xenophobe."

Penelope's mother marches toward Hank and shoots out her thick, callused hand. "Barbara Halpern. So very, *very* nice to meet you." She smiles and bats her false eyelashes.

Hank shakes Barbara's hand. "Nice to meet you too. I'm Hank." He nods in our direction. "This is Dan and Charlie."

"Lovely," Barbara says, waving at us. "And, of course, you've

98

already met my highly opinionated daughter, Penelope." She gestures to Penelope, who merely grunts and rolls her eyes.

"Wonderful to make your acquaintance," Hank offers.

"Speak for yourself," Charlie grumbles, snatching a magazine from his bag and snapping it open.

"So." Barbara claps her hands together. "Which way to the Adventure Van?"

"I'm sorry?" Hank says, raising his eyebrows.

Barbara points a stubby finger at us. "My Woodland Trek Adventures, right?"

"Uhh, yeah," Hank says. "That's . . . who we're waiting for."

"Oooooh." Barbara smiles at Hank. "My apologies. Between the backpacks and your rugged, outdoorsy look, I thought you *were* My Woodland Trek Adventures. But I guess we're going to be travel companions instead. Even better! Five days alone together in the Frank Church wilderness . . ." She turns to Penelope. "And you said there wouldn't be anyone your age going on this trip. Exciting, huh?"

"I'm bursting with jubilation," Penelope says. She drags her backpack over to an adjacent bench, unzips the top, and tugs out a dog-eared copy of *Infinite Jest*.

"Holy cannelloni," Barbara says. "You brought that behemoth with you? No wonder your bag's so stinkin' heavy."

Penelope sighs, ignoring her mother.

I watch her as she leans back and cracks open her gigantic book, wondering if my life has taken an incredibly lucky turn — or if my plans for scaring away Hank have just been spectacularly shat upon.

* * *

Over the next half hour, the five of us—six, counting Baby Robbie—sit in baggage claim and continue to wait.

And wait. And wait. And wait.

I use the excuse of needing to pacify Baby Robbie to stand well away from Penelope, so as not to assault her pert little nose with my moldering odor. It's also the perfect opportunity to devour all of the snacks I bought at the newsstand well away from any curious eyes.

Meanwhile, Charlie and Penelope continue to read as a way of violently ignoring each other. And Hank gets his ear chewed off by Barbara, who sounds like she's training for the Ironman World Championship: apparently she bikes thirty miles a day, has hiked the Pacific Crest Trail, has kayaked the Outer Hebrides, *and* has climbed Mount Kilimanjaro. I'm out of breath just listening to her:

" . . . and the *views*, oh-my-God!" Barbara says. "The mountains. The clouds. The colors. It was like I was standing in heaven. Seriously. I could have died right then and there and been, like, 'Thank you, world! Good night and good-bye!' I mean, you could see forever. *Literally*, forever. I mean, look at that." She turns her phone toward Hank, then toward me, then toward Charlie, who doesn't look up from his magazine. "Is that something or is that something?" She stares at her own picture, looking wistful. "Gorgeous. Best time of my life. Well, unless you count the time Pen and I ran the rapids at Cataract Canyon." She twists around to look at her daughter. "Wasn't that a hoot and a half, Pen?"

Penelope doesn't say anything. Doesn't even blink.

Barbara turns back. "Definitely a hoot and a half. Talk about an adrenaline rush. And the endorphins! Better than sex. *Literally*. I mean, don't get me wrong, Hank." Barbara slaps Hank's thigh, causing him to levitate. "But this was something else, let me tell you. The rapids, they run for fifteen miles at least. And *fast*. Yowza wowza! This is *not* like some amusement park ride, Hank. 'You may get wet?' Uhhhh, *no*." She howls. "You *will* get *drenched*. I was soaked to the bone. *Literally*. To. The. Bone." Barbara whoops and slaps Hank's thigh again, though this time he merely flinches. "This was like nothing I'd ever experienced before. You have to use every single one of your muscles just to keep your balance and stay inside: your biceps, your quads, your traps, your glutes. It was seriously strenuous. And talk about sore. *Woooosh!* I'm telling you. I could have used some firm hands and a deep, penetrating massage that night."

"Jesus, Mom, really?" Penelope snaps.

"Oh," Barbara says. "Look who's awoken from the dead and decided to join the conversation."

Hank uses this break to leap from the bench.

"I think I'm going to, uh"—he reaches for his belt and unholsters his cherished phablet—"try giving the agents another call." Hank dials, puts the phone to his ear, and forces a smile. "It's ringing." A moment later he frowns. "Voice mail. *Again*." He leaves a rambling message, then clicks off his phone. "Right. So, hopefully they're checking their messages."

Barbara laughs. "No hurry, right? The wilderness isn't going anywhere. Come on. Sit." She pats the bench beside her. "We can use this time to get to know each other before the big expedition. Have you done a lot of camping?"

"Hank's a big-game hunter," I say, feeding Barbara's growing interest in Hank. "He's like a mountain man."

"Oh, really?" Barbara smiles. "That's fascinating. Do tell."

"Yeah, um, maybe . . . later," Hank hedges. He waves his phone. "I'm just going to give my fiancée a ring. Tell her about the delay."

"Oh." Barbara's shoulders slump. "Fiancée. How . . . nice."

"She's Dan's mom," Hank says, as though he feels he needs to explain himself.

Barbara turns and glares at me, like it's my fault Hank is marrying my mother. If only I could tell her that I'm as opposed to the union as she is.

Soon enough, though, she's back to smiling. "So, is this like a bachelor party sort of thing? Sowing a few final wild oats before you tie the noose—knot?"

"Actually," Hank says, "this trip is something we're doing for—"

Just then the skinniest man and woman in the world burst through the doors, careening around, whipping their heads this way and that, looking everywhere but at us.

The man is sporting torn, mud-stained jeans and a see-through orange rain poncho with the hood down. His straggly ponytail is sopping wet. He looks like a drowned chipmunk.

The womanlike creature beside him is missing several of her front teeth, as well as a good deal of her hair. She's draped in a patched-up green rain slicker and wears a pair of too-large, ragged sneakers.

If you looked quickly, you might mistake her for a very large, very weary vulture.

I instantly know these are our greeters. Even though they bear absolutely *no* resemblance to the pretty people on their website.

Here are the folks who will be escorting us to the lake, where we will either find a bush plane and a pilot, or a hell cabin where we will be systematically murdered, chainsawed, and served as slop to these maniacs' pet pigs.

CHAPTER 17

"Oh my God," the man-rodent rasps when he finally notices us. "Please tell me you are the My Woodland Trek Adventures guests." He hawks up something thick and phlegmy, then swallows it, his giant, pointy Adam's apple bobbing.

"We are indeed." Hank holds out his hand. "Hank Langston."

"Monty Zoster," the man says, pumping Hank's hand. "Thrilled to meet you."

Charlie has his camera out and is shooting pictures like he's capturing shots of wildlife.

"Barbara Halpern," Barbara says. She shakes Monty's hand and nods toward Penelope, who still hasn't budged. "And my daughter, Penelope."

"Awesome," Monty says. "I'm so glad you made it. That you're here. And everything."

The bug-eyed lady standing next to him clears her throat loudly.

"Oh. Yes." Monty indicates the woman at his side. "This here's my wife, Fay. We *are* My Woodland Trek Adventures. The two of us." He gestures at himself and the bird-lady. "CEO and COO."

Fay flashes a witchy grin and extends her bony hand. "Pleased to meet you folks." She speaks with a slight lisp, her voice cigarette-and-whiskey gruff. Like Tom Waits wearing a retainer.

Hank takes Fay's hand, then gestures toward Charlie and me. "This is Dan. And Charlie."

"Ah, yes, the birthday boy and his friend," Fay croaks.

As I shake Fay's and Monty's cold and clammy claws, both of them wrinkle up their noses and step away from me.

"Whoa!" Monty coughs and blinks his eyes like he's been skunk-squirted. "OK, then."

Fay makes a move toward Charlie, but he holds his hands up like he's being arrested. "Sorry. I don't shake. Eighty percent of all germs are transmitted by the hands. Kissing is actually more hygienic. It's nothing personal."

"Why don't you kiss them, then?" Penelope says, stuffing her book into her backpack. "If it's *really* nothing personal."

Charlie shoots her a look. "I simply stated that kissing is more hygienic than a handshake. I never said it wasn't a perfectly outstanding vehicle for the transmission of disease."

Monty laughs. "I see. You're one of those germinators. I seen a lady like you on the TLC once. Took twenty showers a day.

Opened doors with her feet. Nutty stuff, that." He knits his brow. "You do know you're about to go on a wilderness excursion, right? Lots of dirty dirt out there."

"Yes, I understand." Charlie pats his backpack. "But I've come prepared."

Hank eyes the Zosters warily. "You're not, er . . . You're not also our guides, are you?"

Fay guffaws, showing off her horrendous orthodontia. "You kiddin' me? We wouldn't be caught dead in the wilderness."

"Not that you all won't have a *terrific* experience," Monty says, jumping in.

"Right, well, anyway," Fay says, "terribly sorry we were late. We practically shit a shar-pei gettin' here—'scuse my French. We had some . . . challenges with our wilderness guide, you see. And between that and the traffic jam and the van issues and the bad weather, well . . ." She takes a deep breath. "Please accept our humblest apologies. We'd be happy to offer each of you a substantial discou—"

"Whoa-no-no." Monty steps in front of Fay and forces a laugh. "What my wife is so eloquently trying to matriculate." He barks up another gob of phlegm. "Is that we are terribly sorry for the inconvenience that this situation has caused you all, but as it could not be helped, and as this was most certainly an act of God, we are not responsible nor required to offer any constipatory reiteration. So . . ." Monty nods. "We sincerely hope you understand."

"It's fine," Hank says, a hint of annoyance in his voice. "We're just glad you finally showed up."

"That's the spirit," Monty says. "Expectorate the positive." He glances at our backpacks. "OK, so, you got your bags, I see. Are you all ready to have the time of your lives?"

"Yee-haw!" Barbara bellows, grabbing her bag and swinging it behind her like it weighs nearly nothing. "Let's get this party started."

"I like your attitude, missy," Fay says, laughing—then breaking into a violent, hacking cough. "'Scuse me." She belches loudly and clears her throat forcefully into her fist, making a sound like a food processor filled with ice cubes. "It's the damn cigars. I gotta quit one of these days."

Monty and Fay make no move to help with our bags, so Hank, Charlie, and I grab our backpacks and our carry-ons. I scoop up Baby Robbie, and we all follow the Zosters out the door—the sorriest wagon train since the Donner Party.

CHAPTER 18

"Here we are," Monty announces, his voice echoing off the concrete beams of the parking garage. He gestures to a dilapidated old Dodge van parked crookedly across two parking spots. "The Adventure Van! Your stagecoach to excitement."

"Oh," Hank says. "Wow."

The long, eight-seat van is white, sort of, though the ubiquitous orange-brown rust stains are staking their claim. On the side the words MY WOODLAND TREK ADVENTURES have been scrawled in Sharpie with what looks like a very shaky kindergartener's hand.

Penelope laughs. "Well, now. You didn't mention we were traveling in such style, Mother. My sincerest apologies for all my doubts about this trip."

"Oh, quiet, you," Barbara says, swatting Penelope's shoulder. "It's not *how* you get there. It's *that* you get there."

"Indeed," Charlie says, snapping a picture of the derelict van. "The promise of which is now very much in question."

The five of us lug all of our bags to the rear doors, me keeping my distance—and my sour stench—from Penelope. Monty grabs the handle on one of the doors and yanks it open, the hinges making a loud, ear-piercing squeak.

"Sorry," Monty says. "Only the one side works. Stupid latch is busted."

"Not a problem," Hank says. He grabs the backpacks one by one and heaves them inside.

"Why, thank you." Barbara touches Hank's arm. "Good to know you're around to carry me out of the woods if I twist an ankle."

Penelope groans and rolls her eyes.

Hank looks incredibly uncomfortable, a contorted smile plastered on his face. But I'm kind of loving this. Finally we see the dark side of being a super stud.

Monty climbs into the driver's seat while Fay rides shotgun. The rest of us head over to the mid-seat doors.

"I have an idea," Barbara offers. "Why don't we have the adults sit in the middle row and the *young* adults sit in the way back? So you guys can talk and get to know each other. Wouldn't that be great?"

"That's a *wonderful* plan, Mother," Penelope says. "I can hardly wait to hear all about their fascinating lives." She then proceeds to climb into the backseat and crack open her book.

I surreptitiously sniff my underarm, wondering if my skunkiness has abated a bit. It has not.

"Actually," I say, my eyes watering. "I think, you know, we should probably sit with our own groups."

"Oh . . . well . . . yes . . ." Hank's eyes dart between me and Barbara: BO or TMI, it's a difficult decision. "And actually, I wouldn't mind getting to know Charlie a little better. Maybe he and I can sit beside each other on this leg of the journey."

"Oh, no," Charlie says. "I wouldn't dream of it, Mr. Langston. This trip was meant as a birthday bonding experience between you and Dan. A nice close and cozy van ride is the perfect opportunity for a little *tête-à-tête.*" He grabs my hand, places the bottle of pomegranate juice in my palm, and looks me straight in the eyes. "You know, a nice *confabulation*?"

Confabulation. Great. As if smelling like a yeasty foot in Penelope's presence wasn't bad enough. Now she's going to see me screaming a rainbow?

"Hey, back there!" Monty calls over his shoulder. "How's about concludifying the seating summit and climbing aboard so we can get a move on. I don't want to point no fingers, but we got some time to make up here."

Hank sighs and clambers into the van. He takes the middle-row window seat. Charlie shoves me forward so I can get in and sit next to Hank, which I do, awkwardly juggling Robbie and ducking out of my sling bag as I crunch over all of the crap on the floor: paper bags, empty cans, Styrofoam coffee cups, dirty clothes, a dancing Santa Claus . . .

Barbara and Charlie climb in the backseat with Penelope, sliding the door shut behind them.

I twist around and give Charlie a death stare, but he just shrugs and pinches his nose.

"Okeydokey. Let's make like a fetus and head out." Monty turns the key. The engine wheezes, clinks, and clangs like a garbage disposal with a spoon caught inside.

"Excuse me," Charlie calls out. "Are we absolutely certain that we wouldn't be better off hiring a car?"

"Life's filled with uncertainties, honey," Fay says. "Sometimes you just gotta grab your dangle-down and hold on for the ride."

"Your engine sounds flooded," Hank offers.

"Nah," Monty says, his fingers twisting the key. "This is normal. She just likes a little foreplay. Come on now, Bessie." He rocks back and forth in his seat like he's revving himself up along with the engine. "Come on, baby. I know ya got it in ya. Giddyup."

Finally, the van roars to life.

"*Woo-hoo!*" Monty slaps the dashboard lovingly. "This old broad's got some life in her yet."

It's clear the second we jerk forward that while the van may have some life left, it sure as hell doesn't have any shocks. We all bounce around in our seats like we're racing over a series of speed bumps.

Now that we're all shut in, my bleu-cheesy stench starts to permeate the cabin.

Hank's nose twitches. He tries his window switch, but it only clicks and whines.

"Can we, uh, get a little fresh air in here?" Hank asks.

"No can do," Monty calls back. "'Lectronics shit the sheets 'bout a year ago."

111

"Lovely." Hank casually places a finger under his nose and turns toward the window.

The rattling of the van shakes my insides like a badly built carnival ride. Between my ever-thickening BO and this violent juddering, I may not need the doctored pomegranate juice to start *confabulating*.

"How far to the plane?" I ask, sounding like someone is beating on my back with their fists.

"Not too far," Monty says into the rearview mirror. " 'Bout an hour and a half if we don't hit no traffic. You just settle in and enjoy the drive."

I stare at the wine-red Pom-Licious sloshing about. If Charlie's plan works, this is going to be one miserable ride.

For me *and* for Hank.

Charlie pokes my shoulder. "Don't be shy, Daniel. *Confabulation* is all about *projecting* how you're feeling. If the stale airport air has dried out your vocal cords, perhaps that juice might offer some relief."

"Perhaps," I say through gritted teeth. "But really, I have to look after Baby Robbie. I don't want my neglect score going up. Maybe the *confabulation* can wait until later."

"Oh my God." Penelope groans. "Is this the word-of-the-day or something? Might I suggest a discussion, a debate, or a colloquy on the merits of using a freakin' thesaurus."

"Let me guess," Charlie mocks. "*Merriam-Webster's Intermediate*?"

"I wouldn't want to tax your limited intelligence," Penelope says. "Perhaps you could begin with *My First Ladybird*."

"*Anyway,*" Hank says, his face practically squashed against the window. "We don't have to force anything, Dan. We'll chat later. When the baby's asleep."

Charlie looks over at Barbara. "Oh, I'm certain Mrs. Halpern wouldn't mind looking after Baby Robbie for a short spell. Would you, Mrs. Halpern?"

"*Ms.*" Barbara smiles. "And no, actually, I wouldn't mind at all. It brings back memories."

"Are you sure?" I say, hoping she isn't. "He can be pretty fussy."

"Not to worry. I have experience with fussy kids." Barbara leans forward, and as she does, her face contorts. "Wowza. They really go for the realism, don't they? Smells like someone's made luckies." She takes the doll from me and checks its diaper. "Oh. Nope. Clean as Cling Wrap. Huh." She starts rocking the doll in her arms, a goofy smile on her face. "There really isn't anything as sweet as a newborn."

"There," Charlie says. "All is resolved. Let the *confabulating* begin."

I glower at him, then turn back around. I open the bottle and raise it to my lips, pausing a second before I take a heavy slug, sucking in my lips as I swallow. Pom-Licious it is *not*. More like Pom-Nasty. It tastes like cranberry juice mixed with grapefruit rind.

I start to cap the bottle, but Charlie does his violent throat-clearing act again.

"I cannot overstate the benefits of complete hydration, Daniel," he says.

I grimace and stare at the near-full bottle of bitterness. I sigh. Take off the cap again. Drink a bit more. God, it's so awful. My tongue shrivels up in my mouth like a salted slug. I don't care what Charlie says; there's no way I can choke all of this down.

"So, Dan," Hank says, turning to me, a smile twisted on his face, "what are your plans after high school?" He takes a few quick breaths through his mouth. "You thinking about college at all?"

I shrug. "Maybe. Probably."

Hank nods. "Great. Any idea"—he coughs, his eyes starting to water—"what you might want to major in?"

"Not sure," I say. "I guess I could try for—"

"Fine arts," Charlie interjects from the backseat. "At least, that's what you told me. Daniel fancies himself quite the *aesthete*. Don't you, Daniel?"

Yes. Right. Of course. *Aesthete*.

"Art, yeah," I say. "I'd like to go for that but, you know, it's a pretty competitive field these days. Plus, I don't even know if I'm any good."

"Well, your mom certainly thinks you have talent," Hank offers.

"Yeah, but she has to say that."

"No, no." Hank slips a thumb under his chin and crooks a finger below his nose, like he's pondering this—rather than fending off my ferocious fragrance. "Not necessarily."

"Yes, necessarily," I insist. "I love her and everything, but she'll lie to me if she thinks the truth would hurt my feelings. I don't want to waste my time if I don't have a shot."

"You should show Hank some of your drawings," Charlie suggests. "Get an objective opinion." He looks at Hank. "You'll tell him the truth, right?"

114

Hank laughs nervously. "Well, I'm no art critic."

"No," Charlie says. "But you *are* a doctor. You deal in cold hard facts." He pats my shoulder. "Come on. Show him. This is the perfect opportunity. This kind of feedback could change the entire course of your life."

"OK now." Hank holds up his free, non-nostril-shielding hand. "Let's not put too much weight on just one opinion."

"You'll be truthful?" I ask, bending over and reaching for my bag, grabbing my dummy sketchbook. "You'll give me your honest opinion? No bullshit?"

"Uhhh, sure." Hank clears his throat. "If that's what you want."

"That's what he *needs*," Charlie says.

"Thanks so much, Hank!" I say, flipping to the first page of my dummy sketchbook. The one that is filled with drawings I did in a single night. Using crayons. In the dark. With my left hand.

Hank takes the pad, looks down at the first picture, and blinks. It's a particularly terrible scrawl of a stick monkey sitting in a stick tree and eating a stick banana. Think early Picasso. *Extremely* early Picasso. Perhaps his preschool period.

"Huh," Hank says. "It's, uh . . ." He blinks again. "Not what I expected. I thought you were into graphic novels. Comic book stuff?"

"I am. It's postmodern primitivism," I explain. "It's a reaction to all of the hyperreal, overly muscularized male and overtly sexualized female superhero characters you see everywhere."

Hank nods. "OK. OK." He turns the page. "That's a good . . . goal. Let's see what else you—whoa!" His head snaps back, and his eyes bug as he stares at a drawing of two dancing stick

115

warriors with spiky headdresses sporting comically enormous erections.

I point to the picture with my pinkie and try not to crack up. "This sketch here is heavily influenced by aboriginal phallic art, where they would overemphasize the dimensions of the genitals in order to celebrate human reproduction."

"Right," Hank deadpans. "Sure. I can see that."

You'd be blind if you missed it.

Hank licks his finger and flicks to the next page.

Here we have a yellow spiral sun in the center of the page surrounded by a swirling blue sky and a few black squiggles that could be birds or flying squirrels or airplanes—or just random marks I made in the dark.

"Interesting." Hank nods. "That's, uh . . . yeah. But, you know . . ." He closes the book and hands it back to me. "I don't really think I'm the person to judge something like this. I don't know anything about art. Seriously. I'm just a dentist. I know teeth. Malocclusions. Gingivitis. Fistulas. That's my area of expertise."

Charlie leans forward and exhales loudly. "I believe you have your answer, Dan. You should give up the art thing. It's not working for you."

"Now wait a minute. I didn't say that," Hank says. "I just . . . don't know if I . . . understand it. That's all. It's over my head. Neo-this and post-that. I'm a Stan Lee guy. You know. *Excelsior! Spider-Man. Iron Man. The Hulk.* That's about my speed, artwise. So you should take my completely useless opinion with a pretty big grain of salt."

116

"Then, you don't think I suck?" I ask, looking at him with puppy-dog eyes.

Charlie pipes up: "And remember, you promised not to lie to him."

"Look." Hank gestures at the sketch pad. "Granted. Maybe this . . . particular . . . thing . . . is not my cup of tea, but—"

I frown. "So you *do* hate it."

"No. Not . . . hate. Not at all." Hank rubs his sweating forehead. "It's just so . . . subjective. For example, I read an article recently about a painting that sold for something like eighty million dollars. I can't remember the artist. But it was this canvas with a big red stripe, an orange swath, and a blue patch. Basically, three fat lines in a row. I didn't get it. But obviously a lot of people—with a lot of money—did. So who the heck am I to . . ." He gestures at my book.

"It's OK," I say, sighing and jamming the sketchbook back into my bag. "It's fine. It's better for me to know now, before I waste my whole life."

Hank pulls his hand down his face. "I don't . . . I'm not . . . explaining this right."

"There's nothing to explain," I say. "Let's just drop it."

I slug back the last splash of the Pom juice. If Hank thought my drawings were bad, wait till he gets an eyeful—and a noseful—of the Jackson Pollock I'm about to pitch into his lap.

CHAPTER 19

My stomach spasms and I vurp.

Orangey acid percolates in my mouth.

It's been around twenty minutes since I finished the juice. Which means—according to the website that Charlie found the "illegal" ipecac syrup on—I'm about ten minutes to launch.

Though it feels like it might come sooner.

Oh, Christ.

I feel so . . . belchy. Like I swallowed a handful of B vitamins on an empty stomach.

I grab the back of my perspiring neck, my head starting to spin.

This is not good. Not good *at all.*

I look over at my soon-to-be stepdad. Staring out the window, listening to something on his phablet—an audiobook or a podcast, from the sounds of the droning chatter leaking from his headphones. Completely oblivious to what's about to happen to him.

I let out another semi-silent burp, releasing some of the gaseous buildup.

I shift in my seat. Take a deep breath. Concentrate on trying to keep my half-digested snacks down. It seems to be working—

Guuurp.

Oh, God.

A giant bead of sweat bobsleds down the center of my back. I've changed my mind. I don't want to do this now. I don't want to hurl in this sealed-tight death machine.

And most of all, I *really* don't want to do it in front of Penelope.

I glance back.

Thank God. Penelope's asleep, her moist lips slightly open. Barbara is oblivious to the world, cooing away at Baby Robbie.

"You're looking a little green around the gills there, Dan," Charlie says, leaning forward and clapping me on the shoulder. "I hope you're not getting carsick. Just continue to breathe, and try to keep your mind clear. *Definitely* do not think about the soiled feminine hygiene product that kid in Missouri found in his Hungry Harley's chili last month. Or, oh, remember the time you bit into that thick, rubbery, urethral artery when you were eating a Doogan Dog? Keep your mind off that, for sure."

"I hate you, Charlie," I gurgle, my stomach a roiling pot of corn chips, tropical fruit, spicy dried beef, chocolaty peanut butter, and pomegranate juice.

Breathe. Breathe. You're fine. You're fine. I start the mental negotiations.

Keep it down and you will have superpowers.

Get through this and you will sell your graphic novel for a million dollars.

Do not throw up and you will get to date Erin Reilly.

But it's a losing battle.

Oh, God. Oh, God. Oh, God. At least let it be quiet. At least let Penelope sleep through the whole awful show.

Charlie leans over, whispers in my ear, "You know what I could really go for right now?"

"Stop," I hiss through clenched teeth.

"A bowl of cold, gelatinous beef brains slathered in warm mayonnaise. Mmm-mmm."

And that's it. My entire digestive system rockets up my throat and out my maw—and there is nothing quiet about it.

"UUURRRRK!"

The chunky spew splashes all over Hank—blanketing his shirt, his crotch, his legs. Spilling onto the seat, the floor, dousing the dancing Santa Claus, coating his cottony beard in multicolored curds.

"Jesus!" Hank springs from his seat, headphones flying from his ears as he attempts to scrabble away. If my thunderous torrent didn't wake Penelope up, Hank's shriek surely did.

"Sorry, sorry, sorry," I splutter, before another surge of swill shoots from my mouth all over Hank, all over everything. "I'm not . . . feeling so well."

120

CHAPTER
20

"We're here!" Monty snaps as he throws the van into park just outside a dilapidated farmhouse. "Everyone get the hell out."

Charlie slides the back door open. The rush of fresh air is a welcome relief. Like stepping out of a muggy, fairground Port-a-Potty into the cool of an old-growth forest.

"Let's go, people!" Monty bangs his hand on the hood. "Move it!"

It took twenty minutes for us to find a gas station following the *confabulation*. Twenty minutes of sitting in my clammy sick—the sharp, tangy, barfy odor overpowering my BO and smogging the van.

Hank and I ran through the rain to the bathroom at the Buddy's Gas & Grub to change clothes while Monty used the dripping windshield squeegee to rake my thick, coagulating hurl off the seat. I also took the opportunity to thoroughly wash my underarms till they smelled liquid-hand-soap fresh. Meanwhile, Barbara bobbed about under the gas station canopy, rocking and singing lullabies to a disconsolate Baby Robbie as Penelope went into the mini-mart and cleaned the Gas & Grub out of all its Little Trees air fresheners.

You would think that fifteen fully unsheathed Bubble Berry Trees would be able to at least somewhat mask the smell of vomit in a sealed-up van.

But you would be wrong.

I do not envy Monty and Fay's long ride home.

Charlie, Barbara, Penelope, Hank, and I take turns stepping from the van. The rain has mercifully abated so we can actually stand outside without getting drenched.

As I shoulder my sling bag, Barbara approaches me, cradling Baby Robbie.

"Thanks for letting me hold him," Barbara says, gently handing over the doll. "It brought me right back to when Pen was a little bundle." She looks over at her daughter. "You remember all those songs I used to sing to you?"

"Remember?" Penelope laughs. "You *still* sing them to me. 'Lavender's Blue.' 'The Circle Game.' 'See That My Grave Is Kept Clean.' Real cozy."

"Oh, you." Barbara grabs Penelope in a powerful side-hug.

Penelope leans her head into her mom's shoulder. I feel a pang, wishing Mom were here with me now instead of Hank. But it only hardens my resolve to follow through with Charlie's and my plan to scare off Hank.

Behind the farmhouse there's a corral with a single skeletal cow grazing apathetically, like it knows it's not long for this earth and doesn't really see the point of eating any more. To the left of the cow sits a large wired coop containing a small flock of fluttering chickens. A further enclosure holds six filthy, patchy, gloomy-looking sheep.

Just beyond the fields is a row of trees and a lake with a dock and a float plane.

"You all have fun now, 'kay." Fay pretends to shoot us with a pair of withered finger guns. "Stay safe and we'll meet everyone back here at week's end."

And with that, Monty and Fay turn, tuck tail, and walk-run back to the van. The tires squeal as they peel away.

"You'd think they'd be a little more reluctant to climb back into that torture chamber," Charlie observes.

Hank eyes the farmhouse warily but then slowly leads us forward. As we walk, Charlie squirts some Purell into the palm of his hand.

"Anyone?" Charlie holds up the bottle of hand sanitizer. "One squirt kills the dirt."

"Actually, it doesn't," Penelope says.

Charlie glares at her as he rubs the gel into his hand. "*Actually*, it does. Very effectively."

"Oh, it's effective all right," Penelope says, "in contributing to the proliferation of antibiotic-resistant superbugs."

Charlie laughs. "Oh, you poor, stupid child. Purell happens to be an alcohol-based hand sanitizer. It does not contain triclosan. *Or* triclocarban. The two ingredients the World Health Organization has named as the main causes of bacterial resistance. Perhaps you should stick to commenting on subjects you know something about. Like obnoxiousness and ignorance."

Penelope cracks up. "*I'm* the ignorant one? Really? Because if you'd truly done your research, you would know that alcohol-based hand sanitizers have been linked to an *increased* risk for outbreaks of norovirus. Not to mention that excessive use of alcohol gel dries out and cracks the skin, which in turn creates a more direct avenue for infection. But, hey"—she claps Charlie on the shoulder—"if you want to be single-handedly responsible for the spread of gastroenteritis while additionally raising your likelihood of contracting flesh-eating disease and MRSA, you go ahead and slather away."

"Please." Charlie rolls his eyes. "You're going to tell *me* about infection? I will have you know that I am a card-carrying member of the Infectious Diseases Society of America. I've read the research and have done the numbers backwards and forwards. And let me tell *you* something, missy." He tosses his tiny bottle of Purell in the air and jauntily—if awkwardly—catches it. "The rewards *far* outweigh the risks."

Penelope sighs and shakes her head. "I suppose if your little delusions give you some measure of comfort, who am I to burst that fragile bubble?"

Charlie grips his fists. "I don't know why I waste my precious breath." He steps up his pace to get away from her.

Penelope smirks.

We reach the weathered and warped front door, the red paint chipping and curling. Hank grabs the tarnished brass door knocker—a cat's head with a mouse hanging from its mouth—and gives it several clicks.

We wait for what seems like an eternity.

No answer.

Hank taps the knocker again, this time a bit more forcefully. "Hello? Anybody home?"

I stand here, cradling Baby Robbie, casually looking over at Penelope but pretending not to. I give a quick, verifying sniff of my now-clean armpit before stepping closer to her.

I lean over and say, "I really like your shirt."

"You'd be stupid not to," she says, staring straight ahead.

"Kenshin's awesome. I love how he's so conflicted over his past."

"We all grapple with our darker predilections, Dan," Penelope says. "Every great character does. Rick Grimes. Two-Face. Jean Grey. Batman. The Hulk. Goku. Some can keep them in check. Others are not so strong-willed."

Oh my God, I think I love this girl.

I mean, I *could* love her, if I didn't already love Erin. Which I do. Of course.

But still . . .

I swallow. Glance sideways at Penelope. So cool. So smart. So . . . cute.

Maybe there's a reason you've never asked Erin out. Maybe fate has held you back. So you could meet Penelope. So you could—

"*Waaaaa! Waaaaa!*" The baby starts to cry and quiver in my arms.

I look down at him.

And see Erin's face. Her smile. The tiny sweater she knitted.

Hear her lilting voice telling me, "Take good care of Baby Robbie."

Wait a second. I'm being tested here. That's what this is. Wrestling with my own dark side, just like Kenshin.

Erin is my destiny. I've known it since third grade. She is my light. My one true love. My . . .

My eyes slide over to Penelope. She pushes her adorkable glasses farther up her cute button nose.

My breath catches in my throat.

My heart hitches in my chest.

Oh boy. This is not good. Not good at all.

CHAPTER
21

The front door suddenly flies open. A giant, red-bearded man with serious bed head stands in the doorway. He smiles big, his cauliflower nose and long droopy ears bright pink.

"Well, hello!" the man bellows, extending his thick, hairy arm. "I'm Clint. Your bush pilot. And you must be my passengers! Come on in! I was just getting to know your guide. First time he's worked this gig. It's a real shame about Tucker, though." Clint shakes his head sadly.

"Tucker?" I mouth to Charlie. He shrugs. We enter.

"Weather's cleared up nice," Clint announces as though everything were normal. As though we weren't following him through a dark and towering maze of junk that wends through his house. "Should be a smooth flight over the mountain." His broad shoulders sway from side to side, clearing the walls of trash by mere inches.

The mountainous piles of crap reach nearly all the way up to the popcorn ceiling. Narrow paths have been cleared to allow passage, like someone carved a labyrinth through a landfill. It's as though everyone in the world has dumped their garage-sale remainders here: newspapers, toys, old telephones, books, bottles, DVDs and CDs, tools, clothes, lottery tickets, broken furniture, lampshades, a cracked wooden reindeer magazine rack, golf clubs, engine parts, flower pots, several scratched-to-hell nonstick frying pans, and, bizarrely enough, the very same dancing Santa that I threw up all over in Monty's van.

I don't know how Clint lives in this mess. I couldn't do it. The claustrophobic feeling is bad enough, but then there's the crushing stench. A disconcerting mixture of deli Dumpster, beef and broccoli, and filthy litter box. With an undercurrent of moldy basement.

Notes to self: Straighten up bedroom. Thank Mom for cleaning. Never get a cat.

"Here we are," Clint says, sliding open the back door.

He steps aside and we all file out onto the porch.

A very tan, very lithe man sits on a folding wooden patio chair. He is barefoot, wearing only cream-colored capris, a blue braided bracelet, and an unbuttoned button-down that shows off his sinewy-smooth chest.

"The travelers arrive." The man smiles and stands. He is tall—taller even than Hank. "Max Roveland." He walks right up to Barbara. "I will be your survival guide this week."

"Lovely to meet you." Barbara's voice flutters as she takes

Max's hand, the palm of which is dark and leathery, like a monkey's paw.

He raises her limp mitt to his sun-chapped lips. "The pleasure is all mine, I am sure."

"Oh. Goodness." Barbara shudders and moans, like she just had a mini-orgasm.

Max turns to Penelope. "And you are?"

"Kind of grossed out, if you must know," Penelope deadpans.

"That's Penelope," Barbara answers, swatting Penelope's arm. "My daughter. She's just shy."

"I've got another name for it," Charlie mutters.

Once all the introductions are made, Max looks at Clint. "Captain Keatley, are you ready to whisk our guests away for the experience of a lifetime?"

"Sure thing," Clint says, rubbing his hands together. "Let's get this show on the road. Anyone need to use the facilities before we leave? It's the last indoor plumbing you're going to see for a while."

"Excellent idea," Hank says. "I think I'll take you up on that."

As soon as Hank starts toward the back door, Charlie turns to me.

"It's time," he whispers.

I blink. "Time for what?"

He grins evilly. *"Evanescence."*

CHAPTER 22

I look down at Baby Robbie cradled in my arms, Erin's face staring back at me. "I dunno, Charlie . . . Maybe we should keep him with us. You know, to torment Hank a bit more. Have him change more diapers. Have Baby Robbie cry all night long."

"Daniel." Charlie grabs my arm. "Listen to me. Nothing will torment Hank more than if the baby goes missing on his watch. It's the ultimate in parental betrayal. He will hate himself. It'll eat him up the entire trip."

"Yeah, but . . ." I bite my lower lip. "I just . . ." I exhale. "You're absolutely sure you'll be able to revive him? When we get home?"

Charlie squints. "I'm moderately confident I will be able to at least partially resuscitate him, yes."

"'*Moderately* confident,'" I snap. "'*Partially* resuscitate.' That doesn't exactly inspire confidence, Charlie."

"Look." Charlie sighs. "The truth is, while I was hacking the doll's software, I noticed that there appeared to be a virtual kill switch in the program."

"A kill switch? What the hell does that mean?"

"It means if the baby dies," Charlie says, "it'll be bricked."

"What? Why?"

Charlie laughs. "I suppose it's meant to stop some meddling student from reviving the baby if, perchance, he allowed his baby to expire."

"Well, can't you just unbrick it?" I ask.

"It's not that easy," Charlie says. "Not without the master program that corresponds with this particular doll's serial number. I could try restoring the entire system, but that will completely wipe all of the baby's data. It'd be pretty hard for Ms. Drizzler not to notice that."

"Well, that decides it, then," I say. "I'm canceling *evanescence*."

"Absolutely not. It's our *coup de grâce*."

"I can't bring a dead doll back to school, Charlie. Ms. Drizzler will fail me for sure. And Erin will never forgive me. She named this baby, for Christ's sake. She crocheted the sweater for him." I tug at the tiny blue sleeve. "And she asked me to take care of him."

"I don't give an elongated excreta," Charlie says. "I'm not about to risk this entire mission because you're suddenly feeling sentimental about a stupid toy." He lunges for the doll.

"No." I try to spin away, but Charlie's got a grip on the baby's head.

131

We tug-of-war on the lawn, wrestling back and forth, our arms entwined.

The baby starts to howl.

"You're hurting him!" I bark, clenching Robbie's body to my chest.

"And you're anthropomorphizing it!" Charlie spits through gritted teeth.

He yanks the doll violently.

Snap!

Baby Robbie's cries stop suddenly, and Charlie goes reeling backward, tripping over his feet and falling to the grass, landing hard on his ass.

"Oh my God! Oh my *God*!" I look down at the now-headless baby in my arms. Loose wires snake from his neck.

"Everything all right over there?" Clint calls out to us.

"Fine, yes!" Charlie bellows, tucking the baby's head under his shirt. "Just engaging in a little boyish amusement." He gets to his feet and storms over to me.

"You decapitated him!" I growl.

"*Who* decapitated him?" Charlie says. "If you'd just handed him over, this wouldn't have happened."

I take Erin's sweater off the doll and thrust the lifeless body of Baby Robbie at Charlie. We may lose the baby in this war, but I'm not about to let Erin's handiwork get scrap-heaped as well.

"Just fix him, OK?" I say to Charlie. "Before I leave him somewhere to die. *Again.*"

CHAPTER 23

Charlie has somehow managed to rewire the baby's head to its body, securing the whole thing by wrapping it snugly in its blanket.

I carry the swaddled bundle over to Hank, who is bent over his backpack.

"Can you watch the baby while I go to the bathroom?" I ask him.

Hank continues rummaging in his bag. "I'm trying to reorganize a few things. I'm sure Barbara wouldn't mind looking after him."

I glance over at Barbara, standing too close to Max, running her fingers seductively up and down his sweat-beaded glass of lemonade.

"She seems . . . busy," I say.

"And I don't?"

"Look, you don't even need to hold him," I say, gently placing the doll down on a patio chair. "In fact, maybe it's better that you don't. Anyway, he's sleeping. Can you please just keep an eye on him till I get back?"

"Sure, bud," Hank says, returning to his backpack. "No problem."

"Thanks," I say, and head for the back door.

Charlie steps outside as I approach.

"T minus two minutes," Charlie says, speaking low and out of the side of his mouth.

I nod and make my way into the house, navigating the rabbit warren of garbage to find the bathroom, which also happens to be crammed to the rafters with crap: toasters in the bathtub, magazines stacked waist-high on the floor, chains and gears filling the sink. It's a good thing I don't actually need to go, as I'm not sure I could with so much *stuff* watching me.

I wedge myself in front of the toilet, pull the door closed, and count to sixty—just in case anyone followed me inside.

Then I leave.

As I wend my way back through the house, I scan the heaps of junk, looking for a place to hide the baby where he won't be at risk of being crushed.

And that's when I see it. A battered old wooden dresser in the corner of . . . whatever room this used to be. Living room? Dining room? Who the heck knows?

I move to it and pull out the bottom drawer. It's oddly

neat inside. Folded towels and sheets. Nothing Clint ever uses obviously.

And a perfectly soft and cozy place for Baby Robbie to die a slow and agonizing death until we return and Charlie—hopefully—reboots him back to life.

CHAPTER 24

It's turned into a beautiful day. The clouds have cleared. The sky is Twitter-icon blue. All of the trees surrounding us have that lush green after-rain glow. I take a deep breath and catch the scent of Christmas tree pine and a hint of a campfire somewhere off in the distance.

"*Evanescence* seems to have gone off without a hitch," Charlie murmurs as we hump our backpacks toward the lake behind the farm. "Just remember to play up your horrified reaction when you finally realize the doll's gone missing."

"I don't think that'll be a problem," I say, glancing down at my ID bracelet. Baby Robbie has been crying for the last fifteen minutes, and guilt gnaws away at my gut.

We step from the tree-lined path and catch up with the others by the shore. The soft ripples on the lake reflect the sunshine, a thousand sparkling gems dancing across the water.

A banged and battered white float plane bobs gently at the end of a long dock.

"There she is," Clint pronounces as we approach the aircraft. "Put this honey together from parts I got off the interweb. Took me three years to complete. I call her the Keatley Kiwi."

Charlie's got his camera out and is clicking away.

Barbara nods at the plane. "Very impressive, Clint."

"Yes," Penelope says. "Quite the achievement. Though I find it interesting that you'd name your plane after a flightless bird. Were you trying to be ironic? Or just tempting fate?"

Clint laughs. "Neither. As it happens, my great-grandparents were from New Zealand. Trust me"—he pats the plane's wing—"this bird flies like a dream."

"All right, then." Max swings his backpack from his shoulders. "Let's get her loaded."

Clint opens the luggage compartment door, and we all drop our bags beside him.

Charlie breathes deep and says, "Don't you just love the natural world, Daniel?"

"Uhh, yeah," I say, looking at him sideways. "It's great."

"It gives one a certain sense of, oh, I don't know, *liberation,* don't you think?"

"What? Really?" I glance over at Hank, who's helping Clint load the baggage. "Right now?"

Charlie nods. "Yes, right this moment I'm feeling a great sense of *liberation.*"

"I don't know, Charlie," I say, keeping my voice low. "He loves that thing so much. It seems sort of . . . mean."

Charlie crosses his arms. "As mean as breaking your mother's heart? As mean as making you move away from your best friend and the girl of your dreams?"

"OK, fine." I trudge over to Hank as he hoists up a backpack and hands it to Clint.

"Can I borrow your phone a sec, Hank?" I ask. "I want to text Mom a picture of our plane. Make her feel like she's part of the experience."

"Oh." Hank bends down, grabs another bag, and passes it to Clint. "Sure, bud. But, uh, why don't I take it? I'll get a shot of you and Charlie climbing in. She'll like that."

"Yeah," I say, scratching my cheek. "That'd be cool. It's just that . . . I kind of wanted to send her a message, too. Tell her how much fun I'm having and all."

"Great." Hank nods. "Tell me what you want to say and I'll add it to the photo."

"I sort of wanted to make it personal. You know, from me . . . personally. Seems weird you typing that for me. 'Thanks for the present' and 'I love you' and everything."

Hank clears his throat. "Right. OK." He reaches to his belt clip and removes the supersize smartphone. "Just be careful, OK?" He holds the immaculately clean phablet out to me, his fingers gripping the edges, real hesitation in his eyes.

"Yeah, sure, of course," I say, grabbing the phone from him. "Thanks."

I swipe my finger across the screen. Find the camera app

and tap it. Frame the plane. Penelope and Barbara climbing into the back of the cabin. Max getting into the copilot seat.

I pretend to snap a couple of pictures and study them critically. Really, though, I use the time to scroll through Hank's texts, e-mails, and photo albums, looking for anything incriminating. Sexts to and from his buxom, birthday-present-meddling receptionist, Sally, maybe? An active Tinder or Grindr account?

But the only offensive thing on his phone is a text thread from Mom with a bunch of lovey-dovey Boogabear messages. Eww.

I start walking back toward Hank, pretending to type out a message to Mom.

I glance up from the phone to check the distance to the water and then—

I "accidentally" trip, falling forward and hitting the dock hard. I let go of the phone, and it skitters toward the lake.

"Noooo!" Hank shouts, diving toward his beloved phablet.

The huge phone slides across the wooden slats, stopping just short of the edge.

Crap. My stupid luck today.

"I've got it!" I bellow, scrabbling to my feet and leaping for Hank's cell before he can get to it. But instead of grabbing the phablet, I bat it with my knuckles.

The phone sails over the edge and—*bloop!*—falls into the water.

"Oh no!" I say as I watch the gleaming device spiral down until it completely disappears. I look up at Hank, whose face is

Hellboy red. "I'm so sorry, Hank!" I wince. "I am *such* a klutz." I push myself to my feet and brush myself off. "I'm OK, though. So, that's good at least, right?"

Hank says nothing. Just stares down at the lake, blinking into the dark abyss.

CHAPTER 25

The plane rocks softly on the water. It feels more like I'm sitting on a boat than in an aircraft.

Seating is tight in the Kiwi. It's not like a regular plane. There are no tray tables. No seat-back pockets. No reading lights or twistable airflow nozzles or window shades or toilets. It's a bare-bones affair, like you see in the movies—paratroopers headed out to storm a bunker.

Besides the pilot's and copilot's seats, there are two padded benches in the cabin with three sets of lap belts on each, a couple of doors, a few tiny windows. And that's about it.

I wanted to sit in the back row next to Penelope and Barbara so as not to end up beside Hank, who is still silently steaming over the incident with his phone. But when I got to the plane,

Charlie had already commandeered that spot—a choice that I found odd, considering the fact that I no longer smell *and* how much he seems to despise Penelope. I gave him a look, but he just shrugged at me before slipping on his surgeon's mask and rubber gloves.

So now here I am, stuck in the middle row with Hank, who is staring out the window at the dock where his phone took a swim, his jaw twitching like crazy, as though he's one breath away from going full "HULK SMASH!" on me.

"All right," Clint says from the pilot's seat, flipping switches and checking various gauges. "Just a quick hop over the mountains, and the world as you know it will be a distant memory."

Clint pumps a handle, presses a button, shifts a lever, and the engine snarls to life. The propeller stutter-spins a few times before finally catching. A puff of smoke belches from the front of the plane, wisping off into the air and dissipating like steamed breath on a cold day.

My whole body vibrates in time with the engine, my cheeks trembling, my eardrums buzzing. A slick metallic smell of gasoline and oil drifts through the tiny cabin.

Clint grips the throttle to his right and slides it forward. The propeller whirs at a higher pitch, like an empty blender on liquefy. The plane starts to move forward, pulling away from the dock.

"Hold 'em if you got 'em!" Clint shouts as the plane starts to pick up speed. Water splashes up the pontoons, droplets speckling the side windows.

We hurtle faster and faster across the lake, the plane skipping along the tiny waves like a speedboat. It seems impossible that we will ever take flight. But then the engine gets louder and the bush plane races ahead until, finally, Clint pulls back on the yoke and we lift from the water. My stomach drops as we sail into the sky.

I lean over, press my forehead against the cool glass of the window, and watch the world turn miniature below us.

"Pretty amazing, huh?" Hank calls out over the engine.

I turn my head and see him smiling at me, all the anger gone.

"Yeah. Cool," I say.

I can't believe he's actually talking to me again—*smiling* at me. What is this guy, Gandhi or something?

I turn back to the window and watch as we climb higher, putting more and more distance between us and civilization. The land gets thick and dense with trees. Rock formations and rivers appear in the distance. Misty, snowcapped mountains own the horizon.

I feel big and small all at the same time.

"That's where we're headed, bud," Hank says, pointing out my window. "Into the wild. No cell phones needed there, for sure."

My throat suddenly gets tight. There's a twinge in my chest. Some . . . *feeling* is ambushing me. I'm not sure what it is, but I don't like it. I clench my eyes shut and take a breath, stuffing the emotions back down inside.

Someone sneezes behind me.

"Uh-oh," Penelope says, sniffling. "I think I might have contracted an upper respiratory infection."

I twist around and see a masked Charlie leaning away from Penelope.

143

She turns toward him and sneezes hard into his lap. "Oh, God. I'm *so* sorry," she says, her voice all nasal. "This must be a real challenge for you, what with your paralyzing fear of germs and the incredible close quarters of this plane. It's a shame there's no evidence that respirators protect people from airborne pathogens."

Charlie rolls his eyes but remains pressed against the side of the plane. "First, your information about respirators is outrageously inaccurate. Second, I don't for a moment think you're infected with rhinovirus, coronavirus, pneumovirus, enterovirus, or any of the other two hundred–plus viral genera that can cause nasopharyngitis." His face mask pulses in and out with his breath.

Penelope wipes her nose with her hand. "Well, it certainly *feels* like a cold." She coughs loudly without covering her mouth.

"You're immaturity is astounding," Charlie says. "Contrary to accepted wisdom, cough and nasal discharge are *not* initial symptoms of the common cold. It's actually dryness and irritation that herald an infection. But then, I wouldn't expect someone of your subpar intellectual stature to have known that."

Penelope laughs. "I guess you have nothing to worry about, in that case." She slaps his thigh and drags her snotty hand up his leg.

Charlie stares down at his lap, his eyes wide with revulsion. He looks at me for help, but this time it's me who shrugs.

"Excellent choice of seats," I say, before turning back to the front.

Our plane crests a mountain, revealing a majestic valley

144

below. The colors are something out of a freshly cracked crayon box: brilliant blues, vibrant greens, fiery yellows.

"It never fails to blow my mind," Max exclaims.

"She's a stunner, ain't she?" Clint replies. "Hard to look up the ass of things when you've got a view like that to gawk at."

Max looks back over his shoulder. "You picked a good time to visit. Last month this was all blanketed in snow. It was a real long winter up here in the Frank."

"Cold as a witch's titty, too," Clint chimes in. "Been tough on the wildlife, that's for damn sure. Lots of hungry animals out there, I'd imagine."

The plane bucks a little.

"Whoa," Clint says. "Steady there, girl."

We lurch again.

Hank leans forward. "Is that normal, Clint?" he asks.

"She's just clearing her throat," Clint says, adjusting something on the dash. "Been a few weeks since I've flown her. We're almost there. Nothing to worry 'bout."

The plane's engine sputters. Coughs. Squeals.

And shuts off completely.

CHAPTER
26

We are gliding.

It is sickeningly quiet.

So quiet that I can hear my pulse shooshing a million miles a minute in my ears, the blood forcing its way through my constricted veins.

"What the hell's going on, Clint?" Max shouts.

"Give me a sec." Clint's hands are flying around the cockpit, pushing levers, turning dials, pulling knobs. "Everything's fine!"

"You and I have a very different definition of fine," Max says. "The engine's failed."

"Noticed that," Clint snaps, still working the instruments like crazy.

Hank and I turn to each other. His face is as white as a blank sketchbook page.

"What can I do?" Max says. "How I can help?"

"By shuttin' yer trap." Clint cranes his neck, looking out the window—presumably for a safe landing spot.

"You can restart it, right?" Barbara cries, grabbing my bench back and leaning forward.

"Working on it!" he calls out. "Not looking so good, though."

Barbara swallows loudly right by my ear. She's wearing perfume. Something chunky and vanilla. Makes me think of Mrs. Baker, my third-grade teacher.

"OK, OK," Barbara says, leaning back. "Everyone but Clint, close your eyes and visualize. Surround the plane with white light. Imagine it remaining airborne. Picture the engine reigniting, the propeller spinning . . ."

I glance down at my wrist. My Baby-Real-A-Lot ID bracelet, just below my dad's broken Timex, blinks a warning, as if it's reading my level of distress instead of Baby Robbie's.

Penelope nudges Charlie. "And you thought you were going to be killed by a measly microbe." Her voice is shockingly calm. "Fat lot of good your mask and rubber gloves will do you when we hit the ground at two hundred miles an hour."

"Please be quiet," Charlie begs. "I really do not want your voice to be the last thing I ever hear."

"And *I* don't want to die never having kissed a boy," Penelope says.

I smile. It's crazy what the mind dreams up when you're drifting toward certain death. Never kissed a boy. Right. Next Penelope will unbuckle her seat belt and throw herself into my arms, and we'll spend our last seconds on earth locked in a passionate embrace, wishing we'd had more time to explore our obvious animal attraction and our mutual love of all things anime—

"Dan." Penelope clicks off her seat belt, leans forward, and puts her hand on my shoulder.

"Huh?" I say, twisting around.

"Pen, what are you doing?" Barbara says. "Strap yourself in, right now!"

Penelope ignores her mother and looks straight at me. "If you wouldn't mind indulging me before we shuffle off this mortal coil . . ."

My mind stalls, like the plane's engine. I thought I'd just *imagined* Penelope saying she'd never been kissed. And why's she asking me? What about Charlie, who's sitting right next to her in the backseat?

And what about Erin? Can my last moment on earth really be a horrific act of betrayal?

I open my mouth to protest, but I only get as far as "I don't think—" before Penelope grabs my face and presses her warm, soft lips to mine.

All questions—all thoughts of imminent death and infidelity—are instantly forgotten.

If heaven really exists—and I suppose I'll find out soon enough—it can't hold a candle to *this*.

I'm just starting to get the hang of it, my first (and probably last) physical contact with a girl, when Penelope pulls away.

"There," she says, flopping back into her seat and adjusting her glasses. "More clinical than passionate, but it ticks the box."

How can Penelope seem so . . . *normal*? My brain has been short-circuited. My lips tingle, a faint taste of cherry hovering there. An electric feeling runs down my arms. Does she really not feel any of that?

Just then the engine growls back to life, the entire plane vibrating once again.

"Yes!" Clint hollers. "That's what I'm talkin' about! We are back in business, people!"

"Yahoo!" Barbara shouts. "Thank God for the power of visualization!"

Everyone around me cheers, but I can't seem to shake off a vague sense of disappointment.

CHAPTER
27

Clint brings us in for a nice smooth landing on a small lake in the middle of a valley. There is no dock out here in the bush, so he anchors the plane several yards from the shore.

We grab our gear and wade through nearly three feet of nerve-numbing water. My skin tightens and stings, and my junk seeks refuge up inside me as we trudge toward the beach.

"All right," Clint says when we reach dry land. "My job is done for now. I'll be back here Saturday morning, round about ten. This same spot. Don't be late. I've got a vacation planned; don't want to have to leave you out here." He laughs, though I'm not sure that he's joking. "Have fun. And stay safe."

And with that, he turns and sploshes back into the icy water, heading toward his Kiwi.

"OK, people," Max announces. "Let's not stand around getting hypothermia. One of the first rules of survival is 'Cold kills.' And nothing will lower body temperature faster than soaked garments. In fact, it's better to be naked and dry than wet and clothed. How about we all find a bit of privacy to change and meet back here in five?"

But before we can disperse, the float plane's engine coughs and sputters to life, revving loudly before stalling out with a booming gunshot.

"I am no aircraft mechanic," Penelope says, "but that sounds problematic to me."

Clint slides open his window and leans out. "Just a little hiccup!" he shouts to us. "Don't worry. I'll get her started up again."

The six of us go about pulling fresh clothes from our backpacks, then scurry off behind nearby bushes, trees, and boulders.

I choose a secluded shrub and quickly tug off my soaked socks and peel down my wet jeans and boxers. The cool air goose-pimples my clammy legs. I pull off my T-shirt and use it to dry my numbed feet, my cold calves and thighs, and my chilly underlings.

As I stand here swabbing down, I think of Penelope doing the same thing somewhere nearby. I crane my neck, wondering if I can catch a glimpse of her through the trees.

I can't actually see her, but I can *hear* someone changing. There's a snap. A zipper being unzipped. A grumbling as whoever it is wrestles with their waterlogged pants. And somehow I just know it's Penelope. It's like the kiss made me hyperaware of her, able to home in on her like a beacon.

Yikes! Speaking of beacons! I need to change mental gears here. Can't meet back at the lake wielding the Odinsword.

I close my eyes and think of the grossest things imaginable: Rick Chuff's unwashed jockstrap, a vomit-soaked Boogie-Woogie Santa Claus, Alan Moore naked and bending over to pick up a nickel . . .

That's it. There we go. The blood slowly drains back to my heart.

"T-shirt's for the torso," I hear Penelope call out.

My eyes fly open. "Whoa! Hey, now!" I fold over, clutching the shirt to my junk. "Little privacy, maybe?"

"I only mention it," Penelope says, standing by a tree, "because you appear perplexed."

"I'm fine, thanks." I scoot backward, the branches of a bush biting my exposed backside. "I was just . . . thinking."

She laughs. "Is that what the kids are calling it these days? Well, carry on with your . . . contemplation. I'll go let the others know you'll join us when you're through."

"No, that's OK. I'll be right—"

But it's too late. She's already crunching through the bramble, back toward the shore.

My cheeks and ears are burning hot as I scramble to get dressed. What the hell was I thinking, trying to catch a glimpse of Penelope in the buff? I should've just focused on the task at hand, end of story. It was the near-death kiss. It screwed with my head. Made me reckless. And not just that—it made me forget about Erin. My destiny. My one and only.

I burst from the woods and hurtle toward the shore to see

everyone standing and staring at Clint's Kiwi, still bobbing in the middle of the lake.

No one gives me a second look as I scrabble up beside them—no one but Penelope. I pant heavily, my hands on my hips.

"That's some serious ruminating you were doing, huh?" she whispers.

"I wasn't—"

Clang! Clang! Clang!

Clint is standing on one of the plane's pontoons, hanging on to the cockpit window with one hand and hammering on the engine with a huge crescent wrench in the other.

"Oh, Jesus," Hank mutters.

"What's he doing?" I ask.

"It's obvious, isn't it?" Charlie says, snapping a series of photos. "He's using his considerable mechanical knowledge and years of aeronautical expertise to fine-tune his engine."

"Come on, ya bastard!" Clint shouts, striking the gearbox with the huge wrench.

He scoots along the pontoon and climbs back into the plane. He shuts the door, settles into the cockpit, flips a few switches, and . . . the engine splutters to life. The propeller flicks and stutters a few times and then begins spinning evenly.

Clint grins big and gives a thumbs-up. "It's all good!" he shouts as the bush plane pulls away.

The plane picks up speed and then lifts from the water. As it climbs into the blue sky, a stream of black smoke starts to pour from the engine. The Kiwi crests the mountain and disappears.

The six of us wait there. Standing stock-still, listening out: for the plane to circle back, for the sound of a crash, for some sort of sign.

But there's nothing.

"Is it just me," Penelope says, her arms crossed, watching the skies, "or is anyone else getting a serious *Lord of the Flies* vibe right about now?" She smirks at Charlie. "I wonder who's going to end up being our Piggy?"

CHAPTER 28

"OK," Max says, clearly in take-charge mode. "We've all traveled a fair bit today, so I suggest we camp by the lake tonight, smooth the transition from civilization. We've got a plentiful supply of fresh water here," he says, gesturing toward the lake, "so our first order of business should be to build a shelter."

"Why don't you wear shoes?" Penelope asks, apropos of nothing.

"Oh." Max looks down at his brown weathered feet like he didn't even notice. "Well, I like being connected to the earth. To my environment." He wiggles his toes. "Keeps me grounded. Makes me more aware of my surroundings. No encumbrances."

"Yes, but why *really*?" Penelope asks, cocking her head. "Do you think it makes you a more interesting person? Is it an attention-getting thing?"

"Penelope Grace Halpern!" Barbara gasps.

Max holds up a hand. "It's OK. I don't mind. I suppose the real reason I go barefoot is because I like how it feels. Simple as that. It reminds me of when I was a child."

"Ahhh." Penelope nods. "OK. Got it. *Puer aeternus.* The narcissist as eternal child."

"I said that it *reminds* me of being a child," Max says, the cords twanging in his neck. "Not that I wanted to *be* a child."

"Speaking of children," Charlie announces loudly, turning to me. "Where's your baby?"

"Baby Robbie?" I say, looking at Hank. "Hank's got him. I should probably get him back from you now so I can feed him."

"What?" Hank blinks at me. "No . . . I thought . . ." His eyes dart this way and that, like he's going to find the Baby-Real-A-Lot somewhere in the nearby brush. "Didn't . . . didn't you take him?"

"*Me?*" I say. "No. You had him last, remember? I asked you to look after him."

Hank shakes his head. "Oh no."

"Wait a second." I stare at him. "You *left* him? How could you do that?"

"I was . . . helping Charlie with his bag," Hank stammers, "and . . . you asked me not to touch him. I just . . . assumed you picked him up. It was a misunderstanding."

"Oh, God. I can't believe this. You said you'd watch him! I'm totally screwed." I look down at my ID bracelet, the LED flashing a cautionary yellow. "Holy crap, my neglect points are through the roof! The poor kid's going to die of starvation!"

"If he doesn't die of a broken heart first," Penelope says sadly.

I glare at her. I can't have her making light of the situation.

I try not to think about how embarrassing this next part is going to be with Penelope watching. I feign a sniffle and squeeze my eyes shut, trying to will some waterworks. But nothing comes.

I remember what Charlie said to do. Something he saw an actor talk about once.

And so I forget about Penelope and this trip and even Baby Robbie. Instead, I think back to the day Dad moved out. I picture him hefting a garbage bag full of clothes over his shoulder like a hobo Kris Kringle. I remember standing in the doorway to our house, waving good-bye and crying. And Dad telling me to buck up, that this wasn't "Good-bye," only "See you later."

I grip his watch on my wrist. I'm still waiting for "later."

A huge surge of missing wells up inside me. I ride the wave . . . and just like that, I start to cry.

"Come on, Dan," I hear Barbara say. "It'll be OK."

"No," I croak. "It won't. He's gone forever." I picture Dad's dented Plymouth Neon backing out of our driveway.

"I'm so sorry, Dan," Hank says. "I'll write you a note. Your teacher will understand."

"You don't know Ms. Drizzler," I rasp, swiping the tears from my face with the back of my hand. "She doesn't give second chances. I'll fail Life Skills, for sure. Which means no dean's list this semester."

As if I've ever been on the dean's list in my life.

I turn away, shaking my head. "All I've got now is his little sweater," I say, tugging the tiny cardigan from my pocket. I stare down at it as I walk off.

"Dan, wait!" Hank cries. He sounds really desperate. I guess my little performance was pretty damn effective.

"I just need to be alone for a minute." I sniffle and continue trudging off.

"Dan," Hank whisper-shouts. "Dan. Stop! Now! There's a bear. Right in front of you!"

"Huh, what?" I lift my head.

And, indeed, there is a bear.

A huge, hulking black beast—just a stone's throw away—plods along the shore, its massive head swaying from side to side, a thick pink scar slashed across its snub nose.

It's walking right toward me.

"Oh shit." I stop in my tracks, a rush of adrenaline shooting through my body. I've seen bears in zoos before, but in the wild like this, up close and personal, it's a completely different story. The animal is gigantic—seven hundred pounds if he's an ounce.

The bear continues lumbering forward, its dark hair stroked by the breeze. Each step of its plate-size paws is eerily silent.

I stumble backward, tripping over my feet.

"No need to be frightened," Penelope says calmly. "*Ursus americanus* almost never feasts on human flesh."

"*Almost* never?" I gasp.

"Everybody stay calm," Max whispers, his hands in the air. "Don't make any sudden movements. Penelope's correct. Black bears are more afraid of us than we are of them."

"Oh yeah?" I gulp. "Then why isn't it crapping its coat right about now?"

"It isn't focused on us yet," Max says, keeping his voice low. "Probably just wants to do a little fishing, maybe establish that this is its lake." Max reaches down cautiously and lifts his back-pack. "Let's all slowly grab our bags and walk away."

"I was under the impression," Penelope says, groping around for her bag while regarding the animal, "that you were supposed to make your presence known to a bear. Create noise. Make yourself appear large."

"Yeah," Barbara says. "That's what they told us when we hiked the Pacific Crest Trail. They said if you retreat, the animal may look at you as prey."

"That's only if a bear is acting aggressively toward you," Max explains. "Now, please. Gather your things and let's leave the bear alone."

Click-click-click-click-click-click!

In the stillness of the wilderness, Charlie's rapid-fire camera shutter sounds like gunshots.

The bear's head jerks up, its ears twitching. Its eyes train on us.

"What the hell are you doing?" Max says.

"What?" Charlie lowers his Nikon. "I may never see another bear in my life."

Max shakes his head, clearly annoyed. "Unless you want it to be the last thing you ever see, we'd better get moving. Fast and quiet, everyone. Let's go!"

We hoist our bags and follow Max, who clears a path through the brush. I look over my shoulder. The bear locks eyes with me, pulling its lips back to reveal huge yellowing fangs.

I swallow and pick up my pace.

159

CHAPTER 29

"So," Max calls out from the front of our procession. "Couple of things to think about as we make our way into the forest. Remember to always keep your core engaged and breathe into your diaphragm." He takes a deep breath in through his nose, his hand on his abdomen.

Barbara stands up tall with her head and neck straight. "How's my form, Max?"

He looks her up and down. "Excellent. Now try to maintain an even cadence. Walk heel to toe, each step about two and three-quarters feet in length and just over a half second apart." Max chops out the rhythm with his hand. "Step, step, step, step, step, step. Just like that."

"Are we going to be walking much longer?" Charlie says, dragging his feet.

"Ideally, I'd like to put four, maybe five, hours between us and our furry friend back there."

"Four or five *hours*?" Charlie grouses. "I'm not going to be able to make that. Fifteen minutes in and my metatarsi are already killing me."

Max laughs. "In the hiking trade we call that lack-of-use cramps. But don't worry. After a another ten miles or so you'll be *wishing* your feet ached only as much as they do now."

"Ah, trail humor. How amusing." Charlie stops. "Perhaps we should put it to a vote. All those in favor of setting up camp right here, right now, raise their hand and say aye." He shoots his hand in the air. *"Aye."*

No one joins him. Not even me. He groans and starts walking again.

"Sorry to inform you of this, Mr. Bungert," Max says. "But out here, I'm in charge. It's my duty to keep you all safe, and I take that responsibility very seriously. So, for now we walk."

Charlie glares at me. "After all I've done for you, a little backup would have been appreciated."

I shrug. "My feet feel pretty good."

Normally, I'd be right there with Charlie. But I'm actually enjoying myself. There's something soothing about being in the wilderness. It clears your head, makes you feel like you can breathe deeper than before.

We're walking single file through a huge field of tiny purple and yellow wildflowers. The colors are so intense, it's like something out of *The Wizard of Oz*. So unbelievably beautiful.

I soak it all in, absorbing the beauty of the surroundings so I can use it later as the setting for a scene in *Night Goblin*. Perhaps the one where Erilin and Stan kiss for the first time. Right after their narrow defeat of the Hobgobblers and a brush with death . . .

Or, no, better yet—the first time they have sex. After they've ridden a safe distance away from the infuriated Night Goblin. They will find a field of flowers, and Stan will spread a downy blanket on the ground, and Penelope will slowly remove her—

Whoa, whoa, whoa. *Penelope?*

My brain just did a search and replace without my consent. Not cool, brain. Not cool at all.

"If my calculations are accurate," Max calls out over his shoulder, "and I'm remembering the map correctly, there should be a river not far from here. We'll find that and then camp nearby."

I take a deep breath of the fresh forest air. It's so clean and crisp. It makes me feel good, strong—like I could hike a thousand miles. Who'd have ever thought it? Apart from my traitorous musings about a certain cute, snarky, bespectacled hiking companion, this trip is turning out to be kind of awesome, actually.

CHAPTER
30

"Ow, goddamn it." I slap the back of my sweaty neck, feeling like I was jabbed with an X-Acto knife. "Something just bit me. Hard."

"Blackflies," Penelope calls back over her shoulder. "The population should be starting to swell around this time. You'll have a nice welt there for a few days. And it'll itch so bad you'll want to dig through your skin with your nails."

"Wonderful," I say, feeling the hot bump starting to grow on my neck.

"Now who's wishing he'd sided with me?" Charlie says. "You'll recall that there were no blackflies back where I suggested we stop."

I give Charlie the finger. After a little more time, I've concluded that this trip is *not* awesome at all. My feet are throbbing, my neck itches with prickly heat and bug bites, my legs are so tired that I'm shocked they still even work, and my Achilles tendons feel like they're going to explode. Add to this the fact that I have to take a wicked pee, and I am seriously starting to hate Mom for getting me into this mess.

"Hey, Max!" I holler. "This looks like a pretty nice campsite right here. Flat and everything. Maybe we should stop and build that shelter you were talking about."

"River's close," Max announces. "Can't be more than another forty-five or so."

My shoulders sag. Forty-five minutes? I don't know if I can walk for that much longer. And I definitely can't wait forty-five minutes to pee.

I veer off the grassy deer trail.

Charlie follows me, panting. "Where . . . are you . . . going?"

"I've gotta take a piss," I tell him, keeping my voice low. "I'll just be a second."

"We can . . . wait for you. Happy to . . . take a break. I'll let Max know."

"No, no, that's OK," I say. "I don't want to slow everyone down. I'll catch up when I'm done."

Charlie narrows his eyes. "This wouldn't . . . have anything to do with Penelope . . . would it?"

"What? Who? Oh, *Penelope* Penelope. *Pshhh.* Don't be ridiculous."

"Everyone micturates, Dan. . . . There's no reason . . . she can't . . . know about it."

"This doesn't have anything to do with her," I say defensively.

"I just . . ." My gaze flits past Charlie to Penelope about twenty yards ahead of us. "I don't want Hank thinking I need a break, OK?"

"Ahh, so this is about maintaining the respect . . . of the father figure," Charlie says. "Despite everything we've done so far . . . to scare him off."

"Think whatever you want," I snap. "But I really need to pee. So either come along and enjoy the free show, or screw off and let me take care of business."

"Fine," he says. "I'll afford you some . . . privacy, lest Hank think you're . . . winded from three hours of relentless hiking with . . . fifty pounds of gear strapped to your back."

"Thanks." I pat Charlie on the shoulder and dart deeper into the underbrush.

I push through some bushes and bound over a rock. The trees aren't dense enough here to hide behind, and despite what I said to Charlie, I really *don't* want Penelope seeing me draining the dragon. I hustle through an obstacle course of downed tree limbs and bramble, stepping over a decomposing tree trunk and coming down on the other side into a web of branches.

My right foot gets stuck, and I nearly twist the hell out of my ankle. I'm about to do a full face plant but miraculously am able to flail my arms and find my balance at the very last second.

"Phew." My heart rabbit-punches my rib cage as I stand there with my hands out in surfer position. I'm not used to recovering before wiping out. Maybe this trip is good for me after all.

I take a deep breath and try to angle my foot this way and that, attempting to extricate it.

But it's trapped in the branches good. Like one of those twisted nails puzzles. And now that I've given the go signal to my bladder, the pressure is reaching the red zone.

I give a quick glance around just to be sure the group is well and truly out of sight. And to make certain there aren't any wolves or cougars sizing me up for supper.

With the coast clear, I yank open my button fly, scoot my pants and smiley-face boxers down, and let nature take its course.

Oh, God. That is, like, the second-best feeling in the entire world.

I watch my pee disappear into the darkness under the webbing of branches. My stream is strong, and it makes a very audible hissing sound on the twigs and dried brush below.

There's a large flying insect flitting around down there. It perches on one of the branches, flicking its wings.

A blackfly, perchance?

I shift positions, take aim, and hit the nasty bastard with the full force of my whiz.

"*Whooo!* Take that, buddy!" I say. "Tell your friends to stay the hell away from me."

The bug darts up and out of the latticework, trying to escape my onslaught.

"Not so fast, fella." I whip my wang back and forth like a samurai sword. "Hah! Yah! Submit to the force of my flow, you little—"

Oh shit.

The bug comes at me fast.

And this is no blackfly.

It's a freakin' black *wasp.*

I swat at it with my free hand, but it has no problem dodging my blow. It lands on my face and sinks its stinger in deep.

"Yowch!"

And then there's another wasp. And another one. And another one.

"I'm sorry! I'm sorry!" I shout, pinwheeling my arms around like a mental patient, feeling hot needles piercing my cheeks, my arms, my—

"Owwwww!"

—dingus.

"Fuck!" I reflexively slap my hand down hard—and punch myself in the junk.

"Uuuuuuuuuuuuuuuuuu!"

I fold over, coughing. I struggle to get my pants up and protect my most sensitive bits, but my jeans are too tight. Or I'm too panicked.

Holy-mother-of-Christmas-morning, that hurts. My eyes fill with tears, but I can still see the angry red welts popping up everywhere I've been stung, including one—big and bulbous—on my schlong. Jeez Louise. I always wanted it to be larger, but not like this.

Meanwhile, I'm still getting jabbed—on the arms, the ears, the elbows—every sting a searing stab.

And that's when the real buzzing starts. First low and distant. Then loud and blistering.

I look up and see a dark cloud heading toward me. Like the scouts have radioed for backup, and they are about to arrive in a big way.

My skin goes clammy. My pulse thrashes in my ears.

I yank up my pants and jerk at my jammed foot.

But it's not coming out.

"Help! Help!" I shout, and as I do, a wasp flies into my mouth.

Plltttth. I spit, and the damn thing stings my lip on its way out.

"Help!" I yell again.

Good thing you got nice and far away from them, huh?

Goddamn it. If I'm going to die out here, it'll be because I've been eaten by a mountain lion or mauled by a bear — not because I was stung to death after peeing on a wasp.

I bend over and yank my bootlace loose. I wrench the boot tongue forward, pull my socked foot free, then run like hell.

"Aaaaaah!" I scream, my wounded wang wailing inside my boxers.

I look back over my shoulder. The wasps are on my tail — a big, zigzagging ball of black specks droning in the near distance.

I turn back around and —

Ooof!

I run right into Charlie, tackling him into the dirt and grass.

"What the hell?" he groans.

"W-wasps!" I cry, looking behind me. "Attacking me!"

"What wasps?" Charlie asks, shoving me off him.

And he's right. There are no wasps. It's like they vanished into thin air.

I turn back around and see Max, Barbara, Hank, and Penelope all peering down at me.

"Have a nice private pee there, Dan?" Charlie says, brushing

168

himself off and examining his camera. "Excellent work not drawing any attention to yourself, by the way." He snaps a series of pictures of me.

"Hey there, Magic Mike." Penelope smirks and points at my crotch. "I do believe your smiley face is showing."

CHAPTER
31

"Don't ever do that again!" Hank says when he returns with my boot. He hurls it down beside me. "You heard what Max said: We always stick together. No matter what. If you need to go to the bathroom, you tell us and we wait for you."

It's the first time Hank has ever yelled at me. And I wasn't even trying to annoy him this time.

"Are we clear about that?" Hank says, his neck red, his hands shaky.

I nod from my seat on a log. "Yes."

And just like that, all of the anger drains from Hank's face. "OK. Good." He takes a deep breath. "Now, how are you feeling? The Benadryl cream helping?"

"Yeah, thanks," I say, glancing down at the sweatpants Hank loaned me. "Still, you know, a little bit . . . tender. But definitely improving."

I thought I'd be able to get away without mentioning the utterly humiliating fact that I'd been stung on my dong. But after the adrenaline subsided, I found the whole "situation" down below getting more and more painful. I tried to ignore it, act casual. And I'd thought I'd been doing a pretty good job—till Penelope asked me why I was walking like a rancher after a three-day cattle drive.

"You sure you've applied Benadryl *everywhere*?" Charlie had asked. "Wasp stings are not something you want to ignore. An allergic reaction can cause permanent neurological damage; a person can lose all feeling in the affected extremity."

The confession came fast and furious after that bit of news. There are places you might not mind losing feeling in. And then there's your Charles Xavier.

"Shall we join the others?" Hank says, extending his hand.

I grab hold and he hoists me up.

We walk over to the stand of trees where Max is explaining to Barbara, Penelope, and Charlie how to build a shelter.

". . . as many of these," Max says, holding up a long, straight stick, "as we can find. A little longer is fine, but this length is best. The straighter, the better." He reaches down and picks up another branch, this one with a fork at the end. "We'll also need six support poles. Again, as straight and thick as you can find."

Barbara looks around. "The weather being as nice as it is, shouldn't we be worried about finding food and water before building shelter?"

"Normally, you'd be right," Max says. "But in the bush, the situation always dictates your priorities. With our little . . . setback"—he glances at me—"we lost some valuable time. If we'd kept pushing on toward the river, we likely wouldn't have had enough light to scavenge by, so right now our priority needs to be our shelter. The temperature drops pretty dramatically in the Frank at night. We're talking into the thirties. That's potential hypothermia territory. You can live three weeks without food. Three days without water. But in the freezing cold, only three hours without shelter." He sizes each of us up. "Barbara, why don't you stay here and help me prep the building site. The rest of you get scavenging. Stay in pairs, and don't stray too far. It's *really* easy to get *really* lost, *really* fast."

Hank turns to me, but before he can ask me to be his stick-finding buddy, I turn to Charlie: "Shall we?"

He frowns. "Don't you think you and Hank should pair off? This could be the perfect occasion for you to share some of your more atypical *predilections*."

"*Predilections*. Right," I say. "I could do that, if you want to spend the next two hours alone in the woods dodging Penelope's sneeze spray."

Charlie sighs. "You make a good point. All right. But if I'm to be expected to lay my hands on Mother Nature's detritus, I need to get outfitted first."

"I think we need to step things up," Charlie says, a bundle of sticks cradled in his long-sleeve-cloaked arms. He is wearing a full-on beekeeper's outfit that he's brought, complete with wide-brimmed hat, screened veil, heavy-duty gloves, and a neck-to-ankle white cotton suit. "It's time to raise the bar."

"What are you talking about?" I squat and grab a thick, forked branch. "We've thrown some great material at him: *emollient, cilia, confabulation, aesthete, evanescence, liberation*—"

"I'm simply saying that I believe we may have misjudged our enemy. His resolve is much stronger than I'd anticipated. Haven't you noticed? Everything we do, Hank responds by being even *more* parental. He's only lost his cool once—when you ran off and got your penis stung."

"What are you trying to say? That everything we've done so far was pointless?"

"Not completely. I think we've laid a fairly decent foundation. Hank's cracks are starting to show. But if we're actually going to pull this off, we have to shift things into a higher gear."

"And how do you suggest we do that?"

Charlie grins at me. It's an evil grin—made all the more unsettling flashed from behind the gauzy black tulle of the bee-keeper's veil.

CHAPTER 32

As Max predicted, the temperature has dropped pretty dramatically now that the sun is down. Big clouds of steam escape my lips with each breath. It's not exactly freezing, but I can definitely feel the bite in my fingers and the tip of my nose.

Charlie and I are attempting to open Max's "emergency provision" canned chili using a couple of sharp rocks we found.

The cans of chili and the bladder of water Max brought are our only backup supplies. He said he doesn't like to use them on the first day but given that we're a short walk away from a river, he feels it's better for us to eat well tonight so we can be fresh and ready to conquer the wilderness tomorrow. "We'll spend most of the day fishing and restocking our reserve supplies with dried and smoked fish."

Amazing how Max can lug emergency rations all the way into the bush but not an emergency can opener. The least he could have done was let us use his knife. But when Charlie and I suggested it, he just laughed.

"If you're not willing to open the cans without tools," Max explained, "then it's not really an emergency."

I pound my stone into the top of the can, making tiny pock-marks in the aluminum but doing no real damage. The same cannot be said of the skin on my palm. I shift the rock to my left hand, flex the fingers on my right, the knuckles feeling like they're locking up.

"I'm sure glad we don't have to live like this all of the time," I say, studying my lack of progress. "It must have sucked being a caveman."

"Indeed," Charlie says. "All those cans of Hormel scattered about and poor Cro-Magnon with no electric opener."

I glare at Charlie. "You know what I mean. Having to get through life without the simplest tools. Like a can opener. A screwdriver. A MacBook."

"If you ask me," Charlie says, "it was a superior existence for them. Everything was more elemental. All the primitives were concerned about was food, water, sleep, and sex."

My gaze flits over to Penelope, who is squatting over a pile of kindling, sending sparks into it by striking the back of Max's carbon steel knife against a piece of quartz. Her jeans pucker just enough at the back to reveal the lacy edge of her red bikini bottoms.

"I would've thought you'd have hated the Stone Age," I say. "All those germs and no hand sanitizer for thousands of years!"

175

"Ah, but I wouldn't have known about the germs, now would I?" Charlie says, slamming his rock into the chili can top. "I do believe Thomas Gray was right when he said ignorance is bliss. However, I've been plagued with an unusually high intellect and thus do not benefit from the blissful state of most of my peers."

I open my mouth to argue but am interrupted by Penelope's triumphant cry.

"Got it!" she calls out, leaning forward, puffing tiny wisps of breath into her mini pyre.

"Gentle, now," Max says as he helps Hank and Barbara layer leaves onto our shelter. "Don't rush. If there's one thing I want everyone to take away from this week, it's that patience pays. Our modern existence may seem to tell you otherwise. That you have to 'get it yesterday.' But this attitude only fosters laziness. Entitlement. The natural world teaches otherwise. Mastery takes time. Endurance, stamina, fortitude, perseverance, persistence, patience. These are the pillars of accomplishment."

"Persistence, my ass," I mutter, slamming my stone down on my chili can. "We are never going to get these open."

"Success!" Charlie shouts, his stone piercing the top of his can, a spray of brown sauce coating his face and his glasses.

"How the hell did you do that?"

He holds up his rock. "It's all in the wrist, my friend."

"OK, Wristmaster." I chuck my can over to him. "Since you're the expert, why don't you finish opening the others? I'll go help Penelope with the fire."

Charlie glances at her. "Do you really think that's such a good idea?"

"What do you mean?" I stand and brush off my stinging hands.

"It means you and I both know why you snuck off to relieve yourself rather than alerting the group to nature's call," Charlie says. "We've got a long list of pranks to pull off, Daniel, but all of them require total commitment on your part. If you're feeling shy, inhibited, or self-conscious because of some harpy . . ."

"I know why we're here, Charlie," I say. "Nothing's going to get in the way of that. Trust me."

CHAPTER 33

A half hour later and Charlie has the five opened aluminum cans sitting in the fire. He's brought a vast supply of seasonings that he's carefully measuring out and stirring into each portion like a mad scientist.

When I suggested we just eat the chili cold from the can, Charlie scoffed at me.

"Can you *really* be that naive, Daniel?" he said. "Have you never heard of botulism? E. coli? It is absolutely imperative this food be heated to the appropriate bacteria-killing temperature. Not to mention adding the correct amounts of antimicrobial spices. Trust me. You and your colon want me working my magic."

Meanwhile, Max is showing us how to fashion a bow and arrow from a bootlace, some sticks, a bit of tree sap, and the top of a can.

"Now, if you don't have the luxury of a can lid," Max says, folding the metal over and pounding it with a stone, "you can chip a small rock to a point." He folds the lid again, does some more pounding. "Or you might look for a shard of bone. Alternatively, you can just sharpen the tip of the wooden shaft and harden it in a fire. But some kind of arrowhead works best because it gives the arrow a little weight, makes it fly farther, straighter, and deadlier."

He bends the metal yet again and hammers it flat.

Penelope's gaze keeps wandering over to Charlie. Finally, she gets up and crouches next to him before the fire. "What the hell are you adding to these, anyway?" she asks, poking one of the chili cans with a nearby stick.

"Could you not?" Charlie says. "You're going to knock it over."

"Not really a student of physics are you, Charlie?" Penelope says, continuing to prod the can. "In order for me to upset this cylinder's equilibrium, I would have to apply substantially more perpendicular force. If you want, I could calculate the can's center of gravity as well as the static equilibrium/torque and learn exactly—"

"What I really want"—Charlie bats Penelope's stick from her hand—"is for you to stop touching my cans."

Penelope laughs. "Well, I guess we know what it takes to upset *your* equilibrium."

I don't know why, but I get a little pang in my chest

179

watching Penelope and Charlie exchange barbs. Is Charlie right? Is Penelope distracting me from my purpose?

I wish I could give back Penelope's stupid potential-plane-crash kiss. I'm sure that's why she's in my head. I'd always imagined my first kiss was going to be with Erin, and Penelope took that from me.

I turn back to the others, tuning out Charlie and Penelope.

I force myself to focus on Max. Watch as he dips the flat end of the metal arrowhead in some melted sap and secures it into the slot he's cut at one end of a stick. He reinforces the tip with some thread he's pulled from his shirt.

"And voilà." He holds up the arrow for us to admire. "After supper each of you will make one. Then, if we have time, I'll demonstrate how to shoot. And if we're lucky, tomorrow we'll bag ourselves some game to go along with our fish."

"Dinner's on," Charlie calls out, the chili bubbling like crazy in the cans. He uses a folded-over stick as tongs and carefully carries a can over to Barbara, placing it on the ground beside her.

"Why, thank you, Charlie," Barbara says, wafting some of the steam toward her nose. "Smells . . . interesting. Nice. Asian, almost. What's in it?"

"Just a few things," Charlie responds, his chest puffed up proud. "Little oregano. Dash of cinnamon. Pinch of ginger. Touch of clove. Bit of garlic powder. For taste, but mostly for their antibiotic properties. Now be extremely careful. That food has been heated to a bacteria-annihilating two hundred and twelve degrees Fahrenheit."

"Just in case any of you were worried," Penelope says, laughing.

Charlie shoots her a withering stare, then proceeds to place a can beside every one of us except Max, who, apparently, doesn't require as much fuel as the average person to function.

"Well, cheers," Max says, raising his handful of nuts and leaves, which he gathered between erecting the shelters and the bow-and-arrow demonstration.

I bring the steaming spoon up to my mouth, tip it toward me, and take my first sip of the food—or try to. The pain is searing and instantaneous, the chili nearly cauterizing my lips shut.

"Jesus!" I shout, jerking my head back, my tongue flicking the burn.

"I warned you," Charlie says. "I'd let it cool if I were you. Though not for too long. Boiling kills botulism bacteria but not the spores. As the temperature lowers, the spores will begin to germinate, grow, and then excrete toxins."

"Yummy," Penelope says. "You ought to write ad copy for Campbell's Soup, Charlie."

"All I'm saying," Charlie states, "is that we should eat the food as soon as possible." He glares at Penelope. "*You*, on the other hand, are welcome to wait until your chili is festering with *Clostridium botulinum*."

"Oh, I don't think you should do that, honey," Barbara says.

"If I wasn't so hungry," Penelope says, staring down Charlie, "I *would* wait. Just to prove how wrong you are."

"Hey, be my guest." Charlie throws his hands in the air. "I'll particularly enjoy when your cranial nerves shut down and you can no longer speak."

Penelope shakes her head. "It's so sad—how you pretend to know so much but really know so little. It's common knowledge that properly heated food can be safely eaten up to two hours after it's been cooked. But then again, what do the World Health Organization, the Food and Drug Administration, and the Centers for Disease Control know about these things?"

"OK, OK," Hank says. "How about we all just enjoy our botulism-free meal and—"

Suddenly, a loud scuffling sound comes from the darkness to our right.

I jump. "What the hell was that? A wolf?"

Max looks over to where the sound came from. "Probably just a squirrel or a fox. Whatever it is won't bother us."

I squint, peering into the dark of the woods. "Are you sure? It sounded . . . bigger to me. Like . . . maybe . . . a wolf."

"It's nothing you have to worry about." Max takes a bite of his roughage. "Most of the wildlife in the Frank will steer clear of humans."

"Unless they're provoked or threatened, or you get in between them and their young," Penelope offers. "Then, all bets are off."

"True enough," Max says. "However, we are not going to do any of those things. Whatever it is may have been attracted by the smell of our food. But it won't come any closer. Not with all of us here and talking."

"Yeah," I say. "But what if it does?"

Max laughs. "I can tell you this: Statistics show that you are ten times more likely to be killed by the neighbor's dog than you are by a wild animal."

"And over a million times more likely to die of a lower

respiratory infection, influenza, nephritis, or septicemia," Charlie says, raising his spoon.

Max blinks at him. "Right." He shakes his head. "Anyway. All this to say, you're actually safer out here in the wild than you are in your own home."

I try to settle back and enjoy my piping-hot chili, but all I can picture is a wolf jumping out of the woods and biting off my face with its spiky fangs.

A boring-ass hockey game, a wasp-stung wiener, and a gruesome wolf mauling.

Worst. Birthday. Ever.

CHAPTER 34

"What are we doing out here?" I whisper to Charlie as we creep from our hut.

"We're upping the stakes," Charlie says, the full moon casting a blue light on his face. He pulls a small red spray bottle from the pocket of his jeans. "As I said."

"What is that?"

"It's our *coup de grâce.*" Charlie starts misting my legs with the spray.

"What the—?" I jump back, raising my arms. "I thought you said leaving Baby Robbie was our *coup de grâce.*"

"This is our backup *coup de grâce.*" He steps close again and starts fogging my entire body.

A wave of cesspool hits me. "Jesus Christ." I gag, jamming my nose into the crook of my elbow. "What the hell are you spraying me with?"

"Stick out your tongue," Charlie demands.

"Absolutely n—"

He lunges at me and squirts the liquid into my mouth.

"Plllugh." I spit and sputter. It's horrible. Salty and warm, like what I imagine ball-sack sweat might taste like. "What the fuck are you doing?"

"Keep it down," Charlie whispers, grabbing my arm and pulling me away from the hut. "You'll wake everyone up."

I lick at the sleeve of my T-shirt, the terrible tang coating my taste buds, trickling down my throat. "What is that crap, Charlie? And why did you spray it in my mouth?"

"It's the doe-in-heat urine," he says, showing me the label. "Deer can smell your breath for five miles."

I blink at him, my skin tingling. "Wait a second. Code word *invigorate*?"

Charlie smiles. "Exactly."

"But we bought that to use on Hank."

"I know," Charlie says. "But after you got stung by the wasps, I started thinking. What would be even better than having Hank get molested by a randy deer? Having *you* get molested by a randy deer and having Hank realize he's doing a terrible job keeping you safe on this trip."

"You *asshole!*" I rub my tongue on my T-shirt, trying to scrub away the putrid taste. My stomach lurches, probably from the foul smell. "I can't believe you just sprayed me with freakin' *deer pee!*"

"Think about it, Dan. If Hank can't protect you, eventually he's going to realize that he's a bad parent. And isn't that the entire point of all of this?"

"Yeah, but—"

"It makes perfect sense. Either Hank will finally give up the idea of being a dad, or when you get home and your mother hears about all of your near-death experiences whilst in his care, she's going to toss him out on his ear." Charlie raises his eyebrows. "It's the perfect plan."

"A wild animal attacking me is the perfect plan?"

"It's a deer, Dan," Charlie says. "It's not going to kill you. Just, you know, rough you up a bit with its hooves." He pinches his fingers together and speed-bags my shoulder, mimicking a rutting deer. "Maybe try to mount you. That's all."

I bat his hands away. "If you *ever* tell anyone you sprayed pee in my mouth, I will murder you in your sleep."

"If this all plays out like I think it's going to," Charlie says, "I imagine instead you will be toasting me at your wedding to Erin Reilly."

He lifts the bottle and quickly blasts my hair with the musky-circus stench.

I belatedly raise my hands to block it. "Jesus. How am I supposed to sleep smelling like this?"

"To be honest," Charlie says, "I don't imagine you'll be getting much sleep tonight."

"What's that supposed to mean?"

"It means that in a very short while, your dinner will not be agreeing with you."

"My dinn—?" Suddenly, I get a massive stabbing pain in my

186

gut, doubling me over. "Holy crap." I grip my belly. It feels like I just ate a plate of glass shards and chased it down with a two-liter bottle of Coke. I look at Charlie. "I thought you said you decontaminated the chili."

"Oh, I did," Charlie says. "That food was one hundred percent microorganisms-free."

I grimace in agony. "Then why do I feel like my intestines are about to explode?"

"That would probably be the bean powder, soy protein, Morton's Magna-Fiber, magnesium citrate, and tetrahydrolipstatin I incorporated into your serving."

CHAPTER 35

"What?" My eyes nearly shoot from their sockets. "*Miscarriage* too? You used *that* on me?"

"I know, I know," Charlie says. "But with the change in strategies, I needed a way to immobilize you. You can't be attacked by a buck if you're running scared. But hunched over a hole, voiding your bowels like a diarrheal dog? Well . . . it's about as close to leg shackles as I could get."

"You bastard." As I step toward Charlie, a quivering squeak escapes from my butt.

Charlie stifles a laugh. "I'm afraid this isn't going to be pretty."

"How could you do this to me?" My gut contracts, causing me to emit another high-pitched sphinc-squeal. "I thought you were my friend!"

"That's exactly *why* I did it," Charlie says. "This is the big push, so to speak. We've worked very hard to get Hank to the edge of the cliff. Now it's time to shove him over."

I'm sweating from head to foot. I feel like I'm going to unload in my borrowed sweatpants.

"I've never hated you more." I whip around and do a butt-clenched hobble toward the shelter.

Charlie hurries after me. "Where are you going?"

"To sleep this off," I say. "All of it."

"Oh, I wouldn't do that if I were you."

I turn on him. "I could care less what *you* would do, you ass nugget."

"Couldn't," Charlie says.

"Couldn't what?"

"You *couldn't* care less. *Could* implies that you do care some."

"How about you go screw yourself? Are you clear on what that implies, Charlie?"

I turn away again, pressing my fingers into my bloated belly as I shuffle over to the shelter. I crouch down and crawl inside, creeping by Hank, Max, and Barbara, who's lying on her back, her mouth slacked open, snoring like a lion with laryngitis. I inch along beside Penelope, mummified in her Wonder Woman sleeping bag.

Finally, I make it to my bedroll and slip inside. I pull the cover up, lie on my side, and hunch into the fetal position. The sharp vinegary stink of deer pee that surrounds me is awful. But the pain in my gut is even worse. Like a giant eel is slithering around inside me, gnawing on my innards.

I try to relax even as my stomach squeaks and growls. People sleep in worse conditions than this. Cancer kids in hospitals. Homeless people on the street. People in war zones. So I have a stomachache. And I smell like an incontinent old man. And I'm trapped in a tiny stick hut with five other people, wrapped up like a polyester burrito.

Big deal.

I can do this. I've slept off food poisoning before. Headaches. Muscle cramps. Various bruises and injuries inflicted by whichever jocks Charlie decided to piss off that day. Eventually I'll drift off and, hopefully, wake up tomorrow feeling—and smelling—like a new man.

Something rustles nearby. I peek over and see the silhouette of Charlie on his hands and knees, cat-pawing his way back to his camping cot. No way Charlie would sleep on the ground. Not with the increased possibility of getting bitten by a "vector-borne illnesses-bearing insect."

I suddenly wish I'd thought to scoop up a bunch of dirt and leaves and sprinkle it into his blankets. Or unload my doctored chili into his cot. Dish him up some soft-serve revenge.

But there was no way I could've managed that, even if I'd thought of it. Not with the agony I'm in. I'm lucky I could make it back to my own sleeping bag.

I close my eyes. Settle in. Take a deep breath—which I instantly realize is a colossal mistake.

Halfway through filling my lungs, a violent, wet cheek-flapper blasts from my ass. I try to squeeze it off, but it splutters on unrelentingly for a good five seconds, sounding like a didgeridoo played into a pot of loose mashed potatoes.

"Huh? Hmm? Wha?" I hear Hank mutter.

I pull the covers tight around my neck to try to bottle up the smell, but it doesn't work. The stink that envelopes me is heinous. Like a provolone-and-salami club left in a filthy urinal. I lie stock-still, every muscle in my body tightened, praying I can avoid further eruptions.

I clasp one palm over my nose and clutch my convulsing stomach with the other, breathing tiny sips of air through my mouth. The poo particles pummel my face, making me gag. Finally I can't take it any longer. I lift the top of the sleeping bag and waft it back and forth, hoping to disperse the stink.

Barbara coughs and I go rigid again. She makes a few sleepy grunting sounds, then starts snoring again.

I breathe in, trying to clear my nasal passages. Relax my body a little.

Another *really* bad idea.

A powerful squall erupts from my rear—deep, resonant, and rumbling. The kind of outburst you might expect from an elephant seal.

Penelope groans awake. She pokes her head out of her sleeping bag and props herself up onto her elbows, her eyes half shut. "Who brought the flügelhorn?"

"Your mom's snoring," I say, softly. "She's been at it all night. Must have some"—I clear my throat—"phlegm or something."

I hear Charlie's barely suppressed sniggers in the corner. I could murder him.

"Yeah, she does that." Penelope drops her head back onto her pillow. "Maybe tomorrow night we can have two shelters," she says sleepily. Suddenly, she bolts back upright, her entire face spasming. "Holy *Christ!*" she whisper-shouts, pinching her nose. "That was no snore. I think . . . I think someone in here shit their pants."

"I bet it was Max," I say, burying my face in the crook of my elbow. "All those nuts and leaves he was eating."

"Some people can't handle their fiber." Penelope retches a little before lying back down. "Let's just pray the tank has been emptied."

"Yeah," I say, tensing everything up. "Hope so."

But—*ohgod, ohgod, ohgod*—it's building again. The pressure.

I visualize pinching off the lip of a balloon. Or covering the mouth of a foaming soda bottle. But my hold is weakening.

No. No. No. Please. No—

Vvvvrrrraaaapth!

My entire sleeping bag puffs up behind me, like a plastic bag catching the air.

Oh, God.

Charlie is cracking up now, not even trying to keep quiet. "No one light a match."

"No kidding," Penelope says. "I think Max might be dying. And he's going to take us down with him. Do you have any of those extra respirators, Charlie?"

"Afraid not," Charlie answers. "And it's not Max who's trying to kill us. It's—"

This time I'm grateful for the snarling jockey-burner that blasts out of me. It's husky and insistent . . . and slightly painful. Like I may have torn something.

"What . . . what's going on here?" Hank mumbles, and sits

192

up. "Who's making all that—" He gags and slaps a hand over his mouth and nose. "Oh, *God*! What is that horrible smell?"

"It's Dan," Charlie blurts.

"Is not." I grit my teeth, another nor'easter threatening to escape my aft.

I quickly roll onto my back, trying to smother the storm. But it does no good. The seal on my gasket is long gone, and the wind whips out wildly and vociferously.

VVVVRRRRAAAAPTH!

A slight, moist discharge follows.

Barbara and Max appear unfazed by the noise and noxious fumes. Everyone else, however, turns and stares at me in the dappled moonlight.

"So it was you all along." Penelope flicks on a tiny flashlight, shining in it my face like I'm in an interrogation room. "Shifting blame is a serious personality flaw, Dan. It belies a much deeper issue. Self-loathing, perhaps? Deep-seated guilt? An inability to accept responsibility for your actions? Which one is it?"

I squint and lift my hand to block the light beam. "I thought we weren't allowed to bring any modern—" I start to say, then breathe in a lungful of air so chunky and toxic that my stomach nearly shoots straight up my esophagus.

I dry-heave and hack, my eyes starting to tear up.

"It's his spastic colon," Charlie says. "IBS. He's had it for as long as I've known him. He's understandably embarrassed by it."

Hank frowns. "Your mom didn't mention that you have a medical condition."

I open my mouth to correct him, but my sphincter cuts me off with a wheezing snorter.

193

Penelope shimmies out of her sleeping bag. "IBS or BS—either way, I'm out of here."

"I think we could all use some fresh air," Hank says, his hand still clamped over his nose. He follows Penelope out of the hut.

Max and Barbara are miraculously still asleep. Why couldn't Penelope have inherited her mother's deep-sleeping abilities?

I glare at Charlie. "I'm going to kill you."

"Yeah, with your stench," he says. "I better go join the others before I'm rendered comatose."

Charlie makes a move to leave, but I lunge for him. Grab his leg.

"Not so fast, buddy," I snarl, grabbing his leg. "You wrought this. Now you're going to stew in it."

He grins at me. "Don't overexert yourself, Daniel. We wouldn't want you to have an accident, now would we?"

Then he pokes me in the belly.

Oh, God.

My stomach gurgles.

Squeezes.

Lurches.

"You dick," I say, letting go of Charlie.

I grab my gut. Leap to my feet. And stumble out of the hut.

Hoping that it's not too late.

CHAPTER
36

I bolt out into the open, buttocks clamped tight, and charge past the others, who seem headed toward the fire pit.

"Dan!" Hank calls out. "Where are you going?"

"Have to . . . check on something!" I shout, not breaking my stride, my socks loose and saggy on my feet as I stumble-run into the moonlit woods.

Oh, Jesus, this is going to be explosive. Goddamn Charlie and his stupid bean powder.

A huge tree twenty yards in front of me becomes my sole focus. The pain in my gut is intense. My intestines are convulsing. Whatever's inside me wants out, and it wants out *right now*.

I take one last leap and make it to the massive Douglas fir in the nick of time.

In a single motion I drop trou, press my back against the tree trunk, squat down, and let go.

"*Oooooooooooooo!*" The relief is immediate and glorious as I splatter the ground with a torrent of the foulest-smelling diarrhea I have ever experienced.

The sputtering is loud and angry, like a faucet with air in the pipes turned on full blast. I scoot my feet a bit wider to avoid spackling them with filth, then hunch over even more, my gut spasming, my anus on fire.

The evil spews and spurts out of me, as though I'm evacuating everything I've eaten for the past month. The thick, eggy stink of it, like a stagnant bog, plugs my nostrils. I clench down and unleash another violent swampy discharge.

"*Uuuuuuuuu.* God." My eyes roll back into my head. "Out, evil spirits! Be gone!"

I contract my stomach muscles hard, blowing out a final sustained stool shower.

I exhale, completely spent.

I glance around in the dimness for some clean leaves to wipe myself with and spot some at the base of the tree. I slowly lower myself down and grab a handful, my thighs trembling from the stress of crouching so long.

Just as I finish cleaning up, I get another knifing pain in my intestines. Oh no. Not again.

I'm about to let loose once more when I hear a rustling sound over to my right, like heavy footsteps in the forest.

"Who's there? Charlie? Hank? I'm still kinda working things out over here. You should probably keep a safe distance."

No response.

Crunch. Crunch. Crunch.

"Hello?" I call out. "I'll be done in just a minute, OK?"

Nothing.

A light breeze sways the branches above me, blessedly shifting my sewer stench away from me. An owl caterwauls somewhere in the distance.

And then I hear it—a wet snuffling sound from just beyond the shrubs. Leaves rustle. A branch snaps.

I squint hard, trying to see through the foliage.

And that's when I remember.

The doe-in-heat urine.

CHAPTER 37

My heart thuds in my chest. My mouth goes spitless.

I have to get out of here, before I'm mounted by a horny stag.

I bear down with everything I've got, feeling like I'm on the brink of giving myself an aneurysm. But it does the trick, sending another powerful spray jetting from my ass, plastering the ground beneath me.

I snatch up more leaves and mop myself up as quickly as possible.

A loud, snotty snort comes from the bushes to my right. Like a bull with a cold.

"Shoo," I squeak, my windpipe constricting. I gulp. "Go away! I'm not interested."

More swishing, more guttural snorting.

"Charlie?" I say. "If that's you trying to screw with me, you can cut it out. I'm in no mood. Come on. Show yourself."

And then, as if on command, a hulking black bear lumbers out of the forest, snuffling along the ground like a drug dog on the scent of a duffel bag full of weed.

I gasp, a jolt of adrenaline spiking through my veins.

The bear looks up, its dark eyes glinting in the moonlight. It sniffs wildly at the air, its scarred nostrils flaring.

Ho-ly *shit*! It's the same bear from the lake! Did it follow us here?

I try not to move. Try not to breathe. Try not to even blink.

But my legs are about to give way. I don't know how long I've been squatting against this tree, but my trembling quads are telling me I'll be dropping to the ground any second now.

I try to remember what Max said about bears.

Don't run. Never run. Under no circumstances should you run.

The beast snorts and paws at the ground. Jesus Christ. I can't believe I'm going to be killed by a bear in a puddle of my own shit soup, with my pants down around my ankles and my junk hanging out.

The burning in my legs is unbearable. My back starts to slip down the tree truck. Inch. By inch. By inch.

I press hard into the tree with the last of my strength, holding my breath, trying to stay as still as I can. *Please just go. Please just go. Please just go.*

But the bear plods toward me. It's just twenty feet away now.

Fifteen feet.

Good God, it is absolutely *massive*.

It's getting closer. And closer. And closer.

Fuck this. I grab my boxers and sweats, yank them up, and run like hell.

The bear takes off after me, just like Max said it would. I can hear the sounds of bushes, branches, and leaves being torn away in its path.

"Help!" I scream. "Bear! *Help!*"

I glance over my shoulder. The rushing beast is gaining ground fast.

"Hank!" I shout. "Charlie! Penelope!"

I pump my arms hard, my stocking feet pounding the ground. Finally, I catch sight of the big branch hut. I burst into the clearing.

Charlie, Hank, and Penelope are huddled around a low-burning fire. They leap to their feet when they see me.

"B-bear!" I gasp, nearly senseless with fear. "Bear! R-right behind me!"

"Jesus Christ!" Hank looks past me, his eyes huge.

Penelope and Charlie leap up and hide behind Hank.

I turn around and watch as the giant creature bounds from the forest. As soon as it sees the four of us, it skids to a halt. It slaps its paws on the ground, grunting and woofing at us. Clearly, it is not pleased by the turn of events.

"Max!" I shout through cupped hands. "Barbara! Help! Get out here!"

"What the hell do we do now?" Charlie says.

"The bear's stopped," Hank says. "It's nervous. We can take advantage of that. Here. Let's get in a line. Make ourselves seem big. Scare it off."

"Interesting theory, Mr. Langston," Charlie says, his Adam's apple bobbing in the moonlight. "However, I do believe I remember a certain bush pilot saying that it has been an extremely long winter here in the Frank. That the animals were having a difficult time finding sustenance."

"If we run away, it'll chase after us," Hank says. "Just like it did with Dan. You want to risk being the one it goes after?"

"Well," Charlie says, pushing his glasses up. "When you put it that way."

The bear lifts its nose, its nostrils twitching.

The four of us stand in a row and link arms. We take a step toward the bear.

The bear slaps at the dirt, warning us.

"Um," I croak, my throat saltine-dry. "It doesn't look very frightened."

The animal takes a step forward.

"Make some noise!" Hank shouts. "*Rah! Rah!* Go! Leave!"

"*Relinquo!*" Penelope yells. "*Ut de loco in inferno!*"

Charlie blinks at her. "You think the bear knows Latin?"

"You think it knows English?" Penelope counters. "Besides, Latin's my reflex language. *Vado! Emigro! Exitus!*"

The animal continues forward, its nose sniffing the air like mad.

"It isn't working!" Penelope cries.

Max stumbles out of the shelter, scratching his head, his eyes half shut. "What the heck's going on out—oh shit!" Suddenly, he's wide awake and in an action-man stance. "Nobody move."

"Tell that to the mountainous omnivore," Charlie says.

"Is it morning already?" Barbara croaks as she crawls from the hut. "I feel like we just—Oh-my-God-a-bear!"

201

Max holds up a hand. "Stay calm. It's just curious. Look at its nostrils go. It's caught a scent. Is someone wearing perfume? Cologne?"

I glare at Charlie, who doesn't meet my gaze.

"It's a bold animal," Max says. "But there are too many of us. It won't attack. Stand your ground."

And yet the bear keeps advancing.

"Keep making noise," Max instructs. "Barbara and I are going to circle around to you. The last thing we want is this animal thinking it's cornered."

Hank roars, "Go away, bear! Go away!"

"*Vanesco!*" Penelope screams. "*Abeo!*"

"*Jah!*" I holler. "*Bah! Wah!* Get lost! This is not the camp you're looking for!"

"Good, good!" Max says, holding Barbara's hand and cautiously leading her in a wide half circle around the camp. "More aggressive! Don't back down."

The four of us go nuts, yelling and howling and shrieking. Stomping our feet. Kicking up dirt.

The bear stops. Tilts its head curiously.

"Excellent!" Max says. "Keep going! Don't let it think you're weak!"

"Hold on, Penelope," Barbara says. "Mommy's coming."

"*Yah! Yah! Yah!*" I shout, my voice going hoarse and phlegmy. "Scram! Shoo!"

Suddenly, the bear rears back and swats its front paws hard on the earth. Its head juts out as it gives a low, angry, guttural growl.

Oh *crap*!

"The bear's just testing you," Max says, stopping in his tracks and holding Barbara back. "It's all a big bluff."

The bear springs forward, its teeth bared and clacking, like Hannibal Lecter about to feast.

The six of us scream bloody murder and scatter.

CHAPTER 38

Hank and Penelope bound into the woods. Charlie stumbles after them, his arms pinwheeling like a mental patient. Barbara stretches out a hand and screams Penelope's name as Max yanks her off into the darkness.

And where do I run? Not away from the camp like all the others. No, *I* race toward the hut—because there's no way a bear will be able to get at me inside a fortress of twigs and sticks.

But even though I know I'm running toward my doom, it's too late to do anything else now. I just have to hope that the bear decides not to—

Fuck!

My foot catches a rock, sending me flying.

I slam hard into the branch shelter, the whole thing collapsing and clattering around me.

I'm swallowed up by sticks, leaves, and shrubbery. I claw at the debris, swiping pine needles from my face. I flip over and look up just in time to see the bear changing course and lumbering toward me, its dark eyes locked on mine.

Again.

The bear clomps forward, its nostrils quivering, its sharp claws scraping the ground as it goes.

I grab a stick and hurl it at the bear from where I'm sitting. The stick goes way wide. *"Yah!* Get out of here! *Yah!"* I grab another one and throw it as hard as I can. *"Yah! Yah!"*

The branch bounces off the bear's shoulder.

But it keeps coming.

I kick the bramble off and scrabble to my feet, the bear closing in on me. I'm about to make a run for it when, miracle of miracles, I spot Max's homemade bow and arrows on the ground. We never did get that archery lesson from him.

I snatch up the bow and one of the crude arrows anyway. I face the bear, my legs weak and wobbly.

I nock the arrow and draw back the bootlace bowstring. My arms tremble from the strain. Or from fear.

I raise the bow and take aim, the shoelace cutting into my fingers.

The bear stops. It growls and smacks at the ground, like it knows what I'm about to do.

"Don't come any closer, you bastard," I say, trying to sound brave and determined. But the arrow clicks and trembles inside the little notch; there's no way in hell I'm hitting this animal. Not even to save my life.

A loud branch cracks to my right.

I spin around to see who—or what—it is. And when I do, the bootlace snaps, thrashing against my forearm.

The bow flies out of my hand and smacks the bear in the nose. Meanwhile, the arrow rockets off to the side and—

"*Uuu!*" Hank grunts and drops to his knees.

"Oh crap!" I stare at the arrow sticking out of Hank's left calf. Blood blooms around the wound, staining the pant leg of his sweats.

I glance over and see the bear dragging its sore nose on the ground.

I run over to Hank. "Oh my God," I say, examining the injury. "It . . . went all the way through. I am *so* sorry, Hank! I was aiming for the bear, but then you startled me and I—"

"It's . . . fine. Just . . ." Hank swallows. He looks up at the snorting bear. "Help me up. We have to . . . get out of here. Before it comes . . . after us."

CHAPTER
39

"Do you need to rest?" I ask Hank, his arm heavy around my shoulder.

It's been slow going with Hank having to lean most of his weight on me as we hobble along, but we've managed to get a fair ways into the forest. If the bear is following us, it's doing so in stealth mode; we haven't heard so much as a rustle from behind us since we left the camp.

"No," he says, his breath labored. "We just . . . need to get as far away as we can."

I grimace, hoping he can't see my expression. My legs are on fire, my shoulders are cramped up, and my back feels like it could snap at any moment.

But there's no way I can complain. Not when Hank's the one with the arrow piercing his calf—an arrow *I* put there. If he can keep going, I sure as hell can.

"I'd like . . . to get to the river . . . if we can," Hank pants.

The damned river. I can hear the sound of cascading water off in the distance, but how far is anyone's guess. I don't know how I'm going to make it there without collapsing.

"Hello?" A voice rasps in the dark. "Who's there?"

"It's Dan," I say. "And Hank. Who's that?"

The bushes rustle and a thin beam of light swings through the dark as Penelope and Charlie lope toward us.

"Thank God we found you," Charlie says when they get to us. "And that you're OK."

"Not exactly," I say, gesturing to the arrow in Hank's leg.

"Holy Christ!" Penelope's eyes bug behind her glasses. "How did that happen?"

"Dan . . . shot me," Hank says.

"He *what*?" Charlie gives me a holy-crap-are-you-*that*-desperate look.

"It was an accident," I explain. "I was aiming for the bear. But the bowstring exploded on me, and the arrow went in the wrong direction. If you want to blame someone, blame Max and his shoddy workmanship."

Penelope crouches down to examine the wound. "That looks extraordinarily unpleasant." She stands. "We need to remove the shaft and clean the wound as soon as possible."

"We'll need . . . water," Hank says, perspiration beading his forehead. "We should head toward . . . the river."

"From the sounds of it, the river's at least a mile away,"

Charlie says. "But there's a stream a couple hundred yards back the way we came." He slips Hank's other arm around his shoulder. "Come on. We'll take you there."

I desperately want to ask Penelope to spell me for a bit, but the combination of guilt and pride makes me bite my tongue. Literally. It's the only thing keeping me from screaming.

Penelope leads the way with her Maglite. Charlie, Hank, and I step-limp our way behind.

"Did you see my mother?" Penelope asks, not sounding terribly concerned.

"Max . . . dragged her off . . . into the woods," I gasp, struggling to keep Hank vertical. "When . . . the bear attacked."

Penelope looks amused. "It's not bear that Max should fear," she says. "It's cougar."

A short but agonizing while later, we find the stream. Charlie and I ease Hank down onto a log.

"Thanks, guys," Hank says, his shirt soaked in sweat. He winces as he props his injured leg on a rock. He grabs the cuff of his sweatpants leg and tears it in two to reveal the full horror of the trauma.

I retch, my stomach turning.

Penelope shines her flashlight on the wound, examining both sides of Hank's leg. "It's fairly clean. The projectile perforated the soft tissue and passed straight through the gastrocnemius. Missed your fibula and tibia completely." She stands. "I've seen worse."

"How do you know all of that?" I ask in awe, still barely able to look at the wound myself.

"I consider myself pre-premed," she says, pushing her glasses up her nose. "I was reading *Gray's Anatomy* when you were still trying to find Spot."

"*Gray's?*" Charlie asks skeptically. "Isn't that a bit antiquated? I'd have thought a serious doctor-in-training would have read Netter's *Atlas of Human Anatomy.*"

"Netter's is excellent," Penelope says. "However, it isn't completely representative of practical anatomy. Not to mention the mistakes. Now Rohen's is another story completely, as it uses actual cadaver photographs."

"I'm all for photographs," Charlie counters, "but don't you think illustrations have the benefit of being able show the borders of structures more clearly?"

"In some cases," Penelope says. "But if I'm going with illustrations, I'm sticking with the Sobatta. The drawings are superior, and they identify all of the anatomical structures by their Latin names, which I prefer."

"Enough!" Hank says, his voice strangled. "Let's get on with this. After I break off the arrowhead, I'm going to need one of you to remove the shaft."

"Wh-why can't you do that, too?" I ask, feeling light-headed.

Hank grimaces. "It's not going to come out without a fight. And to be honest, I'm not sure I'll remain conscious long enough to finish the task."

Oh, God.

Penelope shrugs. "I'll do it. Bloodshed and viscera don't unnerve me. Unlike these two hemophobes."

"I didn't . . . say I wouldn't do it," I croak.

"Me . . . either," Charlie adds weakly.

Penelope shines the flashlight on Charlie and me. "You sure? Because you both look decidedly whey-faced."

"Yeah, well," I say, taking a deep breath. "I shot the arrow. So . . . I should be the one to pull it out."

"I appreciate the gesture, Dan," Hank says, his sweaty face tinted blue by the moon. "But it has to be done quickly, without any hesitation."

"That settles it," Penelope says, pushing me out of the way. "Give me some room, boys. The more time we waste, the greater the risk of infection."

"Well, technically," Charlie says, "the wound's most likely already infected, but—"

"Oh, shut up, Bill Nye," Penelope snaps. "Your pop-science trumpery is next to useless here." She turns to Hank. "You ready?"

Hank takes a deep breath and nods. He grabs the tip of the arrow with both hands and flexes it. "Oh, God." He grimaces as the arrow bows but doesn't snap. *"Rrrrrrrr!"* he groans, bending the shank even farther.

Fresh blood spills from the wound as the jostling arrow tugs at the holes.

"Jesus Christ," Charlie says, turning away. "I can't watch this."

I half close my eyes, but for some reason I can't stop looking, even though my head is full of helium and my stomach is flopping over like a dying fish.

"Aaaaaaaaaaaaaaaa!" Hank gives one last long scream as he bears down and—

Crack!

The wood splinters and the arrowhead breaks off.

Hank's body crumples. He starts to teeter off the log, and I leap over, grab him, and heft him upright.

"Thanks . . . Dan," he mumbles.

"Would you like to wait a minute?" Penelope asks, sounding authoritative. "So you can compose yourself before I commence with the extraction?"

He shakes his head. "No . . . get it . . . over with."

Penelope looks at us. "When I withdraw the projectile, the wound will start to hemorrhage. One of you needs to be ready to perform hemostasis. The last thing we want is for him to become hypovolemic."

"And if we were speaking English?" I say.

"We have to stop the bleeding," Charlie explains.

"How do we do that?" I ask.

"Your T-shirt should do," Penelope says. "You're going to want to put a lot of pressure on it in order to initiate coagulation. And no matter how loud Hank begs and screams for you to stop, you do not let up, understand?"

I nod, my chin trembling.

Hank meets my eyes. "It'll be . . . OK, Dan . . . Once . . . it's done."

"I'd offer to do it," Charlie says, retching a little. "But, you know, blood-borne pathogens and everything. Not that I think you've got anything, Mr. Langston."

"It's fine," I say, with false confidence. "I've got it. If you could stand behind him, though, and keep him steady . . . ?"

Charlie gulps. "Oh, uh, right." He moves behind Hank, placing a hand on each of his shoulders. "But make sure you cover that wound immediately. A severed artery can really spray."

"I'll do my best." I pull off my shirt, the night air chilly on my chest. I fold the cloth over a few times to give it some layers. "R-ready," I say to Penelope.

Penelope hunches over Hank's leg. She grabs the tail of the arrow with her right hand and places her left against his calf. All business now.

"I'm not going to lie to you," she says. "This is going to hurt like a motherfucker. But I'll do it as fast as I can."

CHAPTER
40

"Wh-what do w-we do n-now?" I say, shivering like crazy, my arms wrapped around my naked torso.

Penelope, Charlie, and I are huddled up next to each other like penguins, sitting on the ground in front of a passed-out Hank. With the LED light on my ID bracelet now blinking an angry life-support red and the smiley faces on my boxers glowing a bright green, I'm a regular neon advertisement for loserhood.

"We w-wait until he w-wakes up," Penelope chatters back. She's seated on my right, wearing nothing but her red underwear and a white tank top, her milky-white skin glowing in the moonlight.

I mean, *probably* glowing in the moon. I'm doing my best not to look at her. Because when I eventually tell this story to Erin, I don't want to have to censor out parts of it.

It took Penelope three hefty tugs to get the arrow fully dislodged from Hank's leg. He blacked out sometime between the second and third tugs. And who could blame him? If I had to deal with that kind of pain, I would've prayed to pass out the moment the arrow pierced my skin.

There was a shitload of blood. The first big squirt caught Penelope in the glasses, making her look like she'd just staked a vampire. I covered the wound as soon as I could and kept the pressure on. But Hank bled through my shirt and sweats, Charlie's jeans, and Penelope's T-shirt and sweatpants before we were able to stop the bleeding completely. Then we gently cleaned the wound with fresh stream water, using Charlie's undershirt as a final bandage.

Afterward we all rinsed off in the creek, which didn't help with the cold situation.

Now we sit and wait for Hank to come to.

In our underwear.

I shift my position. My ass is starting to feel sort of . . . itchy. Probably because I didn't have time to wipe up properly earlier.

Shifting makes me hyperaware of Penelope's naked arm touching my naked arm. My eyes drift over to her and her long, naked legs, pulled up against her body. Her smooth arms, the moonlight cascading over the soft swell of her—

Whoa-kay! Enough of that. I wrench my gaze away.

"You, uh, think he'll be OK?" I ask the stream. "It s-seemed like he lost a l-lot of blood."

"It's n-not the blood l-loss you have to w-worry about." Charlie, seated to my left in his not-so-tighty-whities, rubs his arms vigorously. "It's s-septicity. That's what'll k-kill him. There are at least thirty different types of bacteria that'll c-cause a wound to become gangrenous: staph, strep, klebsiella, E. coli. The list goes on. If he's l-lucky, it'll be localized and he'll only lose the leg. If he's not so lucky . . ." Charlie shrugs. "Well, you'll pr-probably want to avoid an open casket."

"J-Jesus." A grossed-out shiver runs up my spine.

"Way to be ch-cheery there, Dr. Doom," Penelope says.

"I'm just st-stating facts," Charlie replies.

I look over at Hank. "How long d-do we have before something like that happens?"

"Symptoms usually start to sh-show in a few hours," Charlie explains. "Redness, sw-swelling, oozing pus, fever. If it's not treated, I don't like his ch-chances."

"Shit." A sick feeling balloons in my gut. "M-maybe one of us should go back to camp and g-get some of Charlie's medications. Maybe we can find Max and your m-mom too."

"We're not going to f-find the two of them," Penelope says.

"Why not?" I say. "The four of us f-found each other."

"If I know my m-mother," Penelope says, "and, unfortunately, I know her all t-too well, she will use the bear attack as an excuse to sp-spend the next four days getting to know M-Max better. Much, *much* better."

"Won't she be w-worried about you?" I ask.

Penelope shrugs, her flesh sliding against my flesh. "She s-saw me run off with Hank and Ch-Charlie. Of course, she d-doesn't know that you sh-shot an arrow through Hank's leg, disabling our team captain." She raises her eyebrows. "As for the trip b-back to camp, the potential for getting l-lost in the dark is far too high. Also, there's the p-possibility of another bear encounter to take into account."

"L-loath as I am to admit it," Charlie says, pressing his bony shoulder into mine, "Penelope raises some valid p-p-points."

"Wh-what about Hank?" I say. "Wh-what about infection?"

"You know me," Charlie says. "I t-tend toward the hy-hyperbolic. We cleaned the wound well. Bandaged it up. It's entirely possible he'll be fine until morning. Our m-main concern now should be keeping warm through the night."

"And j-just how do you propose we do th-that?" I ask, blowing into my numbing hands.

"We can make a d-debris bed," Charlie says. "I read about it in one of the s-survival books. First we cover Hank's body with leaves, moss, p-pine needles—wh-whatever we can find. Then we pile up a waist-high mound for us and cl-climb inside. It's good down to t-ten degrees Fahrenheit, which we shouldn't even get close to tonight."

"W-well, w-well, your first g-good idea," Penelope says. "Sh-shocking. You do know, though, that a d-debris bed poses a certain amount of contagion r-risks. Are you sure you c-can handle it?"

"It's not my ideal sc-scenario," Charlie says. "However, if I balance the r-risk of infection with the risk of a f-fatal drop in body temperature, in this case the chance of freezing to d-death is the more likely."

"All right, then. Let's g-get to w-work." Penelope claps her hands and hoists herself to her feet—a bespectacled, nearly naked goddess.

Suddenly, a certain part of me is no longer cold.

I wrench my gaze away again and stare at poor, passed-out Hank to try to keep my smiley faces from bulging.

CHAPTER
41

I am in heaven and hell simultaneously.

I am lying under a pile of leaves next to Penelope—essentially we are in bed together—staring up at a sky teeming with brilliant stars. My left arm and leg are pressed against her right arm and leg. Even through the coarse, scratchy bristles of pine needles, twigs, and grass, her skin feels warm and wonderful. Lithe and lovely. Soft and supple.

One part of me wants to casually roll over and stare into Penelope's eyes, declare my feelings of attraction, and let our bodies do the rest.

And the other part of me is clinging to the edge of the Erin cliff by my chewed-to-the-quick fingernails. The only thing keeping me from free-falling off the precipice is this damn burning itching in my anus. Must be diarrhea rash or something.

It's my penance for indulging in adulterous thoughts about Penelope.

My eyes slide to the side.

Penelope is asleep. So adorable. Such a cute little chin. Such rich, full lips. Such—

Cut it out, Dan!

I lift my head and bang it hard into my moss pillow.

Ow! Crap. Not as spongy as I thought.

I want to reach up and massage the back of my skull, maybe feel for blood, but I don't want to wake Penelope and risk her moving away from me. Breaking our contact. Our connection.

Oh, God, this is so stupid.

Sure, she kissed me once—but only because she thought she was going to die. But it awakened something inside of me. A passion that's burning out of control. Like the fire in my ass.

No. Just . . . no.

I clench my eyes shut and try to avoid thinking about Penelope *or* whatever evil is going on in my sphincter. Erin. I'll think about Erin. But my will is like a sugar cube in boiling water, Erin's face dissolving into Penelope's, until suddenly I'm at risk of breaching the hull of our leafy enclosure.

Between the ill-timed boners, the traitorous lusting, and a wildfire raging inside my butthole, this is going to be the longest night of my life.

CHAPTER
42

"Wake up, Dan. We need to go."

My eyes flutter open, and there's Hank, crouched over me, his hand on my shoulder.

"You're—you're alive!" I croak, my tongue feeling thick and furry.

"Can't get rid of me that easily, bud," Hank says.

A jolt of adrenaline spikes through me. Has he put it all together? Does he think I actually shot him on purpose?

"Ha." I force a laugh and push up onto my elbows. "That's funny. Seriously, though. I'm glad you're all right. We were freaking out last night."

"It's all good," Hank says. "Come on. Let's get a move on. We want to get back to camp."

I make a big production of climbing from the debris bed, using the leafy cover to surreptitiously scratch my burning butt cheeks. *Uhhnnhh.* It feels like someone gave me a cayenne-pepper enema while I was sleeping.

I squint into the morning light. Charlie is pulling on his rinsed-out pants and shirt. Penelope is climbing back into her sweats.

What a shame.

I turn back to Hank. "Are you sure you're OK to walk?"

"Yeah, I'm fine," he says, looking down at his leg. "It still hurts like hell, but at least I can put some weight on it." He nods at the debris bed. "Nice job, by the way. You guys were amazing last night."

"Thanks," I say, grabbing my damp shirt off the branch and pulling it on. It feels gross. Cold and clammy. "The bed was Charlie's idea."

"Really?" Hank laughs. "With all the dirt and everything?"

"Options needed to be weighed," Charlie says. "Sacrifices were made for the greater good. I'll decontaminate when we return to our encampment."

"Speaking of which . . ." Hank looks into the forest. "Does anyone know the way back? I'm afraid I was a little . . . preoccupied when we departed."

"Sure," Penelope says. "Follow me."

A half hour later, we are still tromping through the forest seemingly no closer to camp. Penelope is leaving us in her dust, marching forward with little regard for those of us falling behind.

"Are you sure this was the right way?" I call up to her, my butt burning so badly I can hardly see straight.

"Not a clue," she announces.

"Wait, what?" Charlie stops. "But you said—"

"Somebody had to make a decision," Penelope says, "or we'd still be sitting back there lost in a fog of rhinotillexis and mucophagy."

I look to Charlie for a translation.

"Picking our noses and eating it," he says, rolling his eyes. "Can you believe what a pretentious sesquipedalian she is? It's kind of pathetic."

"Right," I say, watching Penelope march on.

Hank is not looking well. His face is pale and drenched in sweat.

"I think we need to take a break," I call ahead.

But Penelope charges on. Charlie and I get on either side of Hank and help him hobble along.

Fifteen minutes later, Penelope shouts back to us, "Found it! Or what's left of it."

"Holy . . . crap," Hank pants, when we finally catch up to Penelope. "It looks like . . . it was hit by . . . a tornado."

The four of us stand there at the edge of the clearing, staring at the remnants of our camp. There are pieces of backpacks scattered everywhere. Bits of torn clothes, papers, and little plastic medicine bottles flung far and wide. Our sleeping bags ripped to ribbons, fluffs of cotton and polyester strewn to the four winds.

I zombie-walk through the wreckage—furtively digging a finger into my itchy ass crack as I go. I pluck up articles of clothing, one of Max's arrows, Barbara's shattered phone, Baby Robbie's muddied sweater . . .

Under a pile of sticks, I find my sketchbook, dirty and trampled upon but still intact. I flip to the back and find my last drawing of Erin. I mean . . . Erilin. The Desert Princess. *My* princess. I press the baby sweater onto the page, my emotions swelling.

How could I have wavered in my devotion to her? I must have gone temporarily insane. Look at her. How beautiful she is. Those eyes. Her secret smile.

I glance over at Penelope. Back to my drawing. Back to Penelope. There's no comparison. Penelope is just a cute, geeky, super-smart girl who lacks social skills.

But Erin. Erin is the hot sword-wielding maiden of my destiny.

I look down at my ID bracelet. A blue EKG squiggle blipping slower and slower on the screen. Baby Robbie's heartbeat. Decelerating. Weakening. Until at last.

It flatlines.

CHAPTER
43

"Doesn't look like we've got much," I say, dropping my loot on the minuscule pile of salvaged junk by the fire pit.

Besides a few of Charlie's medical supplies and some clean, unshredded clothes for Penelope (lucky her), we didn't find much else. None of our prank stuff seems to have survived. Not that I'm too worried about it now. If this shit show of a trip hasn't convinced Hank that he should keep a healthy distance from the Weekeses, then I don't see how some reeky feet or a viciously itchy crotch is going to make much difference.

"We'll keep looking," Hank says.

"I doubt we'll find much more," Penelope says. "Max and my mother have already been here and left. I'm sure they grabbed most of the usable appurtenances."

"How do you know they've been back?" Hank says, settling down on a log.

"Max's knife is gone," Penelope explains. "And the remnants of their backpacks have been rummaged through. Also, my mom left me this note." She holds up a dirt-smeared piece of paper and reads: "'Penelope. I'm praying you are OK and still with the others. Max and I returned to camp and waited for you all night. We have decided our best option is to return to the lake and hole up there until the plane arrives. If you and the others get this note, please head there as well. Hoping to see you there soon. Much love, Mom.'"

"Why wouldn't they have kept waiting here for us?" Charlie asks. "They must have known we'd come back for our supplies."

"I told you," Penelope says, crumpling the note and tossing it on the ground. "My mom knows a golden opportunity when she sees one."

Hank looks around. "Well, I think we should go through what we've collected and then start heading toward the lake too. It's going to take us a lot longer than it'll take them to get there."

I shift from foot to foot, my ass cheeks feeling like someone is holding a million lit matches to them.

"I think . . ." I croak, trying not to scream. "I think . . . I need to take . . . a bio break."

"OK, but make it snappy," Hank says, picking up the broken pieces of Max's satellite phone and trying to fit them together. "And stay within shouting distance."

"Will do." I dart into the woods, desperate to get my pants

226

off and have a look at the increasingly inflamed situation down below—and maybe violate a tree till my rear is so raw that it no longer has sensation.

I head toward the big Douglas fir I defiled last night, preferring to stick to a familiar route—though I stay well clear of the exact *spot* I contaminated. I scoot down my bloodstained sweats and my boxers and twist around to try to have a gander. I don't see anything out of the ordinary.

But the pain is coming from *inside* my butt crack. I spread my legs, bend over, and—

Holy Hawkman!

My inner thighs, the entirety of my butt crack—everything down there is glowing red. There are clumps of tiny crimson pimples scattered everywhere.

I grab my ankles, straining forward to try to get a better look.

"You do understand that, on a purely physiological level, that's a nearly impossible feat you're trying to perform."

"What?" I bolt back up, my hands clapping over my junk. Penelope stands ten or so yards in front of me. "I'm not . . . doing . . . *that*. I would never . . . I was just . . . I needed to—"

Penelope crosses her arms. "Strange how I keep finding you in these compromising positions."

"I wasn't . . . compromising anything," I say as I yank my boxers and sweats back on. "I'm just . . . itchy."

"Ah, that would be the urushiol," Penelope says. "While I was mercifully spared the sight of your lunar landscape, it doesn't take a Mensa member to piece together the evidence: the enormous pile of excrement and the torn-up *Toxicodendron radicans* at the base of that Douglas fir, accompanied by your less-than-surreptitious attempts to relieve your pruritus ani. It's fairly obvious what's transpired."

"What are you talking about?"

"Poison ivy," she says, matter-of-factly. "I hate to be the bearer of unpleasant news, Dan, but you made a supremely poor choice of wiping material."

"But . . . my hand," I say, holding up my right hand as evidence. "If I'd wiped with poison ivy, wouldn't my hand have a rash, too?"

"You likely rinsed most of the toxin off in the stream last night. But unless you snuck away in the wee hours and gave your glutei a good long soak, I'm guessing the damage there is pretty heinous."

I clench my teeth. I am going to *kill* Charlie! "What the hell am I going to do? I can't live with this pain much longer. I'll go crazy!"

"Untreated, it could last anywhere from two weeks to a month."

"A *month*?!" I reply, my voice strangled.

"Lucky for you, your hypochondriac friend, Charlie, seems to have packed for the Apocalypse." She holds up a tube of something. "Calamine lotion. I figured you could use some."

Ten minutes and a massive Calamine lotion slathering later, I plop down on a log, joining the others around last night's campfire, feeling much relieved. All the stuff we've collected lies on the ground, a pathetic mound of mostly useless crap.

"Before we set out," Penelope says, "I want to be clear that I don't remember the way back to the lake. Does anybody else?"

Charlie and I shake our heads, then the three of us look to Hank.

"You're an outdoorsman," I say. "You can find the lake. Right?"

"To be honest," Hank say, his cheeks reddening. "I . . . I didn't pay close attention on the way here. I'm afraid I let myself be lax because we had a guide."

"OK, but you still know things," I say. "Like, you know which way is north from how the moss grows or where the sun is or whatever, right? We just have to figure out which direction we took from the lake and then head back the other way."

"Of course," Hank says, his eyes searching the sky. "Directions. That's . . . the easy part. Everyone knows that the sun rises in the . . ." He holds out his hands like he's testing us, but I'm not completely confident he knows the answer.

"East," Charlie says.

"Right," Hank says. "And sets in the west."

"Technically, that's a generalization," Penelope corrects. "The sun actually only rises due east and sets due west on two days of the year: the spring and fall equinoxes. Every other day it's either north or south of due east and due west."

"Yes, exactly." Hank points at her. "That's why it's not as precise a gauge as we'd like. And since we don't know which direction we came from, well, then—"

Suddenly, a branch cracks loudly to our left. We all whip our heads toward the sound.

"Max? Barbara?" Hank calls. He sounds hopeful, like he expects them to show up carrying breakfast trays piled high with pancakes, bacon, and coffee.

But when they don't respond, Hank's expression becomes wary.

"Hello?"

The bush we're watching comes alive, leaves rustling, branches shaking.

"Oh crap," I say, vaulting to my feet. "It's the bear. It's come back!"

CHAPTER 44

"Everyone stay calm," Hank whispers, grabbing the remaining arrow and standing. "Get behind me. Slowly and quietly. Don't draw attention."

"What about our stuff?" I whisper back.

"Let the bear have it. It's all crap." Charlie leans forward and slowly plucks his camera from the pile. "Everything but this."

"And these," I say, stealthily grabbing my sketchbook, pencils, the baby sweater, and the Calamine lotion.

The four of us start skulking backward, our eyes glued to the quivering bush.

"Are you sure r-running wouldn't be a b-better idea?" I stammer.

"If it shows itself," Hank explains, "then, yes, we get the hell out of here. But right—"

The bear bounds from the bush.

Hank falls and screams in pain. Charlie trips over him. My foot catches Charlie's leg, and I go down on my back, Penelope landing on top of me.

"Get up! Move!" Hank shouts, scrambling to get to his feet.

For a millisecond it crosses my mind that there would be worse ways to die than with a cute girl splayed on top of me, her face inches from mine.

But then Penelope leaps off me, and I suddenly find the will to live again.

I heave myself up and glance back to check how close the bear is.

Except . . . it's not the bear.

It's . . . a deer. A *baby* deer. A cute little fawn, cocoa colored, with tiny white dots stippling its back. Stumbling around on stick-thin legs.

"Guys! Hold up! It's not the bear." I laugh, tears welling in my eyes. "It's a deer. A tiny baby deer."

The others stop and turn to look.

"Thank Jesus." Hank laughs. "I don't know if my heart can take much more of this."

"Aww," Penelope says. "It's Bambi."

"Shhh." Charlie holds a finger to his lips, tiptoeing back toward camp. "Nobody move. I want to get a picture of this for the paper." He raises his camera to his eye as he moves forward. "Our female readership goes insane for this sort of thing."

He skulks toward the fawn, which has started nibbling on some grass, seemingly unperturbed by our presence.

"Pick up the pace, Ansel Adams," Penelope stage-whispers. "We haven't got all day."

Charlie fiddles with the focus, takes a few shots, then slinks even closer.

"I wonder where its mom and dad are," I whisper.

"Nearby, probably," Hank says, craning his neck to try to locate them. "Thankfully, deer parents aren't as aggressive as, say, bear parents."

Charlie adjusts the focus once more and snaps another series of pictures.

"Jeez, Charlie," Penelope says. "It's a fawn, not the temple of Borobudur."

Charlie scoots just a little bit closer. Any nearer and he could reach out and pet the thing.

He squats to get a fawn's-eye view and clicks a couple more photos. He looks over at us with a big, doofy smile and raises his eyebrows like, *Can you believe how amazing this is?*

And that's when the giant paw shoots out of the bush—swiping the head off the fawn and sending a spray of blood across Charlie's face and camera.

"Holy shit!" I scream, stumbling backward. "Charlie! Run!"

CHAPTER 45

"Where is it? Where is it?" Charlie cries, stumble-running along, tripping over his own feet.

"I think . . . we lost it," I say, puffing and panting, obsessively checking over my shoulder as we tear through the forest.

"The bigger and more pressing question," Penelope says, slowing to a walk, "is where are *we*?"

"We're all . . . safe," Hank rasps, hobbling. "That's all . . . that matters right now."

"Yes, but," Penelope says, "is there any possibility that we're heading in the right direction? *Id est*, toward the lake?"

"Oh, right." Hank stops. He presses his hand against a tree for balance, leaning over to catch his breath. "That's . . . yes. Something . . . I hadn't considered."

Charlie, Penelope, and I gather around Hank's tree.

"Let's just . . ." Hank wheezes, "get our . . . bearings for a second. Is everyone . . . OK?"

"I've got deer blood in my eye, so no," Charlie says, wiping a red smear from his face. "I'm probably going to contract Lyme disease. Possibly hepatitis E. Or worse, granulocytic anaplasmosis."

"You're lucky to be alive at all, Charlie," I say, surprised to find myself still clutching the sketchbook, the pencils, the baby sweater, and the tube of Calamine lotion to my chest.

Charlie shoots me a you're-an-idiot stare. "Not so lucky if my brain starts wasting away from transmissible spongiform encephalopathy."

"Oh, I don't know," Penelope says. "I think a bit of vacuolated gray matter might be just the thing you need to improve your personality."

"And I think," Charlie counters, "that you . . . that you're . . . that maybe . . ." He grabs his head. "Oh, God, it's starting already."

Penelope grins. "You see. A marked improvement."

"OK, everyone. Let's just calm down." Hank swallows and straightens up. "Now." He scans our surroundings. "We need some landmarks. Does anyone recognize any of this?"

The four of us glance around. Trees and more trees. Bushes and downed branches. Dirt and grass and rocks. Nothing even remotely distinctive.

"Perhaps we should retrace our steps," Penelope suggests. "Return to camp so that we can embark from a place of familiarity."

"To be honest," Hank says, rubbing the back of his neck

and blushing, "I'm not really sure which way camp is. We did a sort of serpentine thing." He looks over his shoulder. "Besides, that's twice that we've managed to escape with our lives. I don't think we want to tempt fate by getting anywhere near that bear again."

"What about the supplies?" I ask. "I mean, there wasn't a lot, but there was some stuff we could have used. Penelope's flashlight for sure."

Hank shakes his head. "Definitely not worth risking our necks over. We'll have to get by without them for the next few days."

"This is a nightmare." Charlie removes his glasses and rubs his eyes. "Thank God you've got survival experience, Mr. Langston. That's the only thing keeping me from totally freaking out right now."

A bird suddenly flutters from the bushes. Charlie squeals like a girl and clutches Hank's arm.

"Yes, well, nobody should freak out," Hank says, staring at Charlie's hand. "That's one of the top survival rules: Keep calm at all times."

Charlie laughs nervously and releases his grip on Hank's arm.

"All right," I say, tucking the lotion, tiny sweater, and pencils into my sweatpants pockets and gripping my sketch pad under one arm. "Which direction do you suggest we go?"

Hank points ahead. "Let's continue on this way. And, uh, listen out for running water. Maybe we can find that stream again. I bet if we follow the water downstream, we run into our lake eventually."

Hank grabs a large branch. He stabs it into the ground, testing its strength. Satisfied it'll support his weight, he begins totter-marching forward.

Charlie, Penelope, and I trudge along behind him.

In search of water.

CHAPTER 46

We walk for hours, mostly in silence.

Charlie is clearly suffering from PTSD or something. He kept flinching and shrieking at every sound or sudden movement, till finally Penelope suggested he take some pictures to soothe himself—although, truth be told, I think she just wanted to shut him up. Still, the photography therapy appears to be working, as Charlie seems to have slipped into a sort of meditative state, his camera glued to his glasses.

I've drifted to the back of the pack. I need to clear my head too—to shake off the remnants of the bear attacks and also rethink my plans for scaring off Hank, now that Charlie is dazed and my supplies are lost and this trip has suddenly become much more life-threatening.

Another hour or so goes by, and Charlie slows and joins me at the back of the pack.

"How you doing?" I ask.

"Better," he says. "Now that I've refocused."

"Refocused?"

"Yes. On us. Our situation. And Hank." He caps the lens on his camera. "I believe that we're going to have to go back to basics here. Return to our roots."

I stare at him, confused. "What are you talking about?"

"I'm talking about going *Rocky III* on him." Charlie screws up his face. "Or maybe it was *Rocky V.* Whichever one it is where he's lost the eye of the tiger and needs to rediscover it. The killer instinct." He shakes his head. "Anyway, the point being, I no longer have any of my harassment kit at our disposal. No mayonnaise packets, no personal lubricant, no fake blood, no emetics, diuretics, or laxatives, and no more deer-in-heat urine. Which means we're going to have to extemporize." He scans the forest. "Get creative and use what's around us. What's available."

"Yeah, I don't know." I crane my neck and watch Hank limping along up ahead. "I've been thinking, too, and I'm not sure it's such a good idea to punk him while he's trying to get us back to the lake. We can take up the cause again when we get home."

"You're kidding, right?" Charlie says. "You've got your opponent on the ropes here. You don't let up and allow him to convalesce. You come out swinging. You go in for the kill. The knockout punch. Put him down for the count."

"Yeah, I get it. Rocky. Boxing. But things are kind of effed up right now, Charlie. And personally, I'd really like to get out of here alive. I'm not so keen on making it more difficult for Hank to help us do that."

"Listen to me, Daniel," Charlie insists. "I know we're in deep. You're talking to the guy who nearly got his head pawed off by a killer bear. But that just makes the situation even riper. This is life-and-death we're talking about: Lost in the woods. The bear attack. That little stunt you pulled with the arrow—which was pure brilliance, by the way. Dangerous, but inspired."

"It was an accident," I say.

"Right, yes, of course." He waves this off. "Whatever. It makes no difference. The point is everything is heightened now. If Hank felt a sense of responsibility before, it's tenfold now. That's only going to intensify his feelings of helplessness and frustration. I'm telling you, by the time we board Clint's plane, Hank will have already mentally packed his bags and formulated his 'Dear Jane' letter to your mother."

I shake my head. "I don't know, Charlie . . ."

"Yes you do," he says. "In your gut you know I'm right. What's the point of surviving all of this if Hank still plans to marry your mom and take you away from me—and Erin?"

I sigh. "What did you have in mind?"

Charlie grins. "That's my boy. OK, I've come up with a few ways to adapt some of our original scenarios. But I've also got some new ideas, based on the particulars of our situation—"

"Maybe we should get Penelope on board," I interrupt.

Charlie does a double take. "Excuse me. What? No. Why?"

"Don't you think she's going to figure out what we're up to eventually? And once she does, you know that she'll call us on it. She could ruin everything."

Charlie has been shaking his head the entire time I've been talking.

"Absolutely not," he says. "I don't trust that girl as far as I can throw her—which, as we know, with my carpal tunnel, is not very far."

"I just think that with our lives in the balance here, that she might—"

"Oh my God, you've done what I told you not to do," Charlie says. "You're smitten with her. That's why you want to tell her! So you won't be embarrassed in front of her."

"That's ridiculous." I force a laugh. "I so am *not* smitten with her."

"You know that I only want what's best for you. And what's best for you is that we leave that harridan out of this. She's a wild card, and this is a high-stakes game of Doppelkopf, my friend."

"Doppelkopf?"

"It's a very challenging and complex German card game. With *no* wild cards."

I sigh. "Look, Charlie. All I'm suggesting is—"

"She will destroy everything we've worked for," Charlie says. "I'm going to have to put my foot down on this one. I'm sorry, but it's absolutely imperative that we remain steadfast, strong, and in control of the situation."

A fluffy brown rabbit darts in front of us.

Charlie screams, leaping into the air like he's been anally probed.

"Right." I nod. "In control. Got it."

CHAPTER 47

"It's not the stream," Hank says, standing next to a trickle of groundwater. "But if we follow this little creek, I bet we run into it eventually. Anyway, it's something." He looks up at the late-afternoon sun. "And it's the best we're going to do for today. We'll set up camp here. At least we'll have water to drink."

Charlie scoffs. "Not unless you expect us to risk exposure to cryptosporidium parvum or giardia lamblia."

"I'm sure the odds of that are very small," Hank says. "In fact, *Outdoor Life* recently reported that water in remote locales is much cleaner than previously thought. And I don't think anyone would argue"—he looks around at the vast wilderness—"that we are in a very remote locale."

"What about nourishment?" Penelope asks, grabbing her stomach. "All we've had to eat for two days is a can of chili."

And some of us voided our chili before it could be absorbed for nutrients, I think, glaring at Charlie.

"Yeah, um . . ." Hank looks around. "We might have to forgo eating tonight."

"Seriously?" I say, my belly grumbling. "What about setting up some traps? Like a snare or something? You could show us how."

Hank rubs the back of his neck. "I don't know if that's the wisest use of our time. Even if we managed to catch something, we can't cook it without a fire. And we don't have any way to start one. We should build a shelter for warmth. That's our first priority, just like Max said."

Charlie removes his glasses. "We could use one of these lenses as a magnifying glass." He points to the sky. "Focus the sun's rays on some sock lint or moss or something. Once we've got a flame, we simply add dried twigs, sticks, and then logs. If we have fire, then we have warmth *and* a means for cooking, yes?"

"So you're terribly farsighted, then?" Penelope asks archly.

"No, nearsighted," Charlie says, putting his glasses back on. "Why?"

Penelope rolls her eyes. "Because, mollusk, you can't start a fire with diverging lenses—which are what they use to correct nearsightedness."

"I know," Charlie snaps defensively. "My mind's just a little muddled after nearly being beheaded by a seven-hundred-pound beast. Of course I meant we'd need converging lenses. I don't suppose you're farsighted?"

"Me? No. My glasses are strictly for style. I happen to have twenty-ten vision. Far above the average person. But it wouldn't matter even if I were."

"What? Why not?"

"Oh my God, this is excruciatingly embarrassing for you," Penelope says. "OK, let me impart some basic knowledge of optics: Unless you're, like, legally blind or something, a converging lens isn't going to cut it either. What you *really* need is a biconvex lens—that means it's convex on both sides."

"I know what *biconvex* means," Charlie mutters, his face crimson.

"Outstanding!" Penelope enthuses. "And do you know what has a biconvex lens in it?" She stares at him like he's a dog and she's waiting for him to take the treat she's holding out.

"My camera," Charlie says at last. I've never seen his face so red before. It's nearly the color of the rash on my ass.

"Indeed! I don't suppose you want to smash it, though, so just be sure to open the aperture as wide as possible and point the back end of the lens at your target."

"Right. Good. OK." Hank nods. "So, if you want to take care of that," he says to Charlie, "I'll go see if I can rustle us up some food. It's probably better if I'm by myself. Quieter. Dan, Penelope, maybe you two could start collecting material for our shelter. Just like the other day. Big branches first." Hank looks around and points at a large rock over to our left. "Bring them over there. We'll use that stone as our support."

Penelope and I wander through the forest, searching for building materials. This is now the third time the two of us have been

244

alone in the woods together. You would think that I'd start to become immune to her charms, but I can't help sneaking glances at her low-rise jeans, her form-fitting Squirrel Girl shirt, her—

"What are you thinking about?" Penelope says.

"What? Me? Nothing. Why?"

"I don't know. You seemed deep in thought. I assumed you must be pondering something. Ruminating on the complexities of the human condition."

"Yeah, uh, no." I shake my head.

"You must be thinking *something*," Penelope says. "Personally, I've been trying to piece together the path back to the lake, to see if I could remember anything that might help— landmarks, sun position, whatever. I thought maybe you were doing the same."

"I wish," I say, and I really do. It be awesome if I could be the hero that leads us back to the rendezvous point, to reunite Penelope with her mother.

"OK," she presses. "So if it's not that, then what's on your mind? You seem so intense, the way you're wringing that poor baby sweater."

I look down at the sweater clutched in my right hand. I didn't even know I was holding it. "It's . . . personal." I slip the sweater back into my pocket. "I'd rather not talk about it." Understatement of the year!

"All right. I can respect that."

Penelope crouches down to grab a few branches, and my eyes snap to, laser-focusing on the gaping of her jeans in the back. A ray of heavenly light shines down, spotlighting the glorious suggestion of greater things just a few centimeters below the belt loops. And I swear I hear a chorus of angels start to sing.

I rip my gaze away, my breath snagging in my throat.

Stop it right now. Just stop!

"Why?" Penelope looks up at me.

"Huh? What?"

"Why do you want me to stop?" she says. "Is something wrong with this branch?"

"I didn't . . ." I swallow. "Did I say—"

"'Stop it right now. Just stop!'" Penelope stands, her eyebrows raised. "Yes, you did."

Oh.

Crap.

"I, uh, I . . ." I'm blinking like a madman, trying desperately to come up with a plausible excuse. "I was just . . . talking to myself. In my head."

"And you were castigating yourself?"

"What? No." I glance down, cheeks flaming. "You've got a warped mind, you know? I think you might have a problem."

"*Cas*tigating," she says. "As in reprimanding?"

"Oh. Yeah. Right. Castigating. In my head. That's exactly what I was doing."

"Care to elaborate?" she asks. "Or is it more 'personal' matters?"

"It's just . . . family stuff," I say, picking up an impossibly small twig and throwing it away again. "Hank, actually. My mother's going to marry him when we get back, and I don't think it's a good idea. I just . . . I can't stop thinking about it. Even though I keep telling myself to stop. That's all."

Charlie would not be pleased with me for confessing even this much, but it sure beats confessing to the *other* truth. And it's not like I said I was trying to scare Hank off or anything . . .

"He seems like a decent enough guy," Penelope says, picking up an actual usable stick. "What's your problem with him?"

"I don't know yet," I say. "But there'll be something. There's always something. My mom has about as good a record with guys as Arkham Asylum has of keeping its inmates locked up. In fact, if we lived in Gotham, several of her boyfriends would probably have been escapees."

This makes Penelope laugh, which feels nice. *Really* nice.

"At least your mother is committing to someone. Mine is just satisfied with having a series of meaningless—often quite audible—carnal encounters. I don't even bother learning their names any longer. Though, sometimes, when she's in the throes, I have little choice."

"Earplugs," I say. "That's what I use."

Penelope nods. "Noise-canceling headphones work better. As long as you have something distracting enough to listen to. I'm partial to the *New Yorker* fiction podcasts myself."

We continue walking, picking up branches as we go.

"What about your dad?" I ask. "Is he still around?"

"He is," Penelope says. "Around. Just not twenty-four-seven."

"But you see him?"

Penelope smiles. "Oh, sure. He's great. I love him. We have a lot in common, he and I. Well, except for the fact that he's gay."

"What?" I do a double take. "But didn't he and your mother . . . didn't they . . . *you know* . . . in order to have you?"

Penelope laughs. "What can I say? The mind is a powerful

thing. My father was living in a state of denial. It's a big state, Dan. A lot of people live there."

"I guess. Jeez, that must have been really hard for your mom, huh? When he, you know, finally figured it out?"

"Hard doesn't even begin to describe it. My mother was devastated when he decided to leave. The worst part was that she actually thought she *turned* him gay somehow." Penelope laughs, then bites her lower lip. "Sorry. It's not really funny. But it kind of is, you know? I tried to explain to her that it's not actually possible to turn someone gay, but I don't know if she's ever come to terms with it."

"What about you?" I ask. "Were you mad at him?"

Penelope shrugs. "Not really. A bit like, 'Wow, that's some interesting news.' But how could I be mad? It'd be like getting angry at him for being bald. Sure, I was sad that my mother was sad. But I was also glad my dad wasn't living a lie anymore. I mean, he's an amazing guy. He deserves to be happy. And he loves me. Still loves my mom, even though she can't stand to look at him."

I shake my head. "Sounds like you handled it really well. I'm not sure how I would take that news."

We walk in silence for a while. Collecting more branches.

"How about you?" Penelope finally asks. "Your father? Is he still in the picture?"

"In *my* picture?" I say. "No. He took off when I was ten. Haven't heard from him since. I think he lives in Florida. That's about all I know. Well, and that he's a drunk."

"Ahhh, OK." She nods. "That makes sense now."

"What does?"

"The Hank thing. Why you can't accept him. Why you're against the wedding."

"I already told you," I say. "Because he's going to turn out to be a douche. Just like all the rest of them. Except this time it's going to be even harder for my mom when things go bad. No one's ever gone so far as to propose to her before."

"So, it's your mother you're concerned about?"

"Yeah, of course."

"Not your inability to let go of the prospect of your father coming back?"

"There's nothing to let go of. My father isn't coming back." I instinctively grab my wrist, as if Penelope plans to steal his old Timex.

"But he could. I mean, it's not like he's dead or gay or anything. Your mother and he *could* get back together. Hypothetically."

"But they won't. Even if he did show up, my mom wouldn't take him back. Not after all this time. Not after the way he left." I clench my jaw. "He's a screwup. And an asshole. Why the hell would I want him back in my life? That's just stupid."

"All right, OK," Penelope says, raising a hand. "As long as you're over it."

I blink hard. "Let's just . . . look for branches, OK? It's going to start getting dark soon."

"Yes. Avoidance. Good strategy. Also known as the ostrich approach."

"Right," I say. "And you're *totally fine* with the fact that your

249

dad left your mom—whatever the reason. Doesn't bother you at all. Not even a little, you're so enlightened. That's not burying your head in the sand?"

Penelope looks at me. "You want the truth?"

"Sure," I say.

"Ostriches don't actually bury their heads in the sand," she says. "It's a fallacy."

"OK." I roll my eyes. "Whatever."

"It's true. They wouldn't be able to breathe. They do, however, dig holes in the dirt to use as nests for their eggs, and several times a day the female bird will put her head in the hole to turn the eggs." She laughs. "God, you and Charlie both. No sense of humor. Must be a laughfest when the two of you hang out."

Charlie's right. She is a wild card. Not to mention a head case.

I'm glad I didn't tell her about our plan for Hank. She would have just gone off on some more of her psychobabble. Really, she should turn that microscope of hers on herself.

CHAPTER 48

"Listen, I apologize," Penelope says as we're headed back. "Sometimes I can't help myself. I enjoy goading people. It's, like, a hobby or a compulsion, perhaps. But as my mom says, just because I find something funny doesn't mean everybody else does. Can you forgive me?"

When I don't say anything, she cranes her neck to try to meet my eyes.

"Hello? Yes? No?" she says. "I'm an asshole? I'm a lunatic? Say something, at least."

I'm about to speak, confess that *maybe* there's the tiniest truth to what she was saying about my dad—as much as I hate to admit it—when something skitters behind us.

"Awww, look," Penelope says, pointing off into the bushes. "It's a squirrel."

I smile. "Just like Squirrel Girl." I point to Penelope's shirt. And then I become painfully aware of the fact that we're both staring at her chest. My face prickles with heat.

"See, Dan," Penelope says, breaking the tension and glancing back at the shrubs, "sometimes the universe offers you up just the right thing at the right time."

I look at the squirrel again. It's straight out of a Pixar movie: chubby-cheeked and adorable, nibbling on something in its tiny little paws.

Suddenly, a rock whooshes past my ear and nails the little critter square in the head.

"Holy shit!" I whip around to see Penelope with her fist in the air.

"Got it!" she shouts.

"Why—why the hell did you do that?"

"Supper," she says matter-of-factly.

"But . . . Hank's getting us food," I say, still staring at the lifeless furry form.

"I know, but he didn't seem very confident about it, did he? And I'm really ravenous."

I'm still trying to digest the fact that she just brained a squirrel with a rock. But now the reality of what she's saying kicks in. "You want us to eat *that*?"

"What do you think Hank is hunting—deer? With his bare hands?" Penelope says. "Besides, squirrel happens to be a Victorian delicacy." She starts walking toward her kill. "They serve it at some of the finest restaurants in London."

252

"They serve sausages made out of pig's blood, too," I say. "But I'm not about to tuck into one of those, either."

Penelope hoists the squirrel by the tail. "You'll be singing a different tune when you smell this thing barbecuing over a fire."

"Don't bet on it," I say, cringing as the tiny body sways back and forth. "And you should be grateful I won't be eating it. That thing will barely feed you, let alone all four of us."

"Oh, we're not all sharing this guy." Penelope lays the furry body down gently on the ground and snatches up another stone. She peers up at the branches, cocks her arm, and launches the rock skyward.

"Yes!" Another squirrel topples over and plummets to the ground. "And my mother said Wonder Woman Camp was a silly waste of money."

CHAPTER 49

"Let the feast commence!" Penelope announces as we march into our new camp. She hoists eight dead squirrels over her head.

I stumble over to the big support rock, my forearms aching under the weight of fifteen large branches. I dump the sticks on the ground and return to see that Charlie has gotten a nice fire going. He's also managed to get himself impossibly clean, which is a miracle only Charlie could perform with the supplies at hand.

"Where did you get the squirrels?" Hank asks, crouched over the brook, filtering water through a sand-filled sock, collecting it into a concave stone. I'm sure Charlie had his opinions about the sanitariness of this method.

"Penelope beaned them with rocks," I say. "She's like Squirrel Girl's archenemy."

"Yeah, well." Hank scrunches up his nose. "I'm not sure that we should really be eating those."

"We have to eat them," Penelope insists, tossing the carcasses near the fire pit. "It would be profane to do otherwise. They've given their lives for us."

"Technically," Charlie says, stoking the fire with a long stick, "they didn't *give* anything. You took it from them. Barbarously, by the sounds of it. Which doesn't surprise me."

"Once again, your ignorance is astounding," Penelope says. "Blunt-force trauma to the head happens to be one of the most humane ways to kill an animal. But then, being the simpleton you are, I wouldn't expect you to know that."

Charlie turns away, his clenched jaw twitching like crazy.

"How do you suggest we field-dress them?" Hank asks, regarding the pile of bodies.

Penelope frowns. Not something they covered at Wonder Woman Camp, I presume. "I figured you would know how to accomplish that," she says. "It's just like any other animal, right? Only . . . smaller."

"Generally one has a knife when one is skinning an animal," Hank says.

"It can be done without a knife," Charlie says. "I watched a great deal of survival videos on YouTube before we came here."

"Of course you did," Hank says, a hint of exasperation in his voice.

"I'm happy to talk someone through it," Charlie offers. "But there's no way I'm going to subject myself to the handling of any potential plague carriers."

Hank looks at me as he wrings out his wet sock. "Why don't you take a crack at it, Dan? It'd be good experience for you."

"Me? No way. I practically faint when Mom asks me to handle raw chicken. You're the hunter," I tell him. "Why don't you do it?"

"Actually, now that I think about it," Hank says, turning to Penelope, "it's usually customary for the person who bags the game to prepare it."

"Yeah, no thanks." She shakes her head. "I'm sorry, I have to draw the line at dismemberment. I worry I've already stirred my inner serial killer."

Hank sighs. "OK, fine. But if it proves to be too difficult, I'm stopping. I'm not about to spend the entire night with my hands up a squirrel."

As Charlie instructs Hank in the fine art of disemboweling a squirrel without a knife—which involves squeezing the guts toward the anus, "as though you're icing a cake"—Penelope and I get to work on our shelter. By the time we're done, Hank has each of the eight squirrels skinned, gutted, and skewered on sticks.

"I'm beyond starving!" I say as we all gather around the fire.

"Starving enough to eat squirrel?" Penelope asks, her voice smug.

"Yes, as a matter of fact," I admit. She was right: once I caught smell of the roasting meat, my animal instincts took over. There's no way I'm not devouring *both* my squirrel skewers.

Hank passes me the stone bowl filled with the water he's filtered through his sock. I try not to think about his sweaty, lint-flecked toes as I take a sip. Meanwhile, Charlie hands out the squirrel skewers.

I bring the scorched rodent to my nose for a sniff. "Smells . . . interesting. Kind of like barbecued chicken thigh, but with a hint of, I don't know, underarm odor?"

"It might smell like staphylococcus epidermidis," Charlie says, "but I assure you, there are no living bacteria or parasitic roundworms left in that carcass." He glances at the water bowl. "I cannot, however, say the same for Hank's hosiery-strained refreshment."

I pull off a piece of the hot, charbroiled flesh, pinching carefully so as not to burn my fingers. I juggle the meat in my palm before popping it in my mouth.

"Hot-hot-hot," I huff, my mouth a giant *O*. "But tasty . . . ish."

"Thanks for catching the food, Penelope," Hank says, licking the meat grease from his fingers. "I certainly didn't expect to be eating this well tonight."

"You're most welcome," Penelope says. "And thank you for flaying them. And you, Charlie, for your rudimentary culinary skills. All together we make one reasonably competent mountain person."

Charlie just grunts as he picks at his food.

"You know, there's this great restaurant in my neighborhood," Hank says, chewing with his mouth open. "That serves all sorts of exotic foods. Snails, sweetbreads, horse. And you eat the food blindfolded. So you experience only the smells and flavors." He lifts his charcoal-smeared chin in my direction. "Your mom and I'll take you there sometime. It's an experience."

I cringe. "Yeah, I think I'll pass on that. But thanks."

Hank laughs. "It's actually pretty good. There are all sorts of funky shops and eateries near my house. There's even a super-cool comic book store. I think you're going to like it." Hank looks down. "You know, *if* we end up moving there."

If we end up moving there? What am I, five? Of *course* me and Mom will have to move in with him. There's no way he's going to give up his big swanky house to live in our crappy little hovel. Give me a break.

My rage at Hank rises up all over again. Penelope might be right that I miss my dad—or at least the *idea* of my dad—but that has nothing to do with why I hate Hank. No. It's things like this. Little condescending remarks. That's how it starts with all of the boyfriends. The tip of the asshole iceberg.

That's it. Time to get things back on track here.

"I was wondering," I say, placing my picked-clean skewers down on a rock. "Could you teach me how to fight, Hank?"

Hank's eyebrows arch. "How to fight?"

"Ah, the gentleman's art of *pugilism*." Charlie catches my eye and gives me a slight nod of approval.

"Yeah," I say to Hank. "*If* I'm moving to a new school and all, I figure it might be a good idea to know how to defend myself— you know, just in case. And I was hoping, as my future stepdad, that you might show me how to throw a punch."

My insides are curdling into a little ball of shame. Charlie is right: this is so much more painful to do in front of Penelope. To allow myself to look weak in front of a girl who can knock a squirrel out of a tree with a rock at fifty paces. A girl who, in an alternate universe where I hadn't pledged myself to Erin, could be perfect for me.

But I have no choice.

Times are getting desperate.

"Sure, bud," Hank says slowly. "When we get home, we can practice a few techniques. Maybe even enroll you in a self-defense course if you want. Though I'm sure your new school will be pretty safe."

"How about now?" I press, hating myself. "Just a basic punch."

"Now?" Hank repeats.

"Sure. Why not? It'll be fun," I say. "We've got nothing else to do till the sun goes down. Whaddya say"—I twist the knife—"Dad?"

CHAPTER
50

"This should be interesting," Penelope says, spinning around on her log to watch Hank and me get ready to spar.

"You have no idea," Charlie says under his breath, his camera at the ready.

"Now, obviously this is for self-defense only," Hank says, stepping one foot back and angling toward me. "Violence should always be a last resort. All right, the first thing you want to do is get in a good stance." He winces a little as he adjusts the position of his injured leg. "Your heels are about shoulder-width apart. Your lead foot, your left foot, is in front. Your right foot behind you."

"Like this?" I say, mirroring Hank's position as best I can.

He nods. "That's good. Just point the toes of your back foot away from your body a bit. Turn the front foot about forty-five degrees."

I pivot my feet a little.

"That's right," Hank says. "Excellent."

"Barbecue and a good brawl," Penelope says to Charlie, gnawing off a piece of squirrel. "There's something so Hemingway-esque about it, don't you think?"

Charlie smirks. "I have a feeling this is going to be more *Blood Meridian* than *Old Man and the Sea*."

"Now," Hank says, raising his fists. "Get your hands up. Make sure your thumbs are outside of your fists, otherwise you'll break them."

I clench my hands into fists and hold them up in front of my face.

"Just like your left foot, your left hand leads," Hank instructs me. "You can jab with it"—he demonstrates—"but it's also for blocking. The right hand, the stronger arm, that's what you're going to hit with. All right, so, I'm gonna be you in this scenario. You be the bully or whoever and pretend to take a swipe at me."

I take a weak punch at Hank. He lifts his left forearm, blocking my strike.

"Right here," Hank says, extending his right arm and giving me a light tap on the chin with his fist. "You've got your opening. If you do it correctly, you should only have to do it once. A bully will generally back down if he gets hit, because he's not expecting it. He—or she, it can be a she, I guess—usually only preys on the weak."

"Are you saying it's OK to hit a girl, Mr. Langston?" Charlie asks.

"Well, no." Hank blinks uncomfortably. "You shouldn't ever hit a girl—unless, you know, your life is in danger. Then, I suppose, all bets are off." He laughs. "But, really, come on, when was the last time you were bullied by a girl?"

Charlie and I avoid each other's gazes.

Hank clears his throat. "OK, let me take a shot, and you try to block it."

He swings at me in super-slow-motion. I lift my forearm and block his punch, countering with one of my own, stopping well before I come in contact with his head.

"Perfect," Hank says, nodding. "There you go. That's all you need."

"Yeah, but," I say, "if I'm ever actually attacked, I seriously doubt we'll be fighting in slow-mo. Can we speed it up a little? I'll take a more realistic punch at you, and you block it, then you take one at me, so I can see the block-return-punch thing at a more true-to-life speed."

"Right," Hank says. "Sure. OK. Just tell me when it's coming so I'm ready." He laughs. "The last thing I want is a broken nose here."

"Fight, fight, fight!" Penelope chants, waving a squirrel skewer in the air. She looks over at Charlie. "Come on, Charlie. Where's your spirit? Cheer them on. Fight, fight, fight!"

But Charlie is glued to his camera like he's about to capture a shot of the rare and elusive Philippine warty pig.

I take a deep breath and get into my boxer stance, my heart racing.

This is it. Time to put up or shut up.

"OK," I say, swallowing. "Get ready. It's going to be fast. Here it comes."

I leap at him, taking a powerful swing, putting all my weight behind it.

Hank isn't expecting such a forceful punch, and he jacks up his hairy arm instinctively, blocking my heavy blow expertly, just like I knew he would.

Then, he automatically comes at me with a hard right, firing it out like a piston.

That's when I close my eyes and lunge forward.

Throwing my face toward his fist.

CHAPTER
51

First there's a crunching sound, like someone stepping on a bag of cornflakes. Then a flash of light as my head snaps back, then screaming pain that shoots up my nose and straight into my brain.

"Ahhhhh!" I cry, stumbling back, my hands grabbing my face.

"Holy-crap-what-the-hell-just-happened?" Hank shouts. "You . . . you *leaned into it*! Why-did-you-do-that-you-weren't-supposed-to-do-that!"

"Jesus Christ!" Penelope says, leaping to her feet. "I was just kidding about wanting to see carnage, guys!"

The blood streams from my nostrils like a faucet turned on full blast. My hands are gloved in red.

"That does not look promising," Charlie says.

Click, click, click.

I stare at Hank. "I thick you broke by dose," I say, all nasal.

"Hemorrhaging like that would certainly suggest so," Charlie offers.

Hank snatches up his water filtering sock and gently holds it against my face. "I'm so sorry, Dan, I—you came at me so fast, and I . . ." He's shaking his head, his eyes wide. "I don't know what—I can't believe . . ."

"Why'd you hit be so hard?" I say, my voice muffled by his sock.

"I wasn't trying to! I—I just . . ." Hank stammers. "You came forward and . . . Did you trip or something?"

"You thick it's *by* fault that you hit be?" I say, knowing full well that it was. That this is what I'd intended all along—what Charlie and I had discussed. Though, not exactly this. Not the horrible pain or the busted, bleeding nose. More like a crack on the cheek or a smack to the ear.

At least, that's how Charlie had charted it out in the *pugilism*-planning phase.

"No, of course not!" Hank splutters, still holding his blood-soaked sock to my nose. "I'm not . . . blaming anyone . . . It was an accident, obviously. I'm just . . . trying to figure out how it happened."

"You struck him in the face with your fist," Charlie explains. "There's little mystery to it. We all witnessed the blow."

Hank shoots Charlie a look. "Thank you, Charlie. Yes. I know *what* happened. I'm just trying to discern *how* it happened."

"Baybe it was an unconscious thing," I snuffle. "Baybe you

265

wanted to get be back for accidentally shooting you with an arrow."

"No!" Hank insists, shaking his head. "Not a chance. That's ridiculous. I did not consciously *or* unconsciously attempt to hurt you. I would never do that."

I don't respond. To do so would acknowledge Hank's innocence and accept his apology, which Charlie explained would lessen Hank's remorse. I feel like sort of a dick for leaving him hanging, but I'm not about to throw all of my hard work down the drain.

It's all for the greater good. For Mom. To save her from the avalanche of emotional pain that will come when Hank inevitably disappoints her.

Let's just hope Erin finds guys with crooked noses sexy.

CHAPTER
52

It's difficult to draw when you're rocked by bouts of shivering. The graphite tip of my pencil skitters across the page, the smooth, curved line I'm attempting to make becoming a long, jagged stroke. My skin is all gooseflesh, and my shoulders are scrunched up tight to my neck. I erase the line, shake out my hand, and try again.

I probably should have stayed inside the shelter this morning, warm and protected in our debris bed. But I woke up with what felt like a bayonet in my skull, my nose throbbing, sending pain pulsing across my face.

Also, my ass started burning again. So I was getting it from both ends.

I got up, applied the last dregs of the Calamine lotion to my itchy nether regions, and got to drawing to try to keep my mind occupied.

I shift on my rock, my butt bone sore, my nose a thrumming ache. I touch the bulge on my face. It feels like I've grown a small piece of fruit above my lips.

It took a long time to get the bleeding to stop last night. Once it finally did, I washed up in the brook, using Hank's other sock to dab cold water on the wound in an effort to keep the swelling down. It did not work.

I try to breathe through my nostrils, clogged and wheezy.

The one good thing about having a broken nose is that it's made the poison ivy rash in my ass seem like a feather tickle.

I return to my work. Between the pink-stained sky and the blanket of ground fog acting as a reflector, there is just enough light to allow me to see what I'm drawing.

On the page, a giant Werebear emerges from the Dark Forest, sent by the injured Night Goblin to hunt down Sir Stan and Princess Erilin. The beast silently approaches our sleeping lovers, twisted up in a blanket on the ground, their limbs entwined—

"That's damn good, bud."

I jerk my head up and see Hank looking over my shoulder.

"That's the kind of thing I *thought* you drew." He nods at my drawing. "Comics and stuff."

Ah, crap. He wasn't supposed to see this.

"This stuff is stupid," I say. "It's just to blow off steam. It's so cliché."

"I don't know," Hank says. "I like it. I see that you're incorporating some of our misadventures into your story. Is that Penelope sleeping there?"

"Penelope?" I look down at my sketchbook, at the picture I've drawn of Princess Erilin and Stan. "That's not . . . Penelope."

But it so clearly is.

Hank laughs. "If you say so."

I blink at the dead-accurate image of Penelope, the Desert Princess interloper.

Oh my God, what have I done?

Hank limps over to the log beside me and gestures at it. "Mind if I have a seat?"

"No," I lie, slapping my sketchbook shut. "Go ahead."

Hank settles down with a groan. He glances up at the clear sky.

"Looks like we're in for a nice day," he says. "Once this fog burns off."

"Yeah. I guess."

"It's peaceful," Hank says. "So early in the morning. Like the whole forest is still asleep. The animals. The trees. The fog on the ground . . ."

"Baby Robbie's dead," I say abruptly. "I watched his heart flatline yesterday." I hold up my wrist, flash him my gone-black ID bracelet.

"Jesus, they show you that?" He grimaces.

"I don't know why I'm saving this." I tug the tiny baby sweater from my pocket. "I guess he can wear it in his casket if we have a funeral for him at school."

"Again, I'm *really* sorry about that. And about . . ." He nods at my face, suppressing a wince. "So, uh, how's it feeling?"

269

"Hurts like a bitch," I say. "And it's hard to breathe through." I struggle to snuffle in some air for emphasis.

"I really screwed things up," Hank says, running his hand through his bed head. "I just . . . I feel horrible about this, Dan. About this whole trip. I feel like I've made a mess of everything."

I shrug and stare at my dad's busted Timex, loose on my wrist.

"I really wanted this to be a good thing for us," Hank continues. "A bonding thing, like your mom intended. Boy, did that go south, huh?" He laughs bitterly.

I fake a laugh, too, just to fill the awkward silence.

"When I met your mom," Hank says, "I remember thinking: Here is this amazing woman. Smart, kind, attractive. Someone I felt so lucky to be with. And she had a son. And I thought . . . I thought, 'If this all works out, if this thing clicks and you actually get the chance to be a part of this family, don't you mess it up. Be present. Be involved. Be the kind of dad you wished you had.' That's what I told myself." He shakes his head. "Not exactly going according to plan."

My chest tightens, the back of my throat going thick. I wish it were easier for me to be an asshole—wish it came naturally to me, like it seems to for the Rick Chuffs of the world. Then I wouldn't be sitting here feeling so guilty. So squirmy and greasy. Like I need to bathe in the brook.

"So," I hear myself saying, "you, uh, didn't get along with your dad?"

Hank gives a half smile. "I'll tell you a story." He reaches down and picks up a stick and pokes at last night's ashes. "So, I'm not usually up this early, right? Not a morning person, for sure. I'm more of a night owl. *The Tonight Show, The Late Late Show,* and all that."

"Me, too," I say, and immediately regret it.

"Well, not my dad. He was an early riser. Up at four thirty every single morning. Didn't matter what time he went to bed, four thirty came and he was bounding out of bed—putting on his running shorts, his cross-trainers, so he could go for his morning jog. Rain, snow, windstorm. Didn't matter. Four thirty and he was up and on the road."

"That's pretty dedicated," I say. "Though it sounds like my idea of hell."

Hank chuckles. "Tell me about it. So, anyway, there was this time, when I was about your age. A little younger, actually. Thirteen or fourteen. I can't remember. All I know is that I was desperate to try to connect with him. Show my dad that we had something in common. So, for a few weeks, I joined him in his morning routine. Dragged myself out of bed at four thirty. Did the run with him, nearly throwing up every time. Then we'd have cereal together at the kitchen table: All-Bran and skim milk. No sugar. Tasted like little cardboard rabbit pellets." He laughs weakly. "We'd drink black coffee and read different sections of the paper—all of this in silence. If I'd comment on something I'd read, he might grunt, but that was about it. Eventually, the sun would come up and blink through the window, and my dad would fold his portion of the paper, put his dirty dishes in the sink, and head off to take a shower."

"Wow," I say. "Good times."

"It was depressing," Hank says, flatly. "It was like I was a ghost. Just sort of lingering around him. He never stopped me

271

from coming on the jogs. But he didn't encourage it, either—or even acknowledge it, really. It was just sort of . . . I don't know . . . like I wasn't there. That's about the best I can describe it. I kept at it for almost a month. I figured he'd have to talk to me eventually, right? Ask me how I'm doing? Discuss an interesting news item? But no. Not a word." He looks at me, a bruising in his eyes. "Kind of pathetic, huh?"

"I probably would have given up after the first day," I answer.

"I probably should have."

"Maybe he just liked being alone," I say. "Maybe he liked the quiet before the day started, like you said—the peacefulness, when everyone else was asleep."

Hank pulls his lips in and nods. "I guess I never thought of it like that. And you might have a point, I suppose." He laughs. "Though that doesn't explain why he was so mean and withdrawn the rest of the day."

An uncomfortable silence settles around us as thick as the fog.

"So," Hank finally says. "Your turn now."

"Hmm?" I look at him. "My turn for what?"

He smiles. "This is it, right?" He waggles the stick back and forth between the two of us. "What your mom wanted us to do: get to know each other. We haven't really had the chance to talk up until now."

"I, uh . . ." I blink at him, casting about for an excuse to cut this chat short. How did I let myself get suckered into *bonding* with Hank?

"Look, Dan, I don't want us to be like me and my dad, just

sharing the same space, never really talking to each other. I want us to have a real relationship, you know?" He looks at me, his brown eyes open and encouraging. "So, how about it, bud? What's on your mind? Anything at all: A hope. A dream. A worry."

Do not allow him to manipulate you, I hear Charlie whisper in my mind. *He's trying to use the "we're just pals" play here, the "we've got so much in common" card. Trying to get you to lower your guard so he can smack you in the face again.*

I can't believe that I'm now having to listen to Charlie when Charlie isn't even around.

It's kind of frightening.

And hopefully not permanent.

Still, what "Charlie" is saying makes sense. Hank's trying to smooth everything over—most likely to get me to underplay his horrific parental bumblings to Mom when we get home.

Fat chance, *bud.* I'm not biting.

That's the spirit, Dan, I hear Charlie say. *I think it's time to break out a little* disillusionment.

"A worry?" I say. "OK, well, if you really want to know, I guess what I'm most worried about is . . ." I look up at him with big Bambi eyes. "Being let down by another dad." I blink and force my chin to wobble, like I'm on the verge of tears. "You wouldn't ever do that, right, Hank? You'll always be *one hundred percent* truthful with Mom and me. And you'll stick with us through thick and thin, good times and bad, like the vow says?"

"Of course—"

"I'm serious." I talk to the baby sweater to keep my focus. "I don't think I could stand the disappointment. Not again. And I don't even want to *think* of what it would do to Mom if you guys got married and then you left us like my real dad. It would be the end of her."

I don't know if he's buying any of this. I can't look at him or I might lose my resolve.

"I love your mom very much, Dan," Hank says. "And the last thing in the world I would want to do is disappoint either of you."

Now, Charlie says. *Do it now.*

I look up and stare him dead in the eyes. "I need to hear the words, Hank. Promise me. If you're going to be a part of our family, you'll never lie to us and never let us down."

He nods and gives me a small smile. "OK, Dan. I promise."

And just like that, Hank seals his fate.

CHAPTER 53

We are plodding along like a platoon of soldiers retreating from battle: Hank dragging his injured leg behind him; me with my itchy ass and swollen nose; and Charlie with PTSD, jumping at every swish and crunch in the bushes.

Penelope seems to be the only one who has come this far unscathed—although, technically, she *has* lost her mother. But she doesn't seem too fazed by it.

Just as Hank suspected, the small brook has turned into a stream. That's the good news. The bad news is that dark storm clouds have been slowly gathering overhead, and we only have a couple of days before Clint is due to meet us at the lake. The last thing we need is a nasty downpour to slow us down further.

Just as I'm thinking this, the wind starts to kick up in a big way, whipping leaves and dirt into our faces.

"I don't like the looks of this!" Hank shouts, his first words in hours.

Ever since our little share-time chat this morning, Hank has been noticeably quiet and pensive. Which bodes well for me and my plan, I think.

Suddenly, there is a flash of light to our left. We spin around just in time to see the huge bolt of lightning fracturing the dark sky. A second later, the booming sound of God bowling a strike echoes through the entire forest.

"Don't like the sounds of it, either!" Hank says.

The rain comes instantly, fast and ferocious, the drops swollen and cold.

My clothes are soaked almost immediately. They cling to my body, my shirtsleeves hanging heavy off my arms.

I shove my sketchbook up my shirt, trying to protect it as best I can. Charlie does the same with his camera.

"Come on!" Hank shouts over the sizzle of rain. "We need to find shelter." He starts to stump off as another flash of lightning lights up the sky. *"Right now!"* A crack of thunder explodes, drowning him out.

The four of us dash ahead, edging the stream, tracking the current. A third bolt of lightning spears through the clouds, followed almost immediately by an earthshaking rumble.

"There doesn't appear to be much separation," Charlie hollers, "between the discharge of atmospheric electricity and the rapid expansion of superheated air."

"What the hell does that mean?" I say.

"The time span between light and sound," Penelope explains, "suggests that we are in dangerously close proximity to the lightning. We need to get away from the stream. Electricity travels extremely swiftly through water. If lightning strikes nearby, it could make its way to us in a hurry."

"Over there." Hank points across the stream. "It looks like there's a crevice in the side of the hill. We could hide in there."

Hank steps on a rock in the middle of the stream, using his walking stick for balance, and makes his way to the other side. Penelope, Charlie, and I follow his lead.

BOOM!

A blinding blast of light explodes directly in front of us, the ground trembling as sparks fly everywhere.

"Holy shit!" Penelope screams, covering her ears.

"Hurry!" Hank bellows, waving us forward. "We're almost there!"

There are big wisps of smoke snaking around a bush just up ahead. I can smell the wet, singed grass and hear the crackle of burning leaves through the ringing in my ears.

The four of us clamber up the rocks toward the fissure in the hill. My foot slips and Hank grabs my arm just before I take a tumble.

"Thanks," I croak, a jolt of adrenaline racing through my veins.

The fissure didn't look so big from a hundred yards away, but up close it's almost like a tall triangular cave.

"Back to the womb," Charlie announces as he steps into the vagina-shaped crevice.

I lean against the side of the cave entrance and stare out at the sheets of rain swooshing down. I am exhausted. Drenched to the bone. And so, *so* sick of these brushes with death.

"We need to strip," Charlie says, starting to peel off his wet shirt. "Immediately. Naked and dry is much safer than wet and clothed."

Penelope pulls a face as she hugs herself. "Nice try, Charlie. That kind of chicanery might work on the vacuous girls at your school; however, those of us with above-bovine intelligence aren't so easily inveigled."

"*Barely* above," Charlie says. "And don't flatter yourself. What I'm talking about here is avoiding becoming hypothermic. Did you not listen to Max when we first arrived? Damp and cold do not mix well." Charlie kicks off his shoes and starts to tug off his socks and pants. "A person's core body temperature will drop much more rapidly if the skin remains moist. And your skin *will* remain moist if you stubbornly decide to keep your clothes on." He hops around, a soggy jean leg stuck on the end of his foot, which sort of detracts from his air of superiority.

"I am not getting naked, Charles," Penelope insists. "No matter how much scientific argot you fling at me. So, I suppose I'll be the first one to die."

"Promises, promises," Charlie says.

Hank intervenes. "I think underwear is probably fine."

"Underwear I'll do," Penelope says, yanking down her sweat-pants. "We've basically see each other in our underwear already, anyway. Though, at that time the cover of night kindly spared me the sight of *too* much pale, pimply flesh. I suppose this isn't so different."

But as it turns out, there's a huge difference between

278

basically seeing someone in her underwear in the pale moon-light and *actually* seeing someone in her underwear in the full light of day.

Under normal circumstances I wouldn't say this, but thank God I'm freezing cold.

Hank levels a disapproving gaze at me and Charlie—our mouths agape—then takes off his drenched shirt, his muscled chest coated with dark hair. He starts to wring the water out onto the ground.

"Mr. L-Langston," Charlie says, his teeth chattering. "Shouldn't we c-conserve that? Rainwater is the p-purest water we're going to find out here. We should each d-drink what we can."

"Yes. Right." Hank looks down, embarrassed by the dripping, twisted shirt in his hands. "Of course." He shakes his head. "What was I thinking?" He raises the shirt above his head and squeezes the last trickle of water into his mouth.

Charlie and Penelope do the same with their wet garments. My eyes are glued to Penelope, the water drizzling down her chin, her neck. Good God, I never realized how erotic drinking wrung-out T-shirt water could be . . .

"So!" I cough and spin away, pretending to be shy. "What about a fire?" I ask over my shoulder, inching off my wet sweat-pants and buying myself some time to get things under control. "I mean, you know, a fire would be good, right?" *Come on, now. At ease, soldier!* "To keep warm. And . . . you know . . . our clothes aren't going to dry on their own."

"I concur," Charlie says. "But since we don't have the sun's rays to focus with my camera's *biconvex* lens"—he shoots

279

Penelope a contemptuous look—"I'm thinking that a drill and bow is probably our most practical option right now." He looks to Hank. "Am I correct in that assessment, Mr. Langston?"

"Uhh, yeah," Hank says, nodding. "Bow and drill. Absolutely. You know how to do that one, or do you need me to demonstrate?"

Charlie begins unlacing one of his boots. "If memory serves, we need a bow, which I can fashion from a flexible stick and my shoelace, like Max showed us. Also a firm, straight stick to employ as a drill and a flat wooden base to stabilize the mechanism."

"Perfect," Hank says. "You get started on that. The rest of us will try to rustle up some sort of kindling."

I watch Hank disappear into the dark recesses of the cave, Penelope following close behind. Just a few minutes ago, it had seemed kind of spooky back there, hiding all sorts of creepy-crawly things.

But suddenly it looks like some sort of Tunnel of Love or Temptation Cove. I picture myself accidentally brushing up against Penelope in the dark, maybe "stumbling" and reaching out to catch myself and—*oops, sorry!*—grabbing two glorious handfuls of—

No! That is not—*No!*

I fish around in my pile of clothes to find Baby Robbie's sweater and clutch it to my chest, chanting Erin's name under my breath like an invocation as I slowly step into the depths of cave.

CHAPTER 54

"Tell us something we don't know about you," Penelope says, turning to Charlie.

"Me?" he says. "Why me?"

"We'll all go," Penelope says. "It's just something to kill time."

She scoots up closer to the fire, hugging her naked knees to her chest.

I rub Baby Robbie's sweater. The soggy wool did its trick, keeping me from any bodily contact—accidental or otherwise—with Penelope while we searched the recesses of the cave for kindling. Now if it can just keep me grounded until our clothes dry...

"I'd rather not," Charlie says.

Penelope groans. "OK, fine, I'll go first. Here's something you don't know about me: I've had a short story published online at the *Literary Quadrangle.*"

Charlie scoffs. "I didn't realize this was meant to be a brag-a-thon. In that case, here's something you don't know about me: I actually had to lobby my parents not to skip me ahead two grades. I felt it would make my peers uncomfortable, to be over-shadowed by someone two years younger than they."

"I know that," I say.

Charlie slaps his forehead dramatically. "That's right! Dan already knows that. Silly me."

Penelope rolls her eyes. "OK, fine, here's another one: I once kissed a girl at a party on a dare. Though maybe that counts as bragging, too, since I'm guessing you're the only one here who's never experienced the soft, warm pleasure of a lady's osculation."

Danger! Danger! Must. Not. Think. About. Hot. Girl-on-girl. Osculation.

Whatever that means.

And yet there she is: Penelope dressed as slave Leia making out with another girl in a Red Sonja chain-mail bikini.

"There, now," Penelope says. "That isn't so hard, is it?"

Speak for yourself. I shift uncomfortably on the cave floor.

"Now, how about you try again, Charlie," she says.

"How about we contemplate the virtues of silence instead?" Charlie offers. "Challenging as that may be for some of us."

"I'll go next," Hank interjects. "Just to keep things civil." He adjusts himself so he's sitting cross-legged. "OK. Something you all don't know about me. Let's see . . . How about this? The first

282

time I met Dan"—he looks over at me—"I was a nervous wreck. I was terrified he wouldn't like me and that he might be upset because his mom and I were engaged. But he was great about it. And he's been great ever since. I really lucked out."

I slide my eyes away.

"That's interesting," Charlie says. "You say you want Dan to like you, and yet you don't seem to like him. Isn't that strange?"

Hank frowns. "What do you mean? I like him very much." He turns to me. "You think I don't like you?" He sounds genuinely hurt.

"Oh, it's nothing Dan said," Charlie explains. "Just an *observation*." Charlie shakes his head. "I probably shouldn't have mentioned it. Let's just forge ahead with this asinine game of Penelope's."

"No," Hank says. "I'd like to know why you think I don't like Dan. What these so-called observations are."

Oh, Hank. Poor, foolish Hank.

"Well, if you must know . . ." Charlie begins counting on his fingers: "Your mistreatment and eventual misplacement of his Baby-Real-A-Lot doll. The embarrassing comments about Dan's body odor. The negativity about his artwork. The humiliating, vociferous reaction to Dan's carsickness. And then, of course, the vicious strike to his nose. From an outsider's perspective, it could appear that you're harboring some unconscious anger toward Dan. Or jealousy, perhaps. He is, after all, a rival for Sarah's affection."

Charlie gives me a significant look. I sigh internally, no longer as excited to play my part as I was when we first concocted this plan.

I look at Hank, attempting to appear wounded. "Is it true? Are you angry at me?"

"Of course not!" Hank's face and neck are bright red, a noticeable difference from his pale chest and shoulders. "Those were accidents and misunderstandings and—"

"Perhaps," Charlie says. "But if you believe Sigmund Freud, there are no such things as accidents."

Penelope rolls her eyes. "He was talking about slips of the tongue, you imbecile."

"Listen," Hank says, leaning toward me, an intense look in his eyes. "I promised to tell you the truth, and here it is: When your mom first told us about this trip, I wasn't exactly . . . thrilled. I thought it would be kind of awkward, since we hardly knew each other. And hard work, too—not the greatest way to spend a week's vacation time. However, the closer we got to the date and the more time I spent with you, the more excited I got about it." He shakes his head. "All these things Charlie listed—they're crazy! Even if I *did* hate you—and I don't!—there's no way I could've planned even half of that stuff. Nobody could. It's just been a run of bizarrely bad luck. Honestly."

I wrench my gaze from his, guilt and shame eating away at my insides. My eyes happen to catch Penelope's. She's staring at me with a look that's almost as intense as Hank's—and as much as I wish I could pretend it's because she's suddenly overcome by lust, I can tell it's not that.

"Let's just forget it, OK?" I say. "Charlie's just trying to make trouble. It's what he does."

"I beg to differ," Charlie says indignantly. "I was simply pointing out the facts and my *observations.*"

"I think we've had enough of your *observations*," I say firmly. "My turn. Something you don't know about me . . ." I look down at my wrist. The dead ID bracelet. Dad's Timex. "This watch"—I tap the glass face—"was my father's."

"This is not news, Daniel," Charlie says. "At least not to me."

Penelope turns on him. "For someone who didn't want to participate, you sure have a lot to say about everyone else's contributions."

"It's not whose watch it is," I say, "but why I wear it, even though it hasn't worked in years. That's what you don't know." I take the watch off and let it dangle from my fingers. The black leather band is cracked and peeling, the buckle worn smooth. The time is permanently stopped at 11:09 and the date frozen on the seventh. "He wore this watch all the time. I always remember seeing it there on his hairy wrist. When he taught me how to play chess. When he dealt out a game of gin rummy. When he drunkenly read Dr. Seuss to me at bedtime. It's a piece of junk, really. Anytime anyone complimented him on it, he'd say, 'This old thing? I've had it for thirty years. Cost me two bucks at a garage sale. Proves you don't have to spend a lot to get a lot.'" I can hear his voice clear as day. "It still smells like his aftershave, too." I bring the watch band to my nose and breathe in the ghost of Dad's scent. "A little bit, anyway. Inspired by Polo. 'Why buy the real thing when the cheaper imitation smells exactly the same? A lot of suckers in this world, let me tell you.'"

"So you wear it to remember him," Hank says. "That's nice."

I shake my head. "No. I wear it to remember him leaving. It fell off his wrist when he flung his garbage bag full of stuff over his shoulder—hit the driveway hard and stopped working. When

I picked it up and tried to give it back to him, he told me to chuck it, that he was going to get himself a new watch. 'A new watch for a new life.'" I look down at the scratched face. "Every time I look at this, I'm reminded of the exact day, hour, minute, and second when I last saw him." I wrap the band around my wrist and reattach it. "How many people in your life can you say that about?"

The cave is quiet, the only sounds the rain coming down outside and the crackle of the fire.

Hank clears his throat. "Wow, Dan. I'm . . . really sorry."

"That's some heavy shit," Penelope says, then turns to Charlie. "You see? Dan just poured his heart out now. Are you really going to sit there and not contribute anything?"

"Nope, not gonna sit here," Charlie says, leaping to his feet and scrabbling backward. "And neither should you!"

Penelope turns to see what he's staring at—

And lets out an ear-piercing shriek.

CHAPTER 55

"Don't make any sudden movements!" Hank says, his hands and arms outstretched.

But it's too late. I'm already springing away, and Penelope is frantically crab-crawling backward, kicking sand and pebbles in the direction of the huge rattlesnake that's slithering toward her, its sharp fangs bared, shaking its rattle like a pissed-off toddler.

"Get it away, get it away!" Penelope cries, her eyes filled with terror. She scrambles backward but can't get to her feet.

I want to help, but my legs know that I hate snakes. The way they freakily glide across the ground. The way they can hold so still, then suddenly strike. The way they can kill you with one bite.

The snake coils, its tongue flicking, its dead doll eyes focused squarely on Penelope.

"Hi-ya!" Charlie shouts, leaping through the air, wielding a flaming stick like a saggy-pantsed ninja.

He swats at the snake.

But completely misses.

"Oh shit," Charlie squeaks, crumpling to the ground. "That's not how I pictured that going."

The snake whips around on Charlie, shaking its tail like crazy, its head bobbing and weaving.

And then the snake attacks—shooting out toward Charlie at superfast speed, its mouth unnaturally wide.

"No!" Penelope cries, her hand covering her mouth.

Charlie raises his branch in defense.

Miraculously, the snake bites the stick, knocking it from Charlie's grasp.

And that's when Penelope, in one fell swoop, grabs a stick, bounds over the fire, and spears the serpent right in the head.

Amazing! I couldn't have drawn it better.

"Oh-my-Christ-thank-you!" Charlie pants. "You saved my life."

Penelope shrugs. "You saved mine first."

"Yeah, but . . ." Charlie struggles to his feet and brushes off his hand. "You actually killed the thing."

She smiles. "Just add it to the long list of things that I can do better than you." She hoists the snake aloft with her stick. "Now, who's hungry?"

CHAPTER 56

The morning sun is warm on the skin, its bright rays drying up yesterday's deluge, filling the air with a fresh, clean smell.

The world around us is quiet, like everything is taking a breath. There is the occasional whisper of wind through the wild grass. The odd bird tweet here and there. But mostly stillness from the natural world.

The same cannot be said for Charlie and Penelope.

It seems saving each other's lives was a real bonding experience for them. They're still insulting one another, calling each other names, but now it's "mewling gudgeon" and "fusty codpiece," delivered with exaggerated Shakespearean accents and a lot of giggling.

"You, my lad," Penelope says, waving her hand in the air, "are a sanguine coward, a bed-presser, a horseback-breaker. Away, you moldy rogue! You filthy bung. Away!"

"Dissembling harlot, thou art false in all!" Charlie counters. "Hag of all despite. To spend another moment beside you, I had rather chop this hand off at a blow, and with the other fling it at thy face."

They fold over in hysterics, like they've just told the world's funniest jokes.

So much for *opposites* attracting. They're basically falling in love with their doppelgängers.

I try to tamp down the flare of jealousy, fondling Baby Robbie's sweater for strength. But I swear, if Charlie ends up getting with Penelope this trip and all I wind up with is a puffy-paged sketchbook, a poison ivy rash on my ass, and Post-Traumatic Hank Disorder, I am going to have to strangle someone.

Hank and I walk beside each other in silence. He stares off, seemingly lost in thought as he gnaws on a piece of leftover snake jerky.

He's been quiet since we left the cave, and I can only hope it's because he's reconsidering the whole parenting thing. I didn't mean to tell the watch story last night. Still, maybe it convinced Hank that I'm even more screwed up by my father's leaving than he imagined and that he's not cut out for this level of responsibility.

"Uhhh, gentlemen," Penelope calls back. "I think we may have a challenge here."

Hank and I catch up to Penelope and Charlie. They're staring at a hole in the ground into which the rolling water seems to disappear.

"Where did it go?" I ask, looking ahead and seeing no sign of a stream.

"Clearly it becomes subterranean," Charlie says, snapping photos of the unusual natural feature. "It could flow underground for miles."

Hank frowns. "Let's check it out. Maybe we'll get lucky and come across it again soon."

A hundred yards. Two hundred yards. Nothing. No water anywhere.

"How do we know we're even going in the right direction?" Penelope asks, looking around. "What if the stream veers off to the right or left?"

I look at Hank, who's searching the grass, sweat beading on his upper lip.

"What do we do now?" I say. "How do we know which way to go? We're running out of time."

"Keep looking." Hank's eyes are darting every which way. "We'll find the stream again. We have to . . ." These last words trail off, like he's saying them to himself. Like they're a prayer he knows won't come true.

Twenty minutes later we're still trekking across dry land.

I sigh and look at Hank. "Are you sure you don't have some trick for finding water—some technique you learned on your hunting trips? Like a dowsing rod or something?"

Hank's been surprisingly spare with his outdoorsy advice this whole trip. Does he think he gets bonus points for modesty or something? At this point, he can be an even bigger braggart than Rick Chuff for all I care if it helps us find our way to the lake in one piece.

"Don't worry," Hank says, his voice falsely cheery. "We just keep heading in this direction." He gestures straight ahead. "Downhill-ish. Keep an eye out. We'll find some sign of the stream eventually. Maybe even come upon the river it feeds."

The tension is thick, like the air has gone heavy and humid, making it hard to breathe. I can tell we're all thinking the same thing.

We are well and truly lost with just a day left to find our lake.

CHAPTER 57

"So be honest," Penelope says to Charlie out of the blue. "Why didn't you want to share something about yourself last night?"

"Truthfully?" Charlie says. "I couldn't think of anything that Daniel doesn't already know about me."

"Really?" Penelope asks skeptically. "I mean, I realize you guys are like, omphalopagus and all. But does he really know *everything* about you?"

I expect Charlie to shut this line of questioning down, like he did last night, but he pauses like he's actually thinking about it. "OK, I suppose not *everything* everything."

"Wait, what don't I know about you?" I ask.

"There are a few things that never seemed worth disclosing," Charlie admits.

"Like what?" Penelope and I ask at the same time. I glare at her. Sure, the dumb game was her idea, but Charlie is my best friend—if anyone has a right to know all his secrets, it's me.

"OK, well, for example . . ." Charlie takes a deep breath. "The week before my parents died, we had quite the altercation. I had come home from school with another fat lip—and I believe a black eye this time, too. My parents wanted to report my assailant to the principal; however, I knew that this would only lead to something worse than a fat lip and a black eye." Charlie pushes his glasses back up onto the bridge of his nose. "Thus, I refused to name names, and so they grounded me. I was to remain grounded until I revealed who had attacked me. Well, that night I was so incensed at the injustice of it all that I prayed for my mother and father to die. And, a week later, they did."

"Whoa," Penelope says. "Really? How did it happen?"

"An automobile accident."

"Jesus."

For a moment, I think that she's going to say something uncharacteristically kind, like "I'm so sorry" or "That must have been awful."

Instead, she says, "Well, no wonder you're such a head case."

Charlie smirks. "Yes. Thank you for that. And your excuse is?"

Penelope laughs. "Touché."

Hank looks over at Charlie. "You know it wasn't your fault, right, Charlie?"

"Of course," Charlie says flatly, fiddling with his camera. "I don't pretend to believe I have some form of telekinesis. Or that there is a God who grants the vindictive wishes of ten-year-old boys. I just find the timing of it all interesting."

"Jeez, Charlie," I say. "I had no idea. That's . . . crazy."

"Coincidental," he corrects. He shrugs. "Now, I certainly hope that fulfills my obligation, as the only other things Dan doesn't know about me happen to be of a much more . . . venereal nature. And I'm sure we're not quite that desperate for conversation, are we?"

"No!" Penelope, Hank, and I respond in unison.

The morning wears on, and we still haven't located the stream.

I glance around to distract myself from the fact that we are totally lost and completely screwed. I don't care how optimistic Hank pretends to be; with no creek or brook guiding our way, there isn't a chance in hell of finding the lake.

I look to the left and see the wind blowing and bending the wildflowers.

I look up and watch the birds flutter around the trees.

I glance to the right and see a bear strolling along through the trees, watching me watch it.

I blink, then stop dead in my tracks.

I can see the telltale slash on its nose.

"Uh, guys!" I whisper-shout. "The b-bear. It f-found us!"

Charlie turns and looks where I'm pointing. The huge black bear has stopped moving and is staring directly at us, sniffing the air like mad.

"What's it smelling?" Hank asks.

"Snake jerky, maybe?" I say.

"Oh Lord," Charlie croaks, emptying the dried snake meat from his pocket. "Mr. Langston, I think perhaps we should—"

"Stand still," Hank insists. "The bear's just checking us out. It's probably attracted by our food, like Dan said. It's not actually interested in *us*—"

And that's when the bear charges—all seven hundred pounds of it hurtling our way, its fur and flesh rippling as it runs, its yellow teeth bared and snapping.

"Run!" Hank screams.

I race toward the nearest tree, dropping my sketchbook somewhere along the way. I launch myself partway up the trunk and start climbing.

I look around. Charlie's climbing a tree, too. Hank and Penelope have bolted into the woods.

Someone has to be shit out of luck, and this time it's Charlie. The bear targets him and starts scaling his tree, as swift and limber as a goddamn monkey.

"Good Christ!" Charlie shouts. "What do I do? What the hell do I *do*?"

But there's nothing either of us can do except watch as the bear closes the distance.

And then I get an idea.

"Charlie!" I call out. "Jump!"

"Are you out of your fucking mind?" Charlie hollers. "I'll kill myself—and my Nikon!"

"It's either that or get eaten!" I yell. "The bear isn't going to leap from the tree."

"Yeah, because it's not stupid."

"Shut up!" I snap. "I mean that it'll have to climb down. And you'll be long gone by the time it reaches the ground."

Charlie looks down from the branch he's inchwormed out

onto, his camera dangling from his neck. "Not if I break my leg! Or my neck!"

Meanwhile, the bear continues making its way toward Charlie, grunting as it goes. Who knew something so big could be so agile?

"Jump, Charlie!" I shout. "It's your only chance!"

Finally, the bear makes it up to Charlie's branch. It starts scooting toward him, swiping out with its razor-sharp claws.

Charlie whimpers and crawls farther out onto the bowing limb.

Oh my God. Charlie is actually going to die—right here in front of my eyes. I swallow a sob and bury my face in my arm.

There's a loud shriek—"*Aaaaaaaahhh!*"—and then a dull thud, accompanied by a howl of pain: "*Owwwwww!*"

I peer over my branch. Charlie is on the ground, his glasses askew, hoisting his Nikon with his left arm, his right arm pressed to his belly. Alive!

The relief is immeasurable, like Thor's hammer has been lifted off my chest.

The bear is still in the tree. It huffs and grunts, clearly pissed off.

"My arm!" Charlie whines. "I think I broke it."

The bear starts creeping back off the branch toward the trunk.

"Get up!" I bellow. "Run, Charlie! *Now!*"

Charlie straightens his glasses and scrambles to his feet. Our gazes meet and hold for a split second—a whole world of emotions conveyed in that one glance.

Then he takes off into the forest.

I watch the bear shinny down the tree like a fat acrobat. It drops to the ground and raises its twitching nose, sniffing the air. Maybe it won't be able to track him. He got rid of his snake jerky, after all. Maybe it'll all be OK.

But no sooner do I think this than the bear lowers its head and charges off in the exact direction that Charlie just ran.

CHAPTER
58

I sit up in my tree, debating what to do next: Do I go down to look for the others and risk running into the killer bear? Do I wait up here until they come looking for me? If I do wait, then for how long? If I climb down, which way do I go? Everyone ran in different directions.

It's probably best to hang tight. Charlie knows I'm up in this tree. He'll tell the others.

If he's still alive.

If any of them are still alive.

Oh, God, what if I'm the only one left? What if I'm lost out here all on my own? There's no way I'll find my way back to the lake — not with a rogue bear hunting me down.

I'm going to die out here.

Alone.

I cup my hands around my mouth. "Hank! Penelope! Charlie!" My throat is raw, my voice like wind through a torn noisemaker. "Hank! Penelope! Charlie!"

Nothing.

I stare down at the ground, thirty feet below. I spot my sketchbook lying in the dirt.

I can't believe I'm going to die at sixteen. That I'm never going to get to kiss another girl. A real kiss. One that matters. Or know what it feels like to touch a breast.

And forget about ever getting laid.

I tug Baby Robbie's sweater from the pocket of my sweats and clutch it in my fist as a wave of dizziness crashes over me. I grip a nearby branch to stop myself from plummeting to the ground.

Get ahold of yourself, Daniel.

It's Charlie's voice in my head again. I've never been so glad to hear his nasally twang in my life!

It's doubtful that the bear has killed everyone. *That's just your imagination running wild.*

Yes. Right. How much can one bear eat, anyway?

Surely someone else has survived. Max and Barbara are out here somewhere, too, don't forget. Maybe they'll happen upon you—though, that's unlikely. They're probably already at the lake, dining on root salad and roasted trout. Still, unlikely is not the same as impossible. And let's not forget about Hank. He's certainly killed far more bears than this bear has killed humans. Granted, he's seemed rather off his game for much of this trip, but surely when the chips are down—as they inarguably are now—he'll come through for you. For all of us.

Charlie's right. There are a lot of scenarios where we get out of this alive. But all of them require me to stay calm and not give up.

I take a deep breath and try to settle my chaotic thoughts.

It must work, because suddenly I'm aware of the throbbing pain in my nose again—and the fact that my poison-ivyed ass has started to itch like a bastard again. What I wouldn't do for some more Calamine lotion right now. Instead, I adjust my position and drag my butt crack along the bough.

"Ooooooooh." What glorious relief! My eyes roll back into my head as I rock back and forth. "Oh, yeah. Get in there. Jesus-Christ-Almighty-that-feels-so-good. Yes. Yes. Yes."

"Listen, when you're through violating that branch there, maybe you could come down and help me look for Hank and Charlie."

I freeze, rocked by successive waves of shock, euphoria, and excruciating embarrassment.

"Penelope! You're—you're alive! Thank God." I breathe a huge sigh of relief. "And, uh, I wasn't, you know . . ." I point to the branch. "It's the rash. I was just trying to—"

"No need to equivocate, Dan," she says, bending over and picking up my sketch pad. "You clearly had an itch that needed scratching. I can make myself scarce if you two need a little more time . . . ?"

"No. Don't go. I'm done." I tuck the baby sweater back into my pocket, then scramble down the tree, my cheeks still flaming. "I'm so glad you're not dead!"

Penelope laughs. "As am I! And I would like to keep it that way. So we should probably get going." She hands me my sketchbook and looks around. "Any idea which way Hank and Charlie ran?"

"Hank ran that way," I say, pointing. I swallow. "And the bear chased Charlie that way." I point in the opposite direction.

"Shit." Penelope starts jogging in that direction. "Do you think he made it?"

"I don't know," I say, my voice shaky, clutching my sketch pad as I run. "He had a decent head start. But he's not the fastest runner . . ."

"Right. Of course." Penelope rubs her cheek. "Well, with any luck, we should be able to catch up to—"

Penelope stops cold, her eyes going wide.

"What?" I say, pulling up beside her.

She holds up a hand. "Don't. Move," she mouths.

I hear a crunch of leaves, then the familiar heavy footfalls. Somewhere behind some bushes, the bear snorts and snuffles, its raspy breathing getting closer.

"It's got our scent," Penelope whispers.

She slowly squats down, never taking her eyes off the bushes. She feels around on the ground and grabs a big rock.

"When I say 'run,'" she says, "get the hell out of here. Just go and don't turn around."

"Wait, what? What are you going to—"

"Run!" she shouts, firing the rock into the bushes.

The bear grunts, then lets out a savage, pissed-off roar.

"Shit!" I turn and bolt, pumping my arms as hard as I can. "Is it close?" I shout to Penelope. "Is it coming for us?"

But there's no answer.

I glance over my shoulder. Penelope's running in the opposite direction, leading the bear away from me.

A second later they're both out of sight.

And then I hear Penelope scream.

CHAPTER 59

I can't believe Penelope just saved my life! Without hesitation. That's twice now that she's risked her own life to save someone else.

Who does that?

Who the hell is *that* selfless?

I jog aimlessly through the forest, replaying the whole scene in my head—what I could have done differently, how I could have protected her, why I didn't I try to save her . . .

I stop jogging and look over my shoulder.

Maybe I should go back, see if I can help her.

And get eaten yourself? Charlie's voice asks incredulously. *Waste her ultimate sacrifice? Make her death be completely meaningless? Yes, that's an excellent plan, Daniel.*

I need to find Charlie—the real Charlie—and Hank. They'll know what to do.

I cup my hands around my mouth and scream, *"Haaaaaank! Charlieeeeee!"*

I scream and walk, scream and walk, for what seems like hours, until my voice is so hoarse, only a dull whistling rasp escapes my throat. The last gasp of a dying man.

I stumble over to a tree and slide to the ground. I lean my head back.

The adrenaline has long since drained from my system, leaving me totally wiped.

I just need to rest for a minute, figure out what to do next.

I close my eyes. I'll start planning after I take a quick break. Just for one . . . tiny . . . little . . .

"Psst!" a voice hisses at me. "Dan. Wake up!"

I jerk my head up. My body is coiled on the cold ground.

I push myself to sitting, shivering. A couple of shaggy shrubs tower in front of me. I don't remember seeing them before I fell asleep. I rub the grit from the corners of my eyes.

"Who's there?" I whisper.

"Dan," a voice calls again. "It's us."

Just then both shrubs start tottering closer to me.

"Ahhh!" I scream, backing up against the tree and raising my sketch pad as a weapon.

"Shhh!" the larger bush commands. "It's Hank and Charlie."

I peer at the bushes, my heart pounding.

Holy crap, it *is* them—covered head to toe in leaves, twigs, and dirt.

I clamber to my feet. "Charlie! You're alive! And you're *filthy!*"

"True on both counts," Charlie says, his injured right arm in a stick-and-vine splint. "The camouflage was Hank's idea. It's an old hunting trick. And the mud helps to cover our scent." He looks down at himself. "You'd be surprised what you're willing to do when you're trying to hide from a seven-hundred-pound beast with bone-crunching mandibles."

"Thank God we found you," Hank says. He looks around, the leaves of his costume swishing. "What about Penelope? Have you seen her at all?"

"Oh my God. Penelope!" It all comes rushing back like a terrible nightmare. I explain what happened—the bear, the rock.

The scream.

"Oh no," Hank croaks, his twig-shrouded shoulders slumping.

Charlie frowns, sending little cracks through his mud mask. "But you didn't actually *see* the bear attack her, correct? So you don't know for certain that she's"—he clears his throat—"you know."

I shake my head. "No, I didn't see it. But the bear was so close, and the horrible sound she made—" I choke back my tears. "It should've been me!"

I can no longer hold the awful thoughts at bay, the weight of hopelessness, grief, and guilt. My body shudders with heavy sobs. Hank shuffles over and engulfs me in his leafy, mud-slathered arms. And I am undone.

CHAPTER
60

Hank is having me cake myself with mud from the river he and Charlie discovered.

"Now that we know where the river is, we can follow it to the lake," he says, using a sharpened stone to cut some branches off a bush. "That's the good news, I guess."

"There is no good news," I say, gently patting some sludge around my tender nose.

"We'll find Penelope," Hank insists. "Don't worry. I'm sure she's fine. She's very resourceful."

"And wily," Charlie adds, weaving branches together for my costume. He forces a laugh. "If anyone deserves our pity, it's the bear."

With Hank and Charlie both occupied, I surreptitiously drip some of the cold mud down the back of my pants. As I'd hoped, it soothes my ass itch quite a bit. Gross but effective.

"Until we have evidence to the contrary," Hank says, coming over and tying a branch to my arm with a piece of vine, "I think it's best to assume she's OK. Maybe lost, maybe frightened, but OK."

I stare at him. "A bloodcurdling scream isn't evidence to the contrary?"

"Circumstantial at best," Charlie says, handing Hank the branches he's woven together. "Certainly not enough to convict the bear in a court of law. You'd need a body for that. Claw marks. Then you'd have a case. But I'm with Hank here. I think she got away. I mean, *I* escaped and she's in much better shape than I am."

I want to believe them, I really do. But that chilling shriek echoes through my head, and I know they're probably kidding themselves.

Hank and Charlie work their magic, and a few minutes later I look like a soldier fighting in the deepest jungle.

Or a kindergartener wearing the world's cheapest Halloween costume.

Charlie pulls his camera out from under his shirt, leans into me, and snaps a selfie. "Bush brothers!" he declares, with remarkable cheeriness. Someone is in deep, deep denial.

"OK," Hank says. "Let's go find Penelope."

It's touch and go for a while, but after about an hour, I manage to lead us to the spot where Penelope beaned the bear.

"She ran this way," I say, following a trail of broken branches and flattened plants. I'm bracing myself for the absolute worst.

We march along, shouting Penelope's name as we go, until the trail of busted foliage peters out.

Hank circles the area. "I don't see any signs of a struggle."

"That's positive," Charlie offers. "I mean, we all saw what happened to that fawn. If Penelope were mauled, there would be some indication: blood, torn clothing, drag marks in the dirt."

A cold chill rockets up my spine as I spot a ragged piece of cloth fluttering on a nearby branch, a long spray of blood on the ground below.

"You mean, like this?" I whisper, pinching the blood-soaked strip of fabric from the branch.

Hank's whole dirt-spackled body sags. "Oh, God. Oh no."

But Charlie is shaking his leaf-covered head. "It's still just circumstantial. There would be a lot more blood if she were . . . if the bear had . . ."

He puts his mud-caked fist in his mouth, stifling a sob.

CHAPTER
61

I am completely numb. I can't process the fact that Penelope is dead. It doesn't make sense. She's too vibrant and ornery and smart-mouthed to die.

"We're going to have to pick up the pace," Hank says when we finally make it back to the river. His voice is weak, weary. "Clint is supposed to meet us at the lake tomorrow morning. Hopefully, Max and Barbara—" The words catch in his throat. "Hopefully, they'll be there too. We'll have Clint call in for a search party. Just as long as we get to the lake in time."

He says this like there is any hope left of finding Penelope alive.

Even though we all know that there's not.

Charlie grabs Hank's arm, making him stop. "What about the bear?" he croaks. It's the first thing he's said since we left the site of the mauling.

Hank looks at him with concern. "What about it, Charlie?"

"Don't you feel it might be prudent to perhaps fashion some weapons?" he asks, glancing around with wide eyes. "Spears or cudgels or something, in case the bear tracks us down again?"

Hank looks up at the sinking sun. "I don't think we have time for that. If we're lucky, we'll make it back to the lake by sunrise." He looks down at his twig-covered body. "We'll just have to hope that our camouflage is enough to keep us safe." He gently removes Charlie's hand from his arm. "Come on. Let's go."

Charlie and I hurry to keep up with a swiftly hobbling Hank, each swish of leaves or snap of a twig making Charlie yip in fear.

"Are you sure we don't have time to make, like, spears or something?" I ask Hank, huffing as I try to match his long strides. "Or maybe it's time we went on the offensive," I suggest, warming to the idea. "If we just kill the bear—if *you* kill it, I mean—we won't have to worry anymore, right? And then even if we *can't* find the lake, at least we can stock up on meat and survive until someone—"

Hank stops abruptly.

"You guys want to make weapons?" he snaps, his expression fierce. "Here." He pulls the sharpened stone from his pocket and slaps it in my palm. "Knock yourselves out. *I'm* going to go find the lake."

Charlie and I share confused, concerned glances.

311

"Hank," I say, as we jog to catch up. "Charlie and I were just trying to help. We're scared. That's all."

"Indeed," Charlie says. "My sincerest apologies. I didn't mean to upset you. I realize that you are the adult here and the wilderness expert. I never should have second-guessed you—"

Hank whips around, his jaw clenched. "I am *not* a wilderness expert. I'm not. I know *nothing* about camping. *Nothing* about hunting. *Nothing* about being a parent. *Nothing.* It was all a big lie. OK?"

Charlie and I stare at him.

I blink, trying to make sense of what he's just said.

"Y-you're not?" I stammer. "I don't . . . But you said . . ."

He shakes his head. "It was a misunderstanding. Your mom saw a bearskin rug in my family room. It came with the house. All of the furniture did. But your mom . . . she got so excited when she saw the stupid thing." He clears his throat. "She jumped to conclusions. And I didn't correct her. I should have, but I let it slide. I guess . . . I guess I liked the idea that she thought I was this man's man, instead of just a boring old dentist. I certainly didn't expect it to go anywhere after that. But then it started to snowball, and before I knew it, I was in so deep that I couldn't figure a way out."

He takes a shaky breath. "I love her so much, Dan. I was scared that if I told her the truth, after going along with the lie for so long, I'd mess it all up." He swallows. "I tried to bone up on some camping particulars, bought some magazines, listened to some podcasts, downloaded survival apps on my phone, but you have to believe me, I never would have agreed to go on this trip with you if I'd had *any* notion that we'd become separated from our guide. I never intended to take things this far . . ." He looks out at the rushing river.

I stand there, saying nothing. The world spins, a million thoughts colliding in my head like bumper cars.

"Oh my God," Charlie says, looking around at the never-ending wilderness. "It's over. We're doomed. We're never getting out of here alive."

"Oh, the misery, the hopelessness of it all," a girl's voice calls out from behind us. "Who are you, Samuel Beckett?"

I spin around to see Penelope pushing through the bushes. She's scratched up and dirty, her shirt ripped at the belly, but she is most definitely still alive.

"'The tears of the world are a constant quantity,'" Penelope quotes.

"Holy crap!" Charlie says, stumbling backward. "W-we thought you were dead!"

"I nearly was," Penelope says, gesturing to her torn shirt. "Thankfully, it's just a flesh wound. Stings like a bitch, though."

"H-how did you find us?" Hank asks, staring at Penelope like she's a ghost. "We looked everywhere for you . . ."

"Just a bit of good fortune," she says casually. "While I wandered around looking for you gentlemen, I happened upon this river. I decided that I would follow it down to the lake in the hopes of connecting with you there—or, worst-case scenario, meet up with my mom and Max and have Clint send out a search party for the three of you. Anyway, I was walking along, contemplating the current state of stem-cell research, when I heard voices. I tracked the sound and caught up to you. Except, at first I didn't recognize you as human." She gestures at our camouflage.

"I thought perhaps I'd inadvertently ingurgitated some hallucinogenic mushrooms. But then I recognized Charlie's nasally whine lamenting the futility of life. That's when I knew it had to be you guys."

She smiles—as though it's the most natural thing in the world for her to be standing there in front of us.

"But . . ." I blink at her. "The bear. It was . . . I heard you scream."

"Ah, right. That must have been when I speared myself on that branch." She lifts her shirt hem, showing us the blood-crusted laceration on her side. "It was quite painful, as I said. But luckily not life-threatening."

"I don't understand," Charlie says, frowning. "Dan said the bear was right on your heels. How did you manage to outrun it?" His voice is heavy with skepticism—like he expects her to rip off her mask and reveal the face of a bear underneath.

She smirks. "You see, Charlie," she begins, sounding like she's talking to an intellectually disabled child, "when the bear first started after me, I came up with a theory regarding our relative turning radiuses. I thought to myself, 'I am like an Aston Martin V8 Vantage Roadster. *Ursus americanus* is a Chevy minivan.' Or so I hoped. To test my theory, I kept making these incredibly sharp turns around trees, changing direction on the fly. The bear had to make wider turns than I did, which slowed it down quite substantially. Eventually, I confused the hell out of it, and the bear gave up."

"That's . . . freakin' brilliant," I say.

Penelope laughs. "Don't sound so surprised! You are looking at the winner of a tertiary scholarship at the Intel International

Science and Engineering Fair. Although how I didn't receive top honors still remains a mystery to me." She cocks her head to one side. "So, I'm feeling a little like bear bait in my current state of dress." She looks at Charlie. "Might I entreat your assistance in getting properly festooned, good sir?"

CHAPTER 62

Somehow Penelope manages to make the whole Swamp Thing look seem hot. She's taken the lead, apparently unencumbered by her injury or the awkward bulk of the outfit.

We hike into late afternoon. The shadows of the trees, rocks, and bushes stretch out long and thin on the ground, looking more and more like funhouse-mirror versions of themselves with each passing hour.

Penelope's Jean Grey–like resurrection initially distracted me from Hank's devastating confession. But as the hours have passed, I've gone over and over his words in my head, like watching an endless loop of the Viper getting killed by the Mountain on *Game of Thrones: He's fine, he's fine, he's fine—BLAMMO! Teeth knocked out, skull crushed, the Viper is dead!*

I wish I could be as happy as Charlie about Hank's revelation, but I can't seem to muster his level of enthusiasm.

"Well, we did it, my friend," he said, not long after we set out again. "We got him to crack."

"Yeah, I guess," I said, a knot in my throat.

"I bet he gets out of Dodge as soon as we get back. The shame! The embarrassment! The feelings of inadequacy! I would *not* want to be him right now."

I nodded and swallowed. "Yeah, no. Me neither."

"You were right about him all along," Charlie said. "Not that I doubted you, of course. But I didn't expect him to be a *total* charlatan. Anyway, your mom should be relieved. Once she gets over the shock of it all, of course."

"Yeah," I said. "She'll be relieved. For sure. . . . Eventually."

"You don't seem that happy about it," Charlie noted.

"I'm just tired," I said wanly.

"Well, lucky for you this saga is nearly at its end."

The miles drag on. Endless and slow.

The warm yellow-orange of the day fades into the cool blue of the moonlit night. Blades of grass and stems of weeds bend in the wind. Tree branches creak overhead.

And still we walk.

"I wonder . . . if it's time to admit," I pant, "that following this river . . . was a stupid idea."

Nobody responds. Everyone's too tired, all effort going into putting one foot in front of the other. My feet are swollen and blistered, and my legs are burning up.

"I'm just saying . . . we spent one day walking . . . into the

317

woods. We've spent the last three and a half . . . trying to get out. I'm no math genius, but the numbers . . . don't really add up."

"Rivers . . . don't run . . . in a straight line," Hank says, every word sounding like an effort. "And it has to . . . feed into the lake . . . eventually."

I don't have the energy to argue, to point out that this place is probably called the River of No Return for a reason, that we shouldn't be following someone who's lied to our faces since the moment we met him.

And so we keep walking. Hour after hour. The moon arches across the dark, star-speckled sky until the black starts to dissolves into a pale blue.

The morning approaches. Our meeting time with Clint is now just a few hours away.

The ribbon of water continues to course through the valley, into the distance, seemingly flowing forever—with no sign of the lake anywhere.

Just as the sun starts to peek over the horizon, Charlie's foot catches on a root. He stumbles and collapses to the ground, his camera smacking the dirt, his glasses skittering off.

Hank, Penelope, and I stagger over to him. Charlie's half-closed eyes are red and rheumy.

"Charlie?" Hank says, handing him his glasses. "Are you OK?"

"Can't . . . move," Charlie moans. "Legs . . . dead . . . So . . . tired."

Hank peers into the distance. If there is a lake out there, it's miles and miles ahead.

"All right," Hank says, sighing. "We'll rest here for a bit. Half an hour, maybe. An hour at most."

"Thank God." I drop my sketchbook and start pulling the branches off my arms and legs.

"What're you doing?" Penelope asks, her words semi-slurred.

"There's no way I'm going to be able to rest with all this stuff poking into me," I say, picking the leaves and twigs out of my hair. "If the bear's followed us this far, then let him eat me."

I shuffle off and find a nice patch of spongy moss. As I settle down, I glance at my left wrist. The dead ID bracelet is still there.

But Dad's Timex is gone.

A hot-cold jolt races through my body. I have no clue when I lost it. Running from the bear? Climbing the tree? Putting on the camouflage? Ripping it off?

I stagger to my feet and scan the dirt nearby, kicking at my discarded twigs and leaves. But the watch is not there.

"You OK, bud?" Hank says, lowering himself to the ground.

"Yeah," I say, grabbing my wrist, sniffing back hot tears. "Fine. I just . . . I lost my watch."

"Oh, jeez, Dan," Hank says. "I'm sorry about that. You want me to help look for it?"

I shake my head. "No. I looked already." I pinch the moisture from the corners of my eyes. "Doesn't matter anyway. It was a piece of junk." I move back to the moss I found. I reach into my pocket and find the tiny sweater. I hold it tight in my hand.

I'm too tired to cry. Too tired to care, even. I just want all of this to be over . . .

There is a buzzing sound in my dreams, like someone riding a lawn mower way off in the distance. I feel the heat of the sun on my cheek, like a warm hand caressing me awake.

319

My eyes flutter open. It's bright out, the sun high in the sky. It has to be late morning. Maybe even noon.

Oh, crap! We fell asleep!

I sit up, my body one massive ache.

The buzzing continues, no longer part of my dream, but somewhere here in the real world. I look around, try to locate the noise.

All I see is the river, trees, and grass.

And Hank, Penelope, and Charlie, still out cold.

Hank is snoring, but that's not what I'm hearing. The droning is somewhere else. Somewhere . . .

Above.

I tilt my head back and search the skies. Nothing. Just the sun and a mat of blue with the occasional cottony streak of cloud.

The hum gets softer. Whatever it is, it's moving away from us. I whip my head from side to side. Where is it? Where the hell is it?

"Hey!" I shout. "Guys! Wake up! I hear something! A plane! I think it's a plane!"

Hank is the first to stir. "Huh?" He rubs his eyes. "What did you say?"

"Listen," I say. "You hear that?"

Hank cocks his head, then leaps to his feet. "Where's it coming from? Which direction? Did you see it?"

"I can't tell. I can't see any—There!" I point in the distance. A speck of a plane is flying toward a hill, a wisp of dark smoke puffing from the engine. "It's Clint!" I cry. "The smoke—just like when he left us!"

"Get up! Get up!" Hank bellows at Penelope and Charlie. "We have to go! Now!"

320

"What's going on?" Penelope grumbles, sweeping her mud-matted hair from her face.

"We found the lake!" Hank says. "Dan found it."

"What? How?" Charlie rasps.

"Clint's plane just flew overhead," I say. "He flew that way"—I point—"which must be where the lake is." I snatch my sketchbook from the ground. "Come on. Let's go."

"We can't make it there in time," Charlie says, pulling himself to his feet. "It's got to be at least half a day's walk."

"Then we don't walk," Hank says. "We run. As fast as we can. Now *go!*"

CHAPTER
63

We tear through the forest at what feels like Mach speed: ten, fifteen, twenty minutes of full-out running. The twigs and leaves and vines drop from the others' bodies. I clutch my sketchbook in my hand as branches whip by my face, cutting up my cheeks. The wind whistles in my ears. I imagine my racing legs and pumping arms are a blur, like the Flash.

Hank has dropped his walking stick and is doing a weird sort of limping sprint. Charlie's free arm is flailing about like a chicken wing. And Penelope has gone into full Amazon mode: eyes focused, arms driving, long legs lunging forward in gazelle-like strides.

Charlie stumbles. I grab his good arm and hoist him up before he hits the ground. We are bolting again without missing a beat.

Following the river took us way off course. If I could draw a full breath, I'd point out this little detail to Hank. Instead, I try to focus on the positive: we have a beacon now—and a real possibility that we may be saved.

Just as long as we reach the lake before Clint and the others decide that we aren't going to make it back.

I do not think about the fact that I can no longer feel my feet. I do not think about the fact that my heart feels like it is going to explode in my chest. I do not think about the fact that Max and Barbara may not be at the lake, and if there's no one there when Clint arrives, he might assume he's got the wrong lake or the wrong date and take off.

Instead, I think about cookies.

I think about Mom's marshmallow gingersnaps and about Neil Gaiman, Frank Miller, Kelly Sue DeConnick, Grant Morrison, Emma Ríos, Alan Moore, and Sara Pichelli.

I think about my bed. And our old, soft couch. And our flat-screen TV. And my computer.

I think about our microwave.

And our toaster.

And Frosted Raspberry Pop-Tarts.

I think about toilet paper and clean socks and toothpaste and hot water—all the things I love about living in a civilized world.

But most of all, I think about Erin. And how I am going to make this up to her—my transgressions, my mental infidelities, my irresponsibility with Baby Robbie. I don't know exactly how yet, just that I'm going to make it happen.

"Have to . . . stop!" Charlie groans as he staggers forward. He leans over, his busted arm still in its twig-and-vine sling. "I can't . . . keep going . . . I have to—"

A violent, watery stream blasts from his mouth, splattering his camera, his feet, and the ground.

"Come on, Charlie!" I holler, waving him forward. "We need to hurry!"

"I'm . . . done." He moans and retches again. "Leave me . . . here. Let me just . . . die."

Hank, Penelope, and I jog back to a hyperventilating, hunched-over Charlie. I look around at all the sweaty red faces, feel my own pulse slamming in my head.

"We have to . . . keep going," I rasp. "We can't . . . give up now."

Hank gasps, leaning his back against a tree. "Charlie's in no . . . shape to continue. And we're not . . . leaving him, obviously . . . We'll just have to . . . hope that Max and Barbara . . . made it back . . . If they did . . . they'll make Clint wait for us."

"And if they didn't . . . make it back?" I pant. "If they're out . . . looking for us? Or if"—my eyes flit to Penelope—"something stopped them . . . from getting to the lake?"

"Max will have . . . gotten them to the lake," Penelope says, her hands on her knees. "And my mother . . . won't let them leave . . . without us."

"Worst-case scenario . . ." Hank says, sliding down the tree to the grass, "Clint will send . . . a rescue crew."

Penelope and Charlie seem pretty satisfied with this answer. I want to shake them. How can they stand the thought of waiting for a rescue crew, when we're so close to getting out of here? What if the bear is stalking us at this very minute, and we don't have *time* to wait for a rescue crew?

"No! Not an option!" I shout, five days' worth of fear and exhaustion and anger spewing out of me like Charlie's watery vomit spewed from him. I point to Hank. "You lost the right to call the shots . . . when you admitted to being a big, fat fraud." I shift my finger to Penelope. "And you. You need to stop . . . with this whole self-sacrificing tragic manga-hero bullshit . . . and start fighting for yourself for a change." Finally, I turn on Charlie. "And *you*. How many times . . . have I been there for you? Taken an ass-kicking for you?"

"Always," Charlie wheezes. "You've . . . always been there."

"That's right. And I need you . . . to be here for me now. Because I can't take this anymore. It's like being trapped . . . in a Guillermo del Toro film. I won't make it till a rescue crew comes. So you need to suck it the hell up . . . and haul ass to that lake!"

Charlie nods weakly. "OK, Daniel." He exhales heavily and starts to stand up. "I'll do it . . . I'll keep go—"

He leans forward and dry heaves, nothing but a long string of spittle stretching from his lips to the ground below.

Then he falls forward and does a face-plant in the dirt.

325

CHAPTER 64

Five or six hours—and a butt-load of pep talks—later, we stumble out of the woods and come upon the lake. At last!

Only, there is no plane waiting here.

There is no Max or Barbara or Clint waving ecstatically at our arrival.

There is nothing but a vast stretch of flat, undisturbed water to greet us.

"No," Penelope says, staggering around. "This doesn't make any sense. My mother wouldn't have left without me. She would have made them wait. She may be an emotionally immature narcissist with a raging libido, but she would never abandon me."

"OK, let's all remain calm," Hank says. "Clint probably took Max and Barbara up in the plane to search for us from the sky.

That's what I would have done. Better vantage point from up there. They'll circle around eventually. And when they do, we'll be here to meet them. We should build a fire. As a signal. So they'll see we made it back when they fly back over."

Penelope nods. "Yes," she says, her voice flat. "Good idea. Let's do that."

This is Hank trying to distract us. Trying to keep us busy so we don't think about the facts: That Max and Barbara are either lost or dead. That Clint's smoking, sputtering plane may not even have made it back to the lake. And that we are likely to be stuck here for a very, very long time.

Or at least as long as it takes for the bear to catch up with us and finish things once and for all.

But seeing the look in Penelope's eyes, I figure it's best to play along. And so I join the others in collecting sticks and twigs and dry grass.

"Sun's coming out," Charlie declares after a half hour of scavenging. He shields his eyes as he scopes the sky. "Should be no problem getting a flame going."

"That's right," Hank says, feigning cheerfulness. "We'll make a huge bonfire. One that can be seen for miles." He eyes our pile of wood and kindling. "We'll want five times that much. Let's keep searching."

We tromp back into the bush in search of more fuel for our fire.

And that's when I hear something. A low growling noise. It's not the bear, thank God. But it's definitely an animal. Or several animals. Close by.

"Hey," I whisper-call to the others. "Listen. You guys hear that?"

Uuuuu. Rrrrrr. Uuuuu. Rrrrr.

"Could be bighorn sheep, maybe?" Hank whisper-calls back. "Or a moose?"

Uuuuu. Rrrrrr. Uuuuu. Rrrrr.

"Whatever it is, it sounds like it's in pain," Penelope whispers. "If it's hurt, it could be dinner." She bends down to pick up a large stone.

Rrrrr. Uuuu. Rrrrr. Uuuu.

"Hey." Hank reaches out a hand. "I don't think that's a good idea. It might get spooked and charge us."

Penelope grips her stone tighter. "If we're going to be here for hours or *days* longer, we're going to need something to eat."

Hank looks like he wants to argue but thinks better of it. "OK. But let's be sure to stick together. Just in case."

We all gather close and crouch down as we skulk toward the animal noises.

Uuuuuuu. Uuuuuu. Uuuuuu.

"It sounds like it's stuck in something," I whisper. "Trying to pull itself free."

"Hoof caught in a fissure, perhaps," Charlie says. "Probably broke its leg."

"Shhhh." Penelope presses a finger to her lips, then hefts the rock in her hand, like she's judging how hard and far she can throw it.

We steal forward, a mix of excitement and fear thrumming through me. Up ahead, the branches of a bush are shaking violently.

Uuuu. Uuuu. Rrrr. Rrrr.

Penelope nods, then cocks her arm and—

"Wait!" says Hank suddenly, his face going crimson. "I don't think that's a—"

Too late. Penelope's already hurled the stone with all her might.

Thud!

Then new sounds erupt from behind the bush:

"Ow! What the fuck!"

"What? What happened?"

"Something hit me!"

"What something?"

"I don't know, a rock, I think."

"A rock?"

And that's when Max and Barbara stand up and stumble out of the woods.

Completely, horrifyingly naked.

"What-whoa-no!" I blurt.

Charlie, Hank and I spin away, but not before the ghastly sights of Max's low-hanging fruit and Barbara's floppers and floccus are seared into our retinas.

"Mother?" Penelope asks, her voice containing equal parts shock, relief, and disgust.

"Oh, Pen, thank God you're OK!" Barbara bellows. "I was worried sick about you!"

Penelope scoffs. "Yes, we could hear your wails of despair."

"Oh, that." Barbara laughs. "We were waiting for Clint, and when he didn't show, we got bored. I'm not about to apologize for being a healthy adult, my dear."

"No one's asking you to apologize, Ms. Halpern," Charlie says, his eyes scrunched closed even though his back is turned. "All we request is that you put some clothes on."

"Of course, of course," Barbara says. "Max, honey, fling me my shorts and shirt, will you?" There is the sound of fluttering clothing, then the blessed sounds of zippers zipping.

Slowly, I turn back around. Barbara and Max are fully dressed, thankfully, but it's like I've got X-ray vision or something because I keep picturing them au naturel. I shudder, hoping that this whole incident doesn't ruin sex for me one day.

"Did you guys get my note?" Barbara asks.

Penelope nods. "Yeah, we got your note."

"Well, what took you so long to get here?"

"We had some issues," Penelope says. "Another bear attack. A lightning storm. Oh, and apparently Hank lied about being a mountain man, so there was that."

Hank's face flames. "To be fair, I never said I was a mou—"

"It was basically the blind leading the blind," Penelope says.

"Wait a second," Max says. "Did you say you ran into the bear again? The same one we met at the lake—that destroyed our campsite?"

"Uh-huh," Penelope says. "Though I'd say more *ran from* than *ran into*. Twice, actually."

Max is shaking his head in wonder. "I just can't believe it. I've never heard of such ruthless stalking in a black bear—even a hungry one. If we'd had any inkling that you all were in danger, any at all . . . But, of course, we thought Hank was a skilled hunter."

Hank clears his throat, his face still bright red. "Not to

change the subject or anything, but did you say that Clint *didn't* show up?"

"That's right," Max says. "We saw *a* plane fly high overhead, but it didn't land. Couldn't tell if it was Clint's Kiwi or not."

"Of course it wasn't," Barbara says. "If it was, he would've landed."

"Unless he was having engine trouble," I blurt. "I saw a plane too. There was smoke billowing out of the engine—just like when Clint took off last time."

"That would explain it," Max says. "He probably returned home to get some help. That's what any smart pilot would do."

And, as if on cue, I hear the droning of a plane.

We all turn toward the direction of the sound, which gets louder.

And louder.

And louder.

"Oh my God!" Penelope shouts. "That's him!" She hightails it toward the lake, and we all dash after her.

There it is—Clint's bush plane, cresting the hill in the distance and heading in our direction! A surge of relief wells up inside me as the plane banks to the left.

A puff of smoke wisps from the propeller as it gets closer. Definitely the Keatley Kiwi in all its rattletrap glory.

We're saved! Thank Christ. We're going home. To Mom! To my bed and my computer and my Pop-Tarts! To my beautiful, amazing, glorious Erin!

I watch as the plane tips in the other direction and starts banking to the right. Then to the left again. Then to the right.

"What's he doing?" Charlie asks, his camera raised to his eye. "Is he inebriated?"

"It's probably just really windy up there," Hank says.

And then the small stream of smoke becomes a huge plume of black that pours from the front of the plane.

Suddenly, orange flames shoot from the engine.

The wings tip hard to the right—

And the plane explodes.

CHAPTER 65

All of us stare, our mouths hanging open, as shards of the burning wreckage drop from the sky, splooshing and sizzling into the lake.

Sploosh.

Sploosh.

SPLOOSH!

Charlie is so stunned, he's not even snapping pictures.

"Clint . . ." I mumble, cold inside. "He's . . . gone."

Dark smoke and the stench of burning oil fill my nostrils, then my lungs. I hack and cough, folding over, my throat stinging.

I can't believe I just watched somebody *die*.

And I can't believe *I'm* going to die too—out here in this wilderness, where I never should have been in the first place.

"Look!" Penelope shouts. "Over there! He bailed out."

I look up and see it—the mushrooming rainbow silk in the sky. Clint dangles from the harness below it, his legs swaying this way and that, his arms tugging at the ropes, guiding the chute toward the shore.

Charlie's recovered from his shock and is snapping photos like mad.

The rest of us run down to the shore. Clint comes down hard in the sand, his knees buckling. The fabric of the parachute engulfs him like a massive, multicolored soufflé.

When we reach him, all of us grab at the silk, trying to pull it free.

"Clint?" Hank bellows, grasping a fistful of parachute. "Are you all right?"

There is a muffled moaning coming from somewhere under the chute.

At last we find him, his face sooty, his red-rimmed eyes half shut. Hank and Max each take one of Clint's hands and pull him up. He looks around like he isn't quite sure where he is.

"Well, that was . . . unexpected," Clint rasps.

"What the hell happened?" Max asks.

"Been having a bit of engine trouble of late." Clint coughs, then undoes the buckles on the parachute harness and lets it drop. "I started over this morning, but I had to turn back." He brushes off the butt of his pants. "Thought I'd fixed her up, but I guess it didn't take."

"Thank God you got out," Barbara says.

"Were you able to radio in an SOS?" Charlie asks at the same time.

Clint shakes his head. "I'm afraid not. Whole panel went dead. I was sure I was a goner. Luckily, I had the foresight to strap on my chute before I took off this last time. The chute and this little fella." Clint lifts his shirt and there, swaddled in a dirty towel, is Baby Robbie.

Clint unfastens a strap, removes the Baby-Real-A-Lot, and holds him out to me.

"Oh my God!" I say, running up to him and taking the baby and its bottle. "I can't believe it! I thought I'd never see him again!" I look down at Robbie, his nose so like Erin's that it breaks my heart into a million little pieces. Suddenly Baby Robbie's eyes flutter open. His mouth purses and his tiny fingers clutch the air. "He's . . . he's alive!"

"Sure wasn't when I found him," Clint says. "He was lights out, over and done with. But I opened him up. Tinkered with his wires. Tightened up his joints. Used some spare doll parts I had to change out a couple of loose limbs. Also added a few new computer chips. Little fella can talk a bit now. *And* he has a new killer kung fu grip." Clint laughs. " 'Course, what I'm *not* clear about was how he wound up in my—"

"Thank you so much!" I say, diving in and giving Clint a hug—and cutting him off before he can say any more. "I can't begin to tell you how grateful I am."

"Yes, well." Clint pats my back awkwardly. "It was fun, actually. Restoring the tiny tyke. Enjoyed having the company, to tell the truth. Sweet little bugger—when you get him fed and burped, that is."

I press the power button on my ID bracelet. It lights up like a Christmas tree, showing a strong heartbeat, a yellow smiley face, and all my care scores in the green "pampered" zone.

Incredible.

I pull the filthy, tattered, and torn sweater from my pocket and put it back on Baby Robbie. My eyes start to well. It's stupid, I know, but I've never seen anything more perfect in my life.

We gather up Clint's parachute and drag it over to our pile of firewood.

"All right, we need to make a plan for getting rescued," Max says, switching into guide mode. "This pile of wood is a good start. Should make a nice signal fire." He turns to Clint. "Now, who knows where we are?"

"Besides myself?" Clint asks.

Max frowns. "Yes. Besides *you*, who are stuck here with *us*. Who did you tell?"

Clint shakes his head. "No one. I mean, the Zosters know we're out here . . . somewhere. But, as to our exact location . . ." He shrugs.

Charlie gawps. "Are you telling us that our lives now rest in the hands of those maladroit ignorami?"

"*Ignoramuses*," Penelope corrects. "The word *ignoramus* is a Latin *verb* form meaning 'we do not know' and therefore has no Latin plural noun form."

"Really," Charlie scoffs. "And yet your own beloved *Merriam-Webster* lists it as an acceptable plural form of the word."

Penelope laughs. "So you admit it, *Merriam-Webster* is the superior lexicon."

"Regardless," Hank says. "I'm sure once the ignoram—*Zosters* show up at Clint's place and realize we haven't returned, they'll send someone to find us."

"I wouldn't be so sure about that." Max runs his hand through his hair. "The Zosters are not the most trustworthy people on the planet. Or the most intelligent, for that matter. There's a good chance they'll convince themselves that they just missed us, or that we found our own way back—if only to avoid getting mixed up in a messy situation. And possibly to get out of paying me."

"Oh, I can't believe anyone would do such a thing," Barbara says.

"I'm glad you have such faith in humanity, hun-bun," Max says. "I, however, have had dealings with these . . . ignoramuses and am not so optimistic."

"My mom will call the police," I say, cradling Baby Robbie, "if we don't show up."

"That's all well and good," Max says, "but with two-point-three-six-seven million acres to search, it's going to take some time before anyone finds us."

"What do you suggest, then?" Hank asks.

Max sighs. "We have to be prepared to be here for the long haul. Days, at least. Possibly weeks. Let's start with the basics: shelter, fire, water, food. Who wants to do what?"

CHAPTER 66

I'm on shelter duty with Clint. We have been informed by Barefoot McWrinklenuts that the shelter must be large enough to house all seven of us because "this is the most efficient use of our time, energy, and supplies" and because of "collective body heat" and whatnot.

This has turned out to be a colossal pain in the ass. The structure keeps collapsing, despite the fact that we've been following Max's detailed sand drawing to the letter—well, until Clint stepped on it and left a size-eleven footprint in the middle of the schematic.

I am tired. I want to quit. But I chose this task. It was the lesser of four evils—or at least, that's what I thought at the time.

I could have teamed up with Max and Barbara, who were headed out to scavenge for edible plants together. But I really don't want to spend too much time in their company; Barbara keeps "sneakily" pinching Max's butt, which only serves to sear the disturbing images of them deeper into my mind.

I could've helped Penelope and Charlie to get the signal fire lit. Except that they're all shoulder bumps and Shakespeare insults and etymology jokes now, which makes me feel like a vestigial organ.

Or I could have gone fishing with Hank.

"Come on," he'd said shyly. "I'll show you how it's done. It's the one thing my father actually taught me."

But I'd told him "No, thanks." I didn't give him an explanation—just turned away and sidled up next to Clint, gave him a high five like we were best buds, thanked him again for saving Baby Robbie, and asked him how he wanted to divvy up the hut-building tasks.

I could tell I hurt Hank's feelings. I didn't really care at the time. But I feel sort of bad about it now—and not only because I'm exhausted and sweaty and hate what I'm doing at the moment. It's something else. Something I can't quite put my finger on.

I keep glancing over at him, knee-deep in the lake—casting the fishing line he prepared from vines, gripping the pole he fashioned from a live branch, jiggling the hook and lure he made from one of Barbara's earrings.

He's trying so hard.

Has been trying so hard all along.

With everything.

339

Yeah, he lied to me. And he lied to Mom too. And that sucks. But he didn't really mean it. He didn't set out to deceive us—not like Dad, who'd disappear on payday, stay out all night, and come home the next morning smelling like a recycling bin and saying he had to work late. And not like most of Mom's other boyfriends, who lied in order to get something from us, from her: money, a place to crash, free booze, and pay-per-view porn . . .

And it's not like I've been so truthful with him. I mean, I concocted a whole *list* of lies to tell and pranks to pull, for Chrissakes. And Hank put up with it all. If I'd been in his shoes, I would've taken off after the tiny-testicle talk at the hockey game.

But he didn't leave then, and he didn't leave after I puked in his lap and farted up the hut and *shot him in the leg with a frickin' arrow.*

Though Charlie's right: he probably will leave now.

"Hey, fella," Clint says, breaking my trance. "This shelter ain't gonna build itself."

"Oh, yeah, sorry," I say, picking up a branch. I arrange it on the support pole, then glance back over my shoulder at Hank. He's still standing there, waggling the fishing line, his cheeks red with sunburn, his expression full of hope.

Just then Hank's hands jerk forward, his pole bending. He's got something! A monster one, from the looks of it.

I turn around and watch as he peels his shirt off, then slowly pulls the line in—gingerly, cautiously . . .

He leans forward, the pole in his left hand, his shirt in his right.

Suddenly, he lunges down, water splashing everywhere, and

scoops up a huge fish. Its long, thick body thrashes inside the cloth.

Hank grins hugely. He turns toward shore and sees me watching him. He holds the fish over his head like a trophy and does a little triumphant dance.

I smile and give him a thumbs-up. Oddly, I feel tears pooling in my eyes.

And that's when it hits me.

Hard.

In the gut:

I like Hank.

And I'm going to miss him.

CHAPTER
67

The fish tastes good, but I don't say anything. I just choke it down with my emotions and the bitter greens that Max and Barbara have gathered. Baby Robbie provides a nice distraction, grasping my index finger with his powerful grip and cooing things like "I wuv you" and "Wanna play?" and "Let's be friends to the end."

I don't know how the hell I'm supposed to explain Robbie's newfound dexterity and elocution to Ms. Drizzler, but I'm going to have to come up with something before we get home.

If we get home.

I take another bite of food and glance down at my sketch-book on the ground, then at the fire, at the lake, everywhere but at Hank. I can't look at him. I feel so rotten. How ridiculous is it that I was so worried about him abandoning us that I did everything to push him away—and now I'm all torn up to be losing him?

"This is really something," Clint says, laughing, flecks of salmon flying from his mouth and getting stuck in his beard. "I never eat this well at home! Only fish I ever consume comes in a can with a cartoon fish named Charlie on the label. Ha-ha." Clint swats Charlie's leg. "You think that's where your ma got your name from?"

"I cannot think of anything less likely," Charlie states. "And, just for your information, canned tuna is a *Clostridium botulinum* disaster waiting to happen."

"Not to mention," Penelope adds, "the increased risk of methylmercury poisoning."

"Which"—Charlie gestures with a piece of salmon—"now that I think about it, would actually explain quite a few things about you, Clint."

Clint's brow furrows. "I don't follow."

"Exactly," Penelope and Charlie say in unison. They fold over and crack up.

I hug Baby Robbie closer.

"Owie!" it mewls.

"Sorry," I mutter, relaxing my hold. Great, not even Baby Robbie wants anything to do with me.

"All right," Max says. "I think we should discuss what the next few days are going to look like in terms of setting ourselves up for a rescue."

"No!" Charlie suddenly jumps to his feet and scurries backward.

Max narrows his eyes. "What do you mean, no? It's imperative—"

"N-n-not a-g-g-gain!" Charlie stammers.

"What?" Hank asks. "What is it?"

"It's . . . it's . . . !" Charlie splutters, pointing down the beach.

Six heads turn to follow Charlie's finger.

Oh my God.

It's a bear.

Our bear. Scarface.

How is that possible?

I get to my feet, clutching Baby Robbie tighter than I'm sure he'd like, and join Charlie in backing away.

The bear casually strolls along the shore toward us— like it's been invited for dinner and has brought only its appetite.

"Must have been attracted by the fish smell," Clint says, remaining seated. "Stay cool. It's just curious. Don't blame the critter, tasty food like this. But it won't approach. There's too many of us."

But the bear *is* approaching. And continues to. Steadily. Confidently.

There is something bone-chilling about the animal's calm, as though it has all the time in the world to reach us, like it knows that eventually it will eat each and every one of us.

Some of us today.

Some of us tomorrow.

But eventually it will get us all.

"Owie!" says Baby Robbie.

Oh, honey—you have no idea.

Penelope, Hank, Barbara, and Max all stand up slowly and start stepping away.

Clint laughs and shakes his head. "Just ignore it. You know that, Max. It's Wilderness 101: Wild animals are more afraid of you than you are of them."

How many times have I heard *that* on this stupid trip?

"That bear's attacked us before," Barbara croaks.

"Multiple times," Charlie adds.

Clint looks over at us, still chewing. "That so? Well, you must have done something to provoke it: Left food out? Maybe tinkled near your camp?" Clint stands up with his bark plate and wipes a hand on his jeans. "Black bears don't just come after people for no good reason."

Suddenly, I remember the doe pee. I lift my shirt to sniff it. Is it possible my clothes retained some of the essence of it, even after being rinsed in the stream and soaked by the rain? It was pretty potent. And Charlie did douse me with it. Maybe Clint is right—maybe the bear isn't interested in *us*, just the doe in heat it thinks is nearby.

I quickly nestle Baby Robbie in the sand and start shucking off my clothes.

"Dan, what are you doing?" Hank asks, looking at me like I've lost my mind. And maybe I have. But I'm not going to risk being the reason that any of us gets eaten by this bear.

"It's me!" I shout, standing in my smiley-face boxers, clutching my clothes in my fist. "The bear wants me!"

"What the hell are you talking about?!" Hank cries.

Before anyone can stop me, I hurl my T-shirt and sweats onto the fire, sending a spray of sparks everywhere.

"Hey, now!" Clint says, jumping back, his plate of salmon dropping to the ground. "What's the big idea?"

"M-my clothes," I say, shivering from equal parts fear and cold. "I think . . . I think there was something on them that was attracting the bear. That's why it's been after us."

My gaze shoots to the bear, a football field away. It's still eyeing us but has stopped moving, probably wary of the fire's leaping flames.

"On your clothes?" Hank furrows his brow. "What's on your clothes?"

"Nothing," Charlie blurts, glaring at me. "Dan's just hysterical because of the reappearance of the bear."

"It's pee," I say. "All over my clothes. In my hair. In my *mouth*."

"Urine could certainly attract an animal," Max says. "But how—?"

"It was Charlie," I say.

"Charlie peed on you?" Hank asks.

"He sprayed me with doe-in-heat urine," I confess, my heart thumping hard. "I was supposed to be attacked by a buck, not a bear!"

"I don't understand." Hank shakes his head. "Why would you want to be attacked by a buck?"

"Clearly he would not," Charlie says. "This is obviously a desperate ploy to get your attention, Hank. I did tell you he was feeling rejected by you." He turns and stares hellfire at me. "I think we can now *abandon* this line of discussion."

"No." I shake my head. "I can't. No more code words. No more pranks." I look at Hank. "It was all part of our plan to scare you away." The words come out in a torrent, like water rushing through a broken dam: "The deer pee, the vomiting, the diarrhea, dropping your phone, losing my doll, breaking my nose. All those supposed 'accidents' weren't accidents at all."

Hank's gaze drifts down to his bandaged calf.

"Except that," I insist. "That was a real accident."

"But . . . why?" Hank asks.

"I wanted to get you to take off before you hurt Mom. And me. I didn't want you to get married and then break our hearts. And I didn't want to move and leave my school and my best friend and the girl I've been in love with since third grade."

"Wow," Penelope says. "How sublimely Tom Ripley of you. Have his tactics succeeded, Hank? I ask for personal reasons." She looks sideways at her mom and Max.

But Hank doesn't seem to have heard her. "I don't know what to say, Dan," he croaks.

I shake my head. "I know. I'm so sorry. I lied even worse than you. I wish I could take it all back. It's horrible. And I certainly never meant for us to get attacked by a ravenous killing machine."

"Ah, pshaw!" Clint says, breaking the mood and grabbing a nearby stick. "You all are talking about this bear like it's some kind of psychopath or something. It's just a dumb animal." He marches past us toward the bear, swinging the stick in the air. "*Yah! Yah!* Scat! Get outta here! You can't have my supper, big boy. Go on, git!"

"I wouldn't do that if I were you," Hank says.

" 'Course you wouldn't," Clint calls back, continuing to walk forward calmly, waving the stick around. "And that's why the animal has had the upper hand to this point. It's like a puppy: it'll chase you if you want to be chased."

The six of us stand stock-still as we watch the bear and Clint approach each other like two gunmen meeting at high noon for a shoot-out.

"Oh, Christ," Max mutters.

I cringe and hold my breath.

The bear stops first. It lowers its head and slaps at the ground, then snaps its teeth and lets out a series of loud snorts.

Clint keeps striding forward, saying nothing, staring the beast down.

Barbara's taken to intoning positive thoughts, like she did when our plane nearly went down: "Love, peace, charity," she chants. "Calm, restful waves of energy."

Clint plants the stick right in front of the bear and puffs up his chest. He juts his chin forward and growls at the animal.

The bear blinks and takes a step back.

"Oh my God," Hank says. "It's working."

"Of course," Barbara says, her eyes still shut. "The human capacity for love knows no limits. Keep sending compassion and goodwill their way! Warm, wonderful light. Peace and love."

"Get the fuck out of here, you stupid lummox!" Clint bellows, grabbing his stick and leaping forward. "I'll shove this branch so far up your ass, you'll never be able to walk on all fours again!" He shows his teeth and growls some more.

Barbara's eyes pop open. "Well, that's certainly not how *I* would have gone about things!"

But the bear takes another step back.

Clint raises the stick and brandishes it in front of the bear's face.

"I suppose his approach is working too," Barbara acknowledges grudgingly. "Still, it can be dangerous to fight fire with fire. Love is really the best means of battling aggression."

Clint waves his weapon back and forth, hopping forward and shouting, *"Hah! Hah! Git! Git!"*

The bear lowers its head like a submissive dog.

I stare. "I can't believe—"

Then, all of a sudden, the bear lashes out with its giant paw, smacking the stick right out of Clint's hand.

"Oh shit!" I say.

For an incredibly tense millisecond nothing happens.

Then—

"Run!" Clint screams. "Get in the water! Hurry! Bears can swim, but they ain't that fast." He tears toward the lake, splashes in, and starts to paddle like a maniac.

The bear charges. But not after Clint.

Instead, it comes straight for us.

Max grabs Barbara's and Penelope's hands and yanks them toward the water.

Charlie stumbles backward, panic in his eyes.

"On my back!" Hank shouts, squatting in front of Charlie.

Charlie doesn't hesitate. He leaps up, his legs wrapping around Hank's waist, his one good arm hugging Hank's shoulder.

"Dan, in the water *now*!" Hank orders, piggybacking Charlie toward the lake.

I look at the lake, then at the bear rushing toward us.

There's no way we're all going to make it to the water in time. I can see that. The bear is too close, running like a linebacker returning a punt.

An odd sense of calm comes over me.

I glance over at Clint's crumpled parachute.

I know exactly what I have to do.

CHAPTER 68

I am a coward.

I realize that now. In everything I've done so far in my life—or *not* done—I have been spineless.

I've never stood up to the bullies at school.

I couldn't tell Mom how I was feeling when she got engaged to Hank.

I haven't been able to talk to Erin since third freaking grade.

I couldn't muster the courage to try to save Penelope from the snake or the bear.

And most recently, of course, I was too chicken to go over and talk to Hank when he caught his fish. Too scared to try to patch things up. So, I've done nothing.

Until now.

I am thinking all of this as I place Robbie on a bed of leaves and grab my sketchbook from the sand. I turn toward the bear and scream, "Hey! Hey! Over here!"

I fling the pad like a Frisbee. It slices the air, sailing thirty yards and finally opening with a flutter before landing in the water at the bear's feet.

The animal stops. Turns. Looks at me.

Then I snatch up the parachute and shove my arms through the harness straps.

And sprint.

Right at the bear.

"Noooo!" Hank shouts, waist deep in the lake, Charlie still clinging to his back.

"Daaaaaan!" Penelope screams from where she wades.

But it's too late. I'm committed.

I pump my arms and legs, thinking again of the Flash. I have to get up enough speed to inflate the chute. I need to make myself look big and scary.

The bear stops in its tracks, watching me race toward it.

But I'm not feeling the resistance I'd expected to feel. I glance back as I run—and nearly topple over.

The parachute strings are all tangled up. There's no way for the rainbow canopy to billow out as I'd planned.

Which means I'm screwed.

I stutter-step to a panicked halt just a few feet from the bear.

It grunts and sniffs the air, its scarred nostrils flaring. Surely I no longer smell of deer pee. All I have left on is my boxers, and

Charlie didn't spray those. The bear can't possibly be attracted to me now, right?

As if in response, the bear stretches its neck and roars—its spittle flecking my cheeks, its meaty breath hot and musky.

I gulp.

We stare at each other.

Then it rushes me.

"Fuuuuuck!" I squeal, cutting sharp around the bear and hauling ass, just like Penelope described.

And it works. It takes a moment for the bear to adjust its huge body so it can make the turn and come after me—which gives me an extra couple of seconds to channel my inner Barry Allen.

I put everything I have into my legs. I run faster than I have ever run in my life. Even faster than when we were trying to get back to the lake to meet Clint's plane.

My thighs burn, my feet kick up sand.

Then, all of a sudden, I'm barely moving.

The bear must have grabbed my chute!

I have to get free of this harness. Let the bear chew up the silk. Maybe I can get away before it realizes what's happened.

I slip my arms from the straps, drop the harness, and take off, feeling suddenly weightless.

I glance back and see that the parachute has somehow inflated. It's huge—a bright, beautiful, giant jellyfish.

The bear snarls at the parachute, which blows toward it in the wind. The beast smacks at the ground and snorts and growls. But the chute keeps advancing.

353

The bear gives one last, loud snort—

Then turns and dashes off into the forest.

I collapse to my knees, out of breath, out of energy, adrenaline leaching from my nearly naked body.

"Dan!" Charlie calls out, his camera fused to his eye. "Holy crap! You did it! You scared off the bear! That was absolutely genius!"

I try to get to my feet, but I can't move—can hardly get air into my lungs.

Moments later everyone's by my side, helping me to my feet and cheering like I've just won the Indy 500. I want to smile, to wave off the praise like it was nothing—like I do this sort of thing all the time.

Instead, I fold over and hurl a surge of partially digested salmon and field greens all over everyone's feet.

CHAPTER 69

I sleep like a corpse. There are no dreams. No thoughts. Nothing.

When I wake the next day, it's actually a surprise: I feel like I've been resurrected from the dead. My mouth tastes chalky and sour, my eyes are crusty, and my head feels like it's wrapped in cotton. It takes me a long time to get my bearings, to remember where I am and all that's happened.

I crawl from the empty hut, the early morning light stinging my eyes. Penelope and Charlie are restocking the signal fire while Hank, Max, and Barbara are stretching the rainbow parachute out on the beach as wide as they can, securing the edges with large stones so it doesn't blow away.

"Should we write a message on it?" Barbara asks. "Help or something?"

"I'll do it," I say. I walk to the campfire and grab a burnt stick. I'm wearing an extra pair of Max's shorts and one of Barbara's pink T-shirts that reads KISS ME, I'M BOOTYLICIOUS—if Erin could see me now . . .

I strap on the baby carrier that Clint made me out of the parachute harness and some vines, Baby Robbie cooing as I tromp across the sand.

Barbara turns to Max. "Care to join me in a little more harvesting?" she asks.

Max gives her a knowing wink. "I think I can muster up the energy for bit of reaping."

The two of them laugh, grasp hands, and bound off into the woods together, ensuring that I will go nowhere near the forest for the next two hours.

"I'll see if I can catch us some lunch," Hank says, turning and limping back to our hut.

I climb into the middle of the parachute and use the burnt end of the stick to write SOS in giant letters. Then I draw a huge Werebear with snarling teeth and razor-sharp claws underneath—so whoever sees this knows we're not kidding.

"I like it," Clint says, giving me a big smile. I crawl off the parachute, and Clint offers me a hand up.

"I'm going to do a little scavenger hunt," he says. "See if anything of use survived the plane crash. Wanna come?"

"Thanks . . ." I say, glancing over at Hank as he wades into the lake. "But I think I'm going to take Hank up on that fishing lesson."

Clint nods. "Sounds like a lot more fun. And a much better use of your time. Can't imagine I'm going to find much out there."

356

Clint shuffles off.

I stand there, waiting—for what, I don't know. For my legs to carry me forward. For this weird shyness to dissipate. What if Hank is pissed at me? What if he hates my guts and tells me to get lost?

But I'm done being a coward, and so I force myself to move.

"Hey," I say, when I reach the water's edge. "Can I . . . Could you teach me how you do that?"

Hank smiles big. "Sure thing, bud," he says. "Let's get a pole set up for you."

He joins me on land, and we find the perfect branch: a live one with good bend. We gather up some strong vines for the line and a thorny twig to use for my hook. Hank baits the twig with a small piece of salmon skin.

"That should do just fine," he says, admiring our work. "Now brace yourself. The water's pretty icy."

I take a deep breath and we wade together into the lake. The cold water burns my toes, sending a chill rocketing up my spine.

Hank stands beside me. He shows me how to hold the fishing rod with two hands. How to cast the line and how to tug it gently so the hook dances under the water, enticing the fish.

"That's right, good," Hank says as I jiggle my fishing pole.

"It's really cool that you know how to do this," I acknowledge, nodding at our makeshift supplies.

"Thanks," Hank says. "Of course, this is nothing compared to scaring off killer bears."

"Yeah," I say, glancing down, my face flushing as I remember him screaming at me not to charge the bear. "I-I'm sorry I didn't listen to you. It just—it looked like the bear was going to catch up to us, and it was my fault he was after us, so I knew I had to do something—"

Hank reaches over and adjusts my hands on the fishing pole. "All I care about is that you're OK," he says. "Though, I'm not ashamed to admit that a little bit of pee escaped me when you ran toward that animal."

I laugh.

"I mean, your mom may—or may not—forgive me for misleading her about my hunting skills," Hank says. "But she would never forgive me if I let you get eaten by a bear." He looks at me, his eyes filling with tears. "That was the scariest moment of my life—watching you take on that animal." He blinks and shakes his head, like he's trying to dislodge the memory.

I blink, too, and look away. We stand there for a bit, the two of us, fishing together in silence. It feels nice. Peaceful. Good.

"You think you can ever forgive me?" I ask, breaking the silence.

"For scaring the crap out of me?" Hank says.

"For everything. I was wrong about you. I didn't even give you a chance. I'm really sorry. I was so convinced that you'd turn out to be a jerk that I tried everything I could think of to get you to act like one. Only you never did. Because you're *not* a jerk. In fact"—I glance at him—"you're the best boyfriend that Mom has ever had." I shrug. "Of course, that's not exactly saying a whole lot. But still, I'm really sorry for all the crap I pulled and . . . I don't want you to go. I want you to marry Mom."

I look over at him, a sad smile tugging the corner of his mouth.

"I get it, Dan," Hank says. "Believe me, if anyone understands dad challenges, it's me. I accept your apology—if you accept mine."

"Oh my God, yes, for sure," I blurt, relief flooding me.

Hank laughs. "Great. Now let's just hope your mother forgives me."

"You don't have to tell her," I say. "About you not being a hunter, I mean. I won't say anything. She never has to find out."

Hank smiles. "That's nice of you, Dan, but I am going to tell her. I can't go on pretending to be someone I'm not. Your mom deserves better than that. Heck, she probably deserves better than me." He glances at me. "If she *does* still want to marry me once she knows the truth, though, will you still be my best man?"

I nod, feeling my chest tighten. "If you'll still have me."

"Nothing would make me happier," he says. "Of course, a best man needs to make sure everyone's on schedule. Which means you're going to need something"—he unclips his giant man-watch from his wrist—"to keep the time." Hank holds the watch out to me.

I shake my head and swallow. "No way, I couldn't . . ."

"I'd really like you to have it."

I reach out and take it from him. I stare down at the clear cobalt-blue face, the second hand gliding smoothly around the dial.

Hank clears his throat. "I know it's not any sort of replacement . . . for what you lost or anything . . ."

"No," I say, my eyes getting hot, my throat scratchy. "It's way better."

And not just because it works.

I slide it over my hand and clip the latch, feeling the weight of it on my wrist.

It feels solid.

Like something that'll last.

We fish until our legs go numb but catch nothing.

No plane comes that day.

Or the next.

Or the next.

Hank and I go to the lake each morning, only ever catching enough fish to keep us fed but not enough to keep us full. Charlie and Penelope tend the fires and cook. Clint keeps the shelter sturdy and solid. Occasionally he wanders off to check for supplies from his obliterated plane, but so far he's found only scrap metal.

And Max and Barbara disappear into the bush every day, returning hours later with armfuls of greens and big smiles.

Three days after we were supposed to have returned home, we hear the sound of an engine in the distance. We shout and race around, shielding our eyes and trying to spot the plane. But it must be flying over another part of the wilderness, because we never do see it.

The next day we hear the plane again, but again we don't catch sight of it.

And then we hear nothing.

And nothing.

And nothing.

CHAPTER
70

It's been seven days since we set the first signal fire, and though no one is saying it, I can tell that everyone is starting to lose hope.

For a short time—after the bear was gone and we'd heard that first plane—it felt kind of like an adventure. We weren't stranded with no hope of rescue, like Robinson Crusoe or Oliver Queen. We worked as a team and got into a rhythm, fishing and hunting and gathering roughage and kindling during the day and telling stories over the campfire at night. Probably the sort of thing Mom had pictured from the get-go.

But now food is getting harder to come by.

And it's been four days since we heard a plane.

And tempers are starting to flare.

I spend most of my time fishing with Hank, drawing in my mangled sketchbook, and tending to the newly vocal Baby Robbie.

"I've got it," Charlie says, sitting down next to me as I rock back and forth, snuggling and feeding the doll inside the make-shift carrier.

"Got what?" I ask.

"The solution to the Baby-Real-A-Lot dilemma—you know, how to explain his many upgrades." He grins like the Cheshire cat and pushes his glasses up on his nose. "It came to me as I was trying to squeeze the last dregs of power from my camera's battery by overriding its OS. I don't know why I didn't think of it before."

I'm tempted to tell him that the last thing in the world I'm worried about is my Life Skills grade. But instead I force a smile and say, "OK. What do you got?"

"A simple e-mail to Ms. Drizzler," Charlie says. "I can make it appear to be from InfantWorks with the subject 'Automatic Software Update.' Something to the effect of this being version four-point-oh-one-two or some such. Pushed out to all of the units via Wi-Fi, adding improvements to the doll's operating system in an effort to make the baby-rearing experience more realistic than ever, blah, blah, blah. Very official, unverifiable, the whole nine yards."

"That's a great idea, Charlie," I say brightly. "You think she'll buy it?"

"Why not?" he says. "If your phone and iPad and electric toothbrush can be updated, why not a computerized doll?"

"Good point," I say, pulling the bottle from the baby's pursing lips.

"Done, done," Baby Robbie coos. "I sleepy."

Charlie looks over at the doll. "I might have to fix that scratchy humming noise it makes when it talks, though."

I look down at Robbie. "What noise?"

"It's probably just a loose wire or something. Sounds like a dishwasher on dry cycle."

I lower my ear toward the doll. "I don't hear anything."

And then I do.

A buzzing noise. A low drone. But it's not coming from Baby Robbie.

I look up into the sky. "It's not the doll," I say. "There!" I point.

A plane flies high overhead.

Charlie scrambles to his feet. "Holy crap, is that—?"

Everyone seems to see it at once.

"The parachute!" Clint shouts from the shore. "Everybody! Now!"

The seven of us—eight, if you count Baby Robbie in his carrier—rush over to the parachute, each grabbing an edge.

And we shake it.

We wave it.

We billow it like crazy—

Until the red search-and-rescue plane starts to descend toward the lake.

CHAPTER 71

"What do you think?" Charlie says, holding up a hot-off-the-presses copy of the *Willowvale Oracle*.

He's grinning hugely, his chest puffed up proud. His scuffed-up camera hangs around his neck, and he's clutching a stack of school newspapers under his cast-sheathed right arm.

It's the first time I've seen him since we got back. His grandparents whisked him straight to the hospital to get his arm examined. He texted me the results: FRACTURED ULNA AND FRACTURED DISTAL RADIUS; NOT DISPLACED SO NO SURGERY NECESSARY. He texted me again when he got home — BLUE ARM CAST AND PAIN MEDS — and said he was going to dash off the "Automatic Update" e-mail to Ms. Drizzler and then spend the rest of the weekend working on a special issue of the *Oracle* so that he could get it out on our first day back.

I shut my locker, Baby Robbie balanced on my left hip, and stare at the front page. I laugh. "Seriously?"

Above a huge picture of me charging the bear—in my glow-in-the-dark smiley-face boxers—is the headline DAN VERSUS NATURE.

"That's a bit much, don't you think?"

"Are you kidding me?" Charlie says. "The public is absolutely devouring this. First bell has yet to peal and I am nearly sold out. You're going to be the hero of Willowvale High by the end of homeroom."

I roll my eyes. "Somehow I find that difficult to believe."

"All right," Charlie says. "Maybe the centerfold shots of you vomiting in the van and your wasp-stung penis *do* detract a bit from your underpantsed act of heroism. But at least I didn't lead with those."

I snatch the paper from him. "You bastard!" My whole body breaks out into a sweat as I shake the paper open to the center page and glance at the photos: more shots of the bear, the burning plane, the baby fawn, the skinned squirrel, Charlie arm in arm with Penelope . . . but none of me in my various stages of embarrassment.

"Ha-ha," I say, shoving the paper back at Charlie. "You got me. Good one."

"What kind of friend would I be if I took advantage of you at your lowest points?" Charlie leans close, his camera bumping my arm. "I do, however, have *all* the photos backed up on six different hard drives *and* the cloud. Don't ever cross me, Weekes. I will destroy you."

I blink at him, wondering if he's kidding.

Then he cracks up. "Where's your sense of jocularity, Daniel? I am, of course, being facetious."

"Heh," I say weakly. I'm not exactly sure what I think about this new, cockier Charlie. As if the old version didn't get us into enough trouble...

Charlie's phone chimes.

"Let me guess," I say. "Could it possibly be thy leman, thy adoreth, thy one true love... eth?"

"As a matter of fact, it is," Charlie says, messaging back with just the one hand.

"So, what, you guys planning the wedding already?" I say. "Going to get married and have a gaggle of super-obnoxious genius babies?"

Charlie laughs. "Not us." He slides his phone back into his pocket. "But it does appear as though Barbara and Max may be heading to the altar rather soon."

"It boggles the mind," I say, shaking my head, "how both you *and* Penelope's mom managed to hook up on that trip."

"Speaking of affairs of the heart, how are things between your mom and Hank?" Charlie asks, his expression concerned.

I wince. "Yeah, that." My gaze drops to the linoleum tiles on the floor. "Not so good. It's funny how quickly incredible relief can turn to extreme outrage. There was a lot of yelling when Hank and I came clean. Then there were tears. And more yelling. I'm not sure who she was more disappointed in. She hasn't talked to either of us since Saturday night. But she did take off the engagement ring, so . . ."

"Oh, Dan. I'm sorry," Charlie says. "I feel somewhat accountable. If I hadn't goaded you into testing Hank's parental limits—"

"It's not your fault," I say. "I went along with it. And Hank did what he did, so . . ." I trail off again and shrug.

"Yes, well . . ." Charlie clears his throat. "Small consolation perhaps, however I'm fairly certain that *your* love life will improve now that I've made you famous."

I scoff. "Infamous, more like."

"Regardless," Charlie says. "I would be beyond astounded if you are not chatted up by a large segment of the female portion of our student body today."

"Yeah, but there's only one girl I want to talk to, and—"

I stop short, because there she is, behind Charlie, stepping up to her locker with her friends; the only girl I've ever really cared about. God, she's even more gorgeous than I remembered. I can't believe I ever thought, even for a second, that I wanted to be with anyone else.

It's Erin.

It's always been Erin.

I give Baby Robbie a soft squeeze, remembering the promise I made to myself as the search-and-rescue plane flew us back to civilization.

Wish your dad luck, buddy.

Suddenly, the doll is yanked from my arm.

"Owie," Robbie cries.

Rick Chuff waves Baby Robbie in the air. "How frickin' adorable. *Dolly Has Two Daddies.*"

"Cut the crap, Rick," I say, hoping Erin isn't seeing this. Not only do I not want to be pummeled in front of her, I also don't want her seeing me failing to protect our baby. "Give him back."

"Or what?" Rick laughs, shoving me against my locker. "You gonna throw a jockstrap at me? I told you I was going to get you. And now the day of reckoning has come."

Just then Baby Robbie grabs hold of Rick's fat lower lip, pulling it out impossibly far.

"I wuv you," the doll says.

"Ow! Fugg!" Rick shouts, trying to pull the baby off. He grips Robbie's arm, looks like he's going to break it. "Get your hupid bahtard off of may rip!"

As Charlie gleefully snaps picture after picture, I speak soothingly to Baby Robbie, "It's OK, buddy, it's OK, you can let go now," patting his back and continuing to reassure him till finally he releases Rick's lip.

"Well, well, well!" Charlie chortles, waving his newspapers in the air. "My good man Daniel here takes on a seven-hundred-pound death-dealing beast whilst ''Roid Rage' Rick is vanquished by the tiniest of toy toddlers." He shakes his head. "Now you tell me, folks," he says, appealing to the students who've gathered in the hallway, "which of these men is deserving of your veneration and plaudits?"

Rick presses his hand to his lip, then stares down at the blood on his fingertips.

"That's it," Rick growls, glaring at me. "Today. You. Die."

All right. Here we go. My moment to shine. I hope you're watching now, Erin.

I turn to Charlie and press the doll into his free hand. "Keep him safe," I say.

I clench my fists and go over everything that Hank taught me—legs apart, arms raised, left hand forward, right hand back, thumbs on the outside . . . I take a deep breath and spin back to Rick—

BAM!

The pain rockets up my sinuses as Rick's fist destroys my nearly healed nose.

There's a scream, a flash of light, and a trickle of warmth over my lips.

Then the world tilts and tunnels, and I am gone.

CHAPTER 72

Streams of light start to leak into my vision, like sunbeams through the clouds.

The agony comes next—sharp and strong. My face feels like it recently collided with Harley Quinn's mallet.

"Uuugh," I groan, my eyelids fluttering open.

Everything is so bright and white. There's a figure nearby, but it's smeary and out of focus.

I try to sit up. A warm hand touches my shoulder.

"Don't move," a voice says.

It's a voice I would know anywhere.

"Am I . . ." I croak, my tonsils stinging. "Is this heaven? Am I dead?"

Erin laughs. "No. But you probably have a concussion. And your nose is definitely broken."

"Again?" I ease my head back down. "Crap." I reach for my face, but Erin grabs my arm.

"I wouldn't do that if I were you," she says. "The nurse will be back in a minute."

She places my hand on my stomach, her touch warm and wonderful and electric. When she releases my wrist I instantly feel cold, like I've lost something essential to my very existence.

"What . . . What are you doing here?" I rasp, my vision clearing a bit. "I mean, I'm glad you're here. *So* glad. But why . . . ?"

Erin laughs again. "I couldn't very well abandon you after what you did for Baby Robbie. That was incredibly brave—and incredibly foolish. But I guess you're the foolishly brave type, huh? Taking on killer wasps and wild bears and the school's biggest jerk."

"You saw the paper." I wince as I recall the front-page picture of pale, scrawny me in my ridiculous boxers.

She nods. "The whole school saw it. It's pretty amazing! I can't believe what you guys went through! I would kill to have an adventure like that."

"Really?"

"Are you kidding? It's like something out of Dragon Age or *Thirty Days of Night*! Scary but cool."

She touches my shoulder, and a warm, happy glow washes over me again. Erin. My Erin. Gorgeous Warrior Princess. Lover of high-fantasy role-playing video games and obscure horror films. Knitter of adorable little sweaters—

"Oh my God, Robbie!" I say suddenly, trying to sit up. "Is he—?"

"He's fine." She holds up the doll. "Though I should probably make him a new sweater." She tugs at the torn and tattered wool. "This one has seen better days. Oh, and hey . . ." She scrunches up her face. "Did you update his programming or something? He couldn't talk and grab things when I was taking care of him."

"Oh, yeah, that." I laugh—then wince as a fresh wave of pain radiates from my nose. "Sort of. I mean, *I* didn't, but . . . It's a long story," I finish lamely.

Erin smiles. "Maybe when you're feeling up to it, you could tell me. I'd love to hear it. And all about your time in the wilderness too."

"Really?" I say, afraid I'm hallucinating. "You'd . . . you'd want to hear about that stuff?"

"Are you kidding? Totally! I have a feeling that article left a few things out."

"Maybe one or two things," I say, vowing never to let her find out just how *much* Charlie left out.

"Hey," Erin says. "Why don't I put my number in your phone, and you can text me when you're feeling up for company? I'll treat you to a mochaccino."

"O-OK," I say, digging frantically in my jeans pocket and finally wrestling out my phone. I watch in stunned disbelief as Erin—Princess Erilin herself—adds her number to my list of contacts.

"All set," she says, handing my phone back to me. "Just relax now. Your parents should be here soon. Your friend Charlie called them a while ago."

Suddenly I feel overcome with exhaustion. I press my head back against the pillow, the world blurring again. I can't believe I'm talking to Erin! And I can't believe *she's* talking to *me*! Why did it take me seven years to get up the courage to do this? This isn't so hard. It's actually pretty easy. And nice! So nice. . . .

I close my eyes and feel myself drifting off. . . .

Time passes. I don't know how long. Then someone rocks my shoulder.

"Dan, honey," a woman's voice says. "Wake up. It's Mom . . . and Hank."

I open my eyes. Mom and Hank are both standing beside the cot. I glance at Mom's hand, which is still on my shoulder.

"Hi," I rasp. "Hey, you're wearing your ring! Does this mean . . . ?"

Mom and Hank look at each other and smile—the big, goopy smiles that I once hated seeing on their faces. Now, though, they fill me with incredible happiness.

"Like you said, Dan, I can't let a great guy like this walk out of my life," Mom says, slipping her arm around Hank's waist. "Besides, I don't even *like* hunting. I was just trying to be supportive of his passions. And hey, now I can get my money back on those *Man vs. Wild* discs."

"Am I the luckiest guy in the world or what?" Hank asks, squeezing my mom to his side. "And don't you worry. You won't have to move schools. Your mother and I are going to find a nice house we can buy together in your neighborhood. I don't really like the decor of mine anyway." He laughs. "But enough about us. How are you doing? Charlie says you got into a little scuffle."

"I didn't get to use the stance," I mutter, raising my fists, Hank's watch sliding up my arm. "Or even throw a punch . . ."

"He was very brave," Erin says, cradling Baby Robbie in her arms. I didn't know she was still here; she and Charlie are standing in the corner of the room. "This big idiot wrestler was harassing him and threatening to hurt our baby—" She shakes her head. "I mean, our class's baby doll. And Dan was going to fight him, but he got sucker-punched! He was very brave," she says again, sounding embarrassed.

"Mom, Hank, this is Erin," I say. "Erin, this is my mom—and soon-to-be stepdad."

"Nice to meet you both," Erin says.

Hank's still staring at Erin, only now he's frowning. "Your face is so familiar. Have we met before?"

Oh crap, my real sketchbook! He asked to see more of my drawings when we got home, and I showed him everything: the Night Goblin, Sir Stan, Princess Erilin.

"I don't think so . . ." Erin says.

Please don't say anything, please don't saying anything. Not now. Not yet. Let me be the one to break the news to her.

"You're not one of my patients . . ." Hank continues. "I'm a dentist," he explains. "But it's not the teeth I recognize. It's definitely the face . . . You're not, like, on TV or anything?"

Erin laughs. "Yeah, right!"

"Huh." Hank shakes his head. "Sorry. It's just so strange. I really feel like I've seen you before!"

Charlie clears his throat and steps forward. "If I may interject. It sounds to me as though you're experiencing a simple case of déjà vu, which neuroscientists have described as a sort

374

of memory-based analogue of an optical illusion located in the hippocampus region of the brain. Occasionally, the pattern-separation circuit misfires, and a new experience—or, as in this case, a face—that's merely *similar* to an older one seems identical. In layman's terms, Mr. Langston, I believe you've experienced a bit of brain flatulence."

Oh, God, Charlie, you're the best.

Hank chuckles. "If there's one thing I learned on our trip, it's not to argue with you, Charlie!"

Mom, Erin, and Charlie laugh. I lean back, wishing I had my sketch pad with me—I'd capture this moment so that I could keep it with me forever.

"I wuv you," Baby Robbie coos from across the room. "I happy. I sleepy."

I smile and let my eyes drift closed. My sentiments exactly, Robbie.

ACKNOWLEDGMENTS

Writing any novel is a leap of faith. You never know exactly how it will turn out (or even *if* it will turn out). All you can hope is that you've set yourself on a decent course and that you have a solid foundation of amazing people who will help you through the dark hours when things get rough. And they will get rough because they always get rough.

I am extremely lucky to have such a group of incredible people on my side, and I would be beyond remiss if I didn't thank them.

I offer my sincerest gratitude to:

Kaylan Adair, my phenomenal editor, who never remembers quite how much she helps me with my novels. I, however, remember quite clearly, and I know for certain that this book would not be anywhere near what it is today without her wisdom, intelligence, and humor.

Jodi Reamer, my amazing literary agent, whose encouragement and support have been unwavering.

All the awesome people at Candlewick Press. I can't tell you how lucky I feel to be a part of the Candlewick family.

Matt Roeser for creating such a kick-ass cover.

Copy editor Erin Dewitt for sifting through the text with her fine-tooth comb. Please accept my deepest apologies for making you look up words like "ball sack" and "fecal-scented."

Ken Freeman and James Fant for helping me kick off this new book.

John Stead, who regaled me with his fascinating wilderness and bow-hunting stories. Also, a big shout-out to his sons, Nick and Michael, who've read all my books.

Sophie Goulet, who introduced me to John over a meal of wild boar and bear.

All of the tireless teachers, librarians, booksellers, and parents who have been so wonderfully supportive to me and my books over the years.

My dad, whom I miss dearly, and whose heart (and watch) found their way into this book.

My mom, who keeps pestering me for "that next novel!"

Robert and Camille for their love and support.

Emily, David, Will, Amy, and Ory. Constant sources of love and inspiration.

And, as always, my wife, Meg, the love of my life, my rock, and my champion.